PROPHECY OF MAGIC

SASHA URBAN SERIES: BOOK 6

DIMA ZALES

♠ MOZAIKA PUBLICATIONS ♠

Copyright © 2019 Dima Zales and Anna Zaires
www.dimazales.com

Published by Mozaika Publications, an imprint of Mozaika LLC.
www.mozaikallc.com

Cover by Orina Kafe
www.orinakafe-art.com

ISBN-13: 978-1-63142-498-4
ISBN-13: 978-1-63142-499-1

CHAPTER ONE

MY BIOLOGICAL MOTHER IS LILITH.

As in, the mother of demons from human legend.

The same Lilith who made herself a god on one of the Otherlands and kept my biological father, Rasputin, in a dungeon, with occasional torture thrown in for good measure.

Yeah, okay.

Getting up, I grab some clothes as I attempt to process all this.

My mother is an ultra-rare Cognizant with double powers—that of a vampire and probability manipulator. She was going to raise me in such a horrible way that Rasputin had to steal me away and hide me on Earth with my non-Cognizant parents. And now, armed with my full name, she's looking for me.

What does she want with me? Somehow, I doubt she's hoping we go to a yoga retreat together.

Not that this is my biggest concern right now. My vision started off with her looking for Nero. She wants revenge for what he did on her world.

He's potentially in more trouble than I am.

Accidentally putting my right foot into the left leg of my jeans, I nearly faceplant. Catching myself on my desk, I finish dressing and locate my phone.

Wow.

I have countless missed calls from Mom, my adoptive—but no less real—mother.

Is she back from her trip? Or does she want to stay in Paris longer?

Oh, and I also have a few missed calls from my adoptive dad—and he definitely should be back from *his* vacation by now.

Great. I got so busy seeking my biological parents, I abandoned my real ones—which is just unacceptable. Mom and Dad are the people who raised me. They should always matter to me more than the virtual stranger that is Rasputin.

And let's not even start on Lilith.

The good news is that Mom doesn't seem to be in panic mode just yet; she'd be calling nonstop if that were the case. Or maybe she's beyond panic mode and in a new phase I haven't seen yet?

But no. Then she'd be over here. That, or have the cops looking for me.

Deciding to deal with the potential life-and-death situation of Lilith seeking revenge first, I call Nero.

He doesn't pick up, so I leave a voicemail urging him to call me back.

Usually my boss is pretty quick to get back in touch, but seconds tick by and nothing happens.

So as not to go crazy, I make my way into the bathroom and do my morning routine.

When I'm done washing up, I text Nero to call me back *now*, and my eyes don't leave the phone as I walk to the kitchen.

No reply.

Felix and Fluffster are both eating oatmeal when I walk in, and the cat is munching on her Fancy Feast. Looking up from her plate, she gives me a look that seems to say, "Another peasant Our Majesty has to patiently tolerate. Our mercy knows no bounds."

Felix is holding a spoon in one hand and a phone in the other. "Maya, I'm really sorry," he says over the food in his mouth. "I wasn't ignoring your calls and texts; I was in a place with no reception. I'll explain—"

Ah.

So I'm not the only one in trouble for going incommunicado. Felix wasn't reachable either—and is now having to explain himself to my almost-eighteen-year-old friend from Orientation.

Oh, and the guilty way he's defending himself makes it official.

He and Maya are dating.

"Sasha," Fluffster says mentally. "You're up early. How are you feeling?"

"One sec," I mumble and email Nero an even more pointed demand to get in touch.

Noticing me, Felix rattles out more apologies to Maya, explains that he can't talk right now, and hangs up.

As I wait for Nero to reply, I grab a bowl and ladle some oatmeal into it.

"Are you okay?" Felix asks, his unibrow quivering as he eyes me quizzically. "You look like you've seen a ghost."

"No," I say after I swallow my first blissful spoonful of nourishment. "I learned something this morning that's really disturbing."

Checking my phone for Nero's reply every few seconds, I proceed to tell them about my vision of Lilith.

A stunned silence follows, with no one but the cat eating.

"I don't know what to say," Felix finally mutters. "That... thing is your mother?"

I grimace. "I know. And now I can't reach Nero. I hope she didn't get to him somehow."

"Nero can take care of himself," Felix says confidently. "This is Earth. Lilith can't do the stunts from her world here."

"But Nero can't turn into a dragon on a whim either," Fluffster says. "Maybe that evens things out?"

"Right," I say, the food feeling like a brick in my belly. "But why is Nero not calling me back?"

"He could be in a meeting," Felix says. "Give him a few minutes before you start to freak out."

"You're right." I spoon more oatmeal into my mouth. "I'll give him until I'm done with breakfast."

As I chew, an idea occurs to me—something I should've done right away but forgot in my panic.

I can look at Nero's future to make sure he's okay.

Eagerly focusing, I end up in Headspace and dwell on Nero's essence. For good measure, I add my very complex feelings for Nero to the summons, mimicking what Rasputin does when he wants a vision about someone. I even go as far as to remind myself that we've had an intimate encounter where Nero pleasured me but didn't give in to his own desire out of fear of losing control and hurting me—whatever that entails.

My work pays off.

A bunch of safe-seeming shapes show up around me, and I reach for the most promising one.

———

I'M BODILESS—WHICH means the vision doesn't include me.

Nero is in his office in the club on Gomorrah. Walking up to the wall, he opens the safe.

Reverently, he takes out the sword he left there yesterday—the sword I came to think of as mine. It's made of something like the technology of the gates, and Lilith used it to kill Nero in one of my visions.

Is he planning to attack Lilith with it? If so, does he

know she's already on Earth? Rasputin did warn him that since she has Nero's blood, she'll be coming for him out of vindictiveness. Then again, Nero said he was going to leave to go look for Claudia regardless. Is that what he's about to do? Go after this woman whom he thought dead but has just discovered is alive?

Is he leaving me without so much as a goodbye?

Nero presses the button on the sword hilt, and the shimmering lightsaber-like blade shows up, illuminating his menacing expression.

Nodding, he presses the button again to hide the blade.

———

I'M BACK at the kitchen table in my apartment.

Felix and Fluffster are talking about something, but my thoughts are with Nero.

This vision explains why he didn't reply to my calls, emails, and texts.

He's probably already on Gomorrah, about to do what I just saw in that vision.

As upset as I am about his leaving, I'm also relieved. From now until the near future in my vision, he's safe. And since he's in his own club on Gomorrah and has that sword, he's better equipped to deal with Lilith.

Still, for good measure, I go into Headspace and focus on Lilith again.

———

EXAMINING MY BIOLOGICAL MOTHER, I notice more resemblances between the two of us, from pale skin to a certain mischievous glint in her eyes.

She's standing next to the Apple store with a new-looking iPhone next to her ear.

Interesting.

She's either adjusting to modernity annoyingly well or has been on a world with our level of technology before.

Soon, this goddess of evil will be texting eggplant emojis to her minions and posting pictures of her disemboweled victims on Instagram… or pinning them on Pinterest for other evil gods (or my new cat) to admire.

"No, that will take too long," Lilith says in an annoyed tone into the phone. "I'll text you what path to take through the Otherlands. If you follow my instructions correctly, you should be here in—"

———

MY VISION CUTS out before I can eavesdrop on more of that cryptic conversation, so I go right back into Headspace—but this time, my vision isn't of Lilith talking on the phone.

It's of her walking out of the Giorgio Armani store in Midtown, dressed as if for a cover of a fashion magazine.

Well, that's reassuring as far as evil priorities go.

How did she even pay for those threads? Does

vampire glamour work when *those* kinds of prices are involved?

"I still can't believe she's your mother," Fluffster says in my head when I come out of Headspace. "Does that mean you've inherited her powers?"

Numbly, I stare at my chinchilla domovoi.

I haven't considered the genetics aspect of this yet.

"It's unlikely," Felix replies in my stead. "Double powers like Lilith's are rare, let alone triple powers."

"But I've always been pale," I say, shifting my gaze to my hands. My fingers, locked spasmodically around a spoon, are so white I could've been an albino. Frowning, I look up. "Does it mean I'm a pre-vamp?"

Felix adds some brown sugar to his bowl and shrugs. "There's no way to know for sure until you've lived a long time without showing any signs of aging. Even then, my understanding is that not all pre-vamps —or at least people who think they're pre-vamps—turn into vampires when they die."

I draw in a calming breath and focus on stirring my oatmeal. "Well, that's just bad terminology then. The suffix 'pre' makes it seem like a sure thing. Given what you're saying, the term should be 'maybe-vamp' or 'hopefully vamp.'" Then something occurs to me. "Wait, no. I'm not a pre-vamp. I've seen myself die in visions before, and I didn't turn into a vampire when that happened. My dead body would just lie there."

"Then you're probably not a pre-vamp," Felix agrees, and I exhale in a mixture of relief and disappointment. As cool as it would be to not die and have all the vampire powers, I don't know how I feel about the blood-drinking thing.

"What about probability manipulation?" Fluffster chimes in. "How can we know if Sasha inherited *that*?"

"There are no physical characteristics like paleness that I know of," Felix says. "Tricksters don't like seers, and Sasha is a seer—which makes me doubt she can be both, but I have no rational basis to prove this."

"Wouldn't I have more luck in my life if I were a probability manipulator?" I ask, remembering all my recent misadventures.

"I don't think that being a probability manipulator prevents all bad things from happening to you." Felix picks up a large spoonful of oatmeal. "The universe is just too chaotic for one person to fully bend it to their trickster power." He shoves the spoon into his mouth.

"You might have a point," I say. "Chester lost his wife and his seat on the Council—though I guess that last one doesn't count since Nero might give it back to him."

"I'd learn more about tricksters if I were you," Fluffster suggests.

"I'll chat with Chester," I say. "He actually owes me some lessons about his power."

"Interesting how he owes you the very thing you need," Felix says over the remnants of food in his mouth. "How *lucky*."

"I have a feeling I'm now going to question every happy coincidence," I say. "Oh, and if I *am* a probability manipulator, I wonder if my TV prediction gave me a power boost in that regard. When that performance was on YouTube, many comments said I just got lucky with my prediction—meaning tons of people *believe* in my luck."

"It's possible," Felix says thoughtfully. "Come to think of it, I wonder if some of the stuff we've attributed to your seer abilities are due to luck… like, say, your stock picks."

The mention of stocks reminds me of Nero, and I check my phone.

Nope. No response. If I want to talk to him about his plans, Claudia, and what's going on between us, I need to catch him in his club on Gomorrah—and since I don't know when the events in that vision will take place, I better hurry.

Then I recall something important I've been meaning to ask Felix. "Can you hide my online presence?" I blurt before I can forget again. "Lilith knows my name, and she might google me."

"I'll do it on my way to work. Speaking of that"—Felix looks at the clock and cringes—"I better run."

"Wait, one more thing," I say. "Can you figure out who Lilith was speaking with on the phone?"

He looks at me blankly, so I tell him about her cell phone conversation in my vision.

"That's not a lot to go on," he says, frowning. "Do you know her number, or the number of the person she called?"

"I'd tell you if I did," I say.

"Right. Sorry. I'll do my best when I have time, but I wouldn't hold my breath if I were you," Felix says.

"Fair enough," I say.

Shoveling the remainder of his food into his mouth, he jumps up and sprints for the door.

I follow his example, swallowing my food without chewing as I jump to my feet. He's already gone by the time I get to the hallway and put on my shoes.

Stepping out, I see Thalia—my non-speaking nun/martial arts trainer/bodyguard—and a guy I've never met before.

A distractingly attractive guy with perfect facial features that make him look like one of the Hemsworth brothers. He has a Mandate aura, which means that unlike some other guards Nero had assigned to me, this guy is some kind of Cognizant.

"Hi, Sasha." The new guy's smile rivals Ariel's in its perfection. "My name is Eric. Nero asked me to help Thalia make sure you're comfortable in your apartment."

"Comfortable?" I look them both over. "Were you instructed to keep me prisoner here?"

CHAPTER TWO

THALIA GRAVELY NODS, then turns away, about to leave.

"No, wait. I need to go somewhere." I instinctively grab her shoulder.

The nun moves as she would on the training mat. Grabbing my wrist, she sidesteps behind me and painfully twists my arm behind my back.

To my shock, Eric grabs the nun's wrist. "No one's allowed to hurt her. Nero was very clear on this. That includes you."

Thalia rolls her eyes but lets me go without a fight. She then takes out her phone and types out:

Sorry, but you're going to have to take a little staycation.

With that, she goes to summon the elevator.

"I'll get you whatever you need," Eric says soothingly as he herds me back toward the door. "Food, movie rentals, magic books—you name it, someone will fetch it for you."

"I have an urgent matter that I need to discuss with Nero," I say, digging my heels in when I'm a foot away from the apartment. "Do you have a way to reach him?"

Thalia shrugs before entering the elevator, and Eric says, "He warned me he'd be unavailable and asked me to apologize to you about this in advance."

"I find that last bit very hard to believe," I say, desperately thinking of a way to bypass Eric.

The elevator closes, taking Thalia away.

"Don't worry," Eric says. "It's not just me and Thalia guarding you. I have people surrounding this building—including the back entrance. No one can come in without me knowing."

Implication being that no one can *leave* without Eric knowing it also.

Well, let's see how good he is at his job then.

I convince myself that I'm going to just run for it—which isn't hard, as I'm itching to do it. Next, I inhale a deep breath and jump into Headspace.

The shapes around me seem unpleasant but not deadly.

Going on instinct, I reach for one.

———

"FAIR ENOUGH," I say to Eric and turn back toward the door, my muscles coiling for a sprint.

"Give me a shout if you need anything," he says.

Without a reply, I leap to the side and sprint for the staircase—just to bump into Eric's hard body.

Wow.

He must have super speed, to get in my way so quickly.

"Please, Sasha," Eric says, steadying me by my arms. "Just go home."

Huffing, I twist away and walk back into the apartment.

—

BACK IN REALITY, I jump back into Headspace and attempt a few more visions of escape. In each, Eric thwarts me, and in some, he carries me home with varying levels of kicking and screaming on my part.

Exiting Headspace for the last time, I enter the apartment and slam the door in Eric's face.

Pacing the hallway, I strain to come up with a way out of this unfortunate predicament.

Could I threaten him with a gun? Bluff my way out?

The problem is that I left my gun in the lab near the JFK hub.

I go into Ariel's room and look for a gun she might've stashed there. She takes her Second Amendment rights very seriously, so I have a chance.

After a long search, I locate a pair of handcuffs in her nightstand, two knives in her closet, and a box of bullets under her bed—but no gun.

I don't want to give up, though. There has to be another way out of the apartment.

I resume pacing until I see Fluffster staring at me quizzically—which is when an idea occurs to me.

I quickly explain the situation to the chinchilla and head for the door.

"Hi, Eric." I smile at the guard when I open it. "I'm sorry if I was cranky earlier. Nero gets under my skin, but I shouldn't take it out on you."

"No sweat." He beams at me. "I don't like this either. I thought I'd be a bodyguard, not some jailer. But I owe Nero a favor, and he said this is to keep you safe, so…"

"Do you want some coffee or tea?" I say as nonchalantly as possible. "Maybe a chair, so you don't have to stand here in the hallway?"

His smile widens. "Coffee would be great, thanks."

"Awesome," I say and head into the kitchen.

Eric enters the apartment without an invitation, so he's not a vampire—not that I thought he was, with that perfectly tanned skin of his.

When he follows me into the kitchen, I hand him an espresso and say, "Oh crap. I forgot to take off my shoes."

As I start to leave, Eric downs the drink on a single gulp and moves to follow me—until Fluffster walks into his path.

"Actually," I say, dropping the friendly tone. "I think it would be best if you stayed in the kitchen."

Using that as his cue, Fluffster changes into his monster form.

He doesn't look as terrifying as when he killed

Harper-the-succubus, but it's enough to raise *my* blood pressure, and I'm not the one in danger.

"Nero told me you might try this," Eric says calmly and sighs. "I was hoping he was wrong about that."

I stare at him in confusion. How powerful is he not to be afraid of a domovoi protecting its own house?

Then again, Nero asked this guy to guard *me*. Given my penchant for making powerful enemies, he would have to be pretty formidable.

With an exaggerated sigh, Eric poofs out of existence in front of my eyes as if he was never there.

I rub my eyes.

Nope. He's gone.

I look at Fluffster. He returns to his cute chinchilla shape and also looks confused.

"Are you invisible?" Arms outstretched, I grope around the kitchen air like a lunatic but find no sign of Eric.

There's a knock on the front door.

I go to open it—and find Eric standing there, looking smug.

"How?" I demand. "You were just in my kitchen."

"I can teleport." Eric's chest puffs up, making him look like a penguin. "If the guards downstairs warn me of danger, I'm supposed to teleport you away to safety." He looks at Fluffster. "I hope your domovoi isn't going to stop me from performing my duties?"

"Of course not," Fluffster says with a swish of his puffy tail.

So a teleporter, huh? Hekima did mention

teleporting power at one of the Orientations. He said it's rare—but I guess if someone knew a teleporter, it would be Nero.

I'm about to pepper Eric with questions about his power when the elevator dings and its doors start to open.

With grim determination, Eric snatches my wrist and tenses—apparently ready to teleport me away from danger.

To my shock, my mother steps out of the elevator.

CHAPTER THREE

MY REAL MOM, that is, not Lilith.

The expression on her face makes me think that she *has* entered a new phase of worrying about me that's beyond her usual 'panic mode.'

Crap. I should've called her as soon as I discovered those missed phone calls.

At the sight of me in the doorway, relief flashes across her face, then morphs into indignation. But before she can say anything, her gaze lands on Eric, and she looks both confused and impressed.

"Don't," I hiss at Eric and try to pull away.

If he teleports me now, he'll break the Mandate and probably give my mom a heart attack to boot.

But it looks like I didn't have to warn him. Something about my mom—most likely her lack of Mandate aura—makes Eric let go of my wrist as if I suddenly developed a bad case of cooties.

"Mrs. Ballard." He hits Mom with a smile so

charming, you'd expect him to save a Disney princess at any moment. "I've heard so much about you."

Wow. Nero really prepared this guy for his duty. Unless he's always prepared my guards so thoroughly, and I just didn't realize it?

Instead of replying, Mom blushes like a medieval maiden who's never seen an attractive man before.

"As I was saying, Eric." I pointedly clear my throat. "Ariel isn't home, but she'll be back before you know it."

"Right," he says and winks at me in such a way that Mom can't see it. "I'll wait here for Ariel so that I can surprise her when she steps out of that elevator. Thank you."

"Yeah." I fight to keep the sarcasm from my voice. "Good thinking." Waving at my Eric-gaping parent, I say, "Come on, Mom, let me make you some of your favorite tea."

She peels her eyes away from my guard and follows me into the apartment.

Once inside, she gives me a disappointed look. "So that man is dating Ariel, not you?"

Is this a prelude to the whole "I want grandchildren" conversation? If so, I have to be careful as *that* topic can take all day—and I don't have the luxury of "accidentally" losing a phone call or having my Skype "cut out."

"He and Ariel belong together," I say, leading her into the kitchen. "In any case, I'm already seeing someone else."

As I speak, I wonder if I'm lying. I almost wish I were Pinocchio, so I could see what would happen to my nose.

Mom sits down at the table, her eyes shining with excitement. "Who? How? Tell me all the details."

If only I could manipulate my enemies as easily as this. I have Mom now—hook, line, and sinker.

"It's still early, so I don't want to jinx it by talking about him." I place my phone on the table in case Nero calls, then put on the kettle. "Knowing you, you'd like him. I'm sure of that."

Of course she would. Nero is the richest person I know, and that carries a lot of weight in my mom's book. Once she learns that and she sees how attractive he is, there will be no end to the baby hints. She wouldn't care that he's my boss or a dragon—not that she would ever learn about the latter.

"That's wise," Mom says, nodding sagely. "Tell me after it's more official."

Yep, that worked as expected. She believes in the evil eye and stuff like that, so the idea of jinxing a new relationship makes perfect sense to her—and the relationship bit is a great distraction from my disappearance.

"I just got back," I say, deciding to really push my luck. "He took me on a romantic getaway, and we left both our phones at home. When I saw your calls a couple of minutes ago, I realized I should've let you know about the trip before leaving, but it was a spur-of-the-moment thing, and I thought you were still in Paris, so—"

"Oh, sweetie." Her eyes gleam brightly. "I understand completely. In fact, it must be kismet because I, too, have met someone in Paris. He was there on business, and the reason I'm back is so that he and I can spend more time together—but I also don't want to jinx things by talking about him too much."

Wow.

Mom has met someone?

That's huge.

And, despite what she says, it's clear she's itching to tell me all about it.

"Is he from New York?" I put a couple of different teabags into Mom's cup and pour in the boiling water. "Is he tall? I'm sure it's safe for you to tell me that much."

"I'll tell you everything when things get more serious," Mom says with a self-discipline even Thalia would envy.

"Can't blame you," I say. "What else is—"

My phone rings.

We both look at it.

The caller is Dad—as in, the man who raised me and Mom's former husband.

Mom's expression is hard to read, but I can guess she doesn't like this.

"I love you both, Mom," I say as I reach for the phone. "I'd never choose him over you, I swear."

"That's nice," she says blandly. "You should take the call, though; I think I know why he's calling."

Confused, I pick up the phone.

"Sasha?" My dad sounds panicky—something that never happens.

"What's wrong?"

"There's a man here not letting me ring your doorbell," he says. "Is everything okay? Your mother—"

"Wait, what? You're at the door? Here in New York?"

"Yes. And—"

"Hold on." I rush over to the door and open it.

Eric, who's blocking Dad's path, looks at me questioningly.

I guess Nero left him a dossier that included my local mom but not my out-of-town dad.

"Let my father through, please," I say. "Ariel should be home any minute now."

"Right." Eric clears his throat and moves out of the way. "Sorry about that. Ariel—my girlfriend—told me someone was prank-ringing her doorbell, so I—"

"Don't worry about it," Dad says. "I'm just glad Sasha is alive."

Alive?

Baffled, I usher Dad into the apartment. "Why wouldn't I be alive?"

"Makenzie," Dad says with exaggerated cordiality as Mom comes up to us.

"Braxton." She nods, her tone cool but not as nasty as I'd expect.

"What's going on?" I look from one parental unit to the other.

"This might be my fault," Mom says, her gaze dropping to her impeccable Louis Vuitton pumps. "I couldn't reach you, and since I knew the two of you started talking, I called him to see if he knew where you were."

Oh. I forgot about the past-panic-mode freak-out. Apparently, when she's worried about me enough, Mom is willing to call the devil himself.

I guess it's touching, in an insane sort of way.

"I jumped on a plane to come find you," Dad says. "But I guess you weren't all that lost."

"She had a good reason for her disappearance," Mom says defensively—even though Dad didn't sound the least bit accusing, just relieved. "It was just a feminine matter." She looks at him challengingly. "You wouldn't understand."

Dad pales.

I bet he just pictured me getting a back-alley abortion or uterine cancer.

"The good news is that I'm totally and absolutely fine," I say before this bizarre conversation turns into a fight—and I don't need seer powers to know that future is nigh.

Is that why I have a bad feeling creeping up, one that reminds me of my usual seer warnings, but not as directed?

I *am* a trouble magnet, so maybe this is my powers warning me about my human parents being so close to me? After all, if Lilith arrived here right now, Eric would likely only teleport *me* away, not them.

That does it. My intuitions aren't something I can afford to ignore, so my parents have to go.

"The good news is that I got to see you both," I say, frantically working out a swift exit strategy. "We should definitely make plans to properly hang out soon—but not right this moment because I have a crazy pile-up of work."

"Oh," they both say disappointedly. It's admirable how they thought they were going to tolerate each other's presence and hang out with me like two civilized adults.

And hey, maybe they could have. I mean, they're still civil, and that's already monumental progress.

"Call me when you're free this weekend," I say to them. "And, Dad, if you have to go back, no worries. I'll fly out to see you as soon as my schedule allows."

To my surprise, Mom smiles approvingly.

Did meeting a new man help her move on? Or is it the bonding experience of "losing me?"

"Right," Dad says to me, then turns to Mom. "We should let Sasha work."

"You have a cat now?" Mom asks, spotting Lucifur—who's looking at everyone with a malevolent expression on her flat face. "What happened to the furry rat creature?"

"Yes. That's Luci." I herd both parents toward the door. "Fluffster is doing well, Mom, don't worry. He and the cat are besties now."

Hearing his name, Fluffster shows up from the living room.

"A chinchilla?" Dad exclaims, and I guiltily realize he's never been to my place or even heard about Fluffster's existence. "You'll have to tell me about that, and the cat, when we hang out," he says.

"And me about the cat," Mom adds jealously.

"I will," I say as I open the door. "I promise."

They reluctantly exit.

"Hello," Eric says to my parents. "Let me summon the elevator for you two."

Before they reply, he does as he offered, and the elevator opens right away. It must have not left since Dad got here.

My parents walk in, and as the doors close, I belatedly realize that having them ride down *together* might not be the best idea. Then again, if a cat and a sort-of rodent can share an apartment, those two can survive a single elevator ride. Still, I make a mental note to use a vision later to make sure they made it out with their sanities intact.

"Crap," I say to Eric as an impromptu idea pops into my head. "I forgot to give Mom something. I'm going to run down and give it to her."

"Of course," Eric says. "We'll go together."

Smart. But maybe he still doesn't get what I'm trying to do. Let's see. "Actually," I say nonchalantly, "maybe you can just catch her for me and give this to her?"

Not letting him reply, I run back into the

apartment, relocate Mom's tea into a paper cup, and rush out to give it to Eric.

"Sure thing." Eric takes the cup and poofs out of existence.

I run for the stairs, but before I'm halfway to the next floor, I spot Eric already standing there, waiting for me with a smile.

Damn him and his teleportation.

How am I ever going to escape?

CHAPTER FOUR

THINKING AHEAD, I pretend not to notice Eric there and run down, smacking into him with a loud plop.

The tea cup flies to the floor, and the shock of the impact gives me a moment to get a little revenge on Eric.

Before he catches on to my sneaky business, I say, "Hey. That hurt."

"You should watch where you're running," Eric says, nonplussed, as he picks up the now-empty cup. "In general, I'd appreciate it if you could avoid unnecessary physical contact with me going forward. I don't want to break Nero's orders, even by accident."

Nero asked him not to touch me? What about my opinion on the matter? Maybe I *want* Eric to touch me. I mean, I definitely don't, but many women would and the restriction is annoying, to say the least. Only *I* should decide who does or doesn't touch me.

"Let's go." Eric gestures for me to lead the way.

"Maybe we got off on the wrong foot," I say when we're halfway to our destination. "My problem isn't with you."

"Don't sweat it," Eric says. "If you stop making my job so hard, I'll call us even."

"Sure," I lie. "Also, I was wondering if you could spare some guards from your retinue to look after my folks?"

Eric clears his throat. "Nero already has people watching them," he says after a pause. "They were here with them; your parents just didn't know that."

I recall Nero saying something along those lines before, but I didn't realize he'd kept on watching over my parents even after the threat of Baba Yaga was neutralized. After I give him a piece of my mind about my incarceration, I'll have to also thank him for looking after them.

I guess his annoying habit of hiring guards to stalk people is a double-edged sword.

When we reach my door, I give Eric a puppy-eyed look and sweetly say, "Listen. I just want to meet Nero in Gomorrah. You can personally take me to him, and if we see any danger, you can teleport me away from it. Once I'm with Nero, I would be safer than—"

"The scenario you describe is something Nero forbade explicitly," Eric says, not unkindly. "It's too dangerous where he's headed."

"Oh, come on. I saved his life not once but twice now," I say indignantly. What Eric is saying supports my earlier "save Claudia" theory, and I don't like that one bit.

The guard gives me a look that seems to say, "I didn't make up the rules, I just follow them."

I decide to try another tack. "What about my work? Nero would want me to—"

"Your offices are being repaired, so you're going to work from home," Eric says. "Then again, I doubt a lot will be required of you in that department any time soon."

No work? Nero must *really* be preoccupied with his quest.

Gritting my teeth, I enter the apartment and slam the door in Eric's face.

As I do so, I realize that it didn't even occur to me to tell my parents about my newly discovered biological origins. Then again, I don't think I'll ever do that. Not only would it upset Mom, but it's all tied up with Cognizant stuff, and talking about it would mean bleeding from everywhere as the best-case scenario.

Blowing out a breath to calm myself, I take out the wallet I pickpocketed from Eric when I bumped into him on the stairs.

Hopefully, there's blackmail material inside.

Sadly, all I find are a dozen movie-ticket stubs to a bunch of recent superhero flicks, a picture of a good-looking elderly woman who is probably his mom, cash, and a slew of credit cards and IDs.

There goes that idea. Unless Eric is *very*

embarrassed of his Costco membership, I have nothing to blackmail him with.

Could I use my skills as an illusionist instead?

Going to my stash of magic paraphernalia, I take stock of the myriad options in front of me.

Fake levitation and coin manipulation would be pretty useless, as would anything involving cards.

The only illusion that might be remotely helpful is the one where I make it look as though I've lost my hand to a knife accident. Once the EMTs come and take me away, I should have ample opportunity to escape—assuming medical professionals would be fooled by this illusion.

The effect *is* pretty realistic, though. When I showed this to Felix on Halloween a couple of years back, he actually fainted—or maybe pretended to faint to make me feel guilty for the prank.

Sniffing the fake blood and examining the rest of the props, I decide this might actually work—and set myself up for the effect by putting on the scratchy blazer I dedicated to the secret hookup of this illusion.

Even if this doesn't work, it might be fun to see the expression on Eric's face. Nero told him to keep me safe and he let me lose an appendage.

Yeah, he'll be freaked out for sure.

I'm already hiding the special prop knife in my secret pocket when I realize a big problem with my plan.

Eric's teleportation.

Even if he buys the "terrible accident" he is to

witness, he might teleport me to some hospital's operating room instead of getting the EMTs involved.

Not good.

Performance magic isn't going to cut it this time.

What I need is some real magic—like a cloak of invisibility or something. Why couldn't my Orientation teacher have been more like Dumbledore?

Wait a sec.

Thinking of invisibility reminds me of yesterday—specifically, how Chester was able to hide his lion, Bert, from humans at the airport by making it unlikely anyone would look at the beast. Though no light bending was involved, the lion was as good as invisible.

The question is, can Chester do that trick remotely?

Probably, I decide after a moment. After all, he was able to mess with Darian's powers remotely, so why not this too?

Yes, that's it. I have to talk to Chester. And while we're at it, maybe he can tell me how to determine if I, too, have probability manipulation powers.

Eagerly, I pull out my phone and dial his number.

The phone rings a while before someone picks up.

"You." Chester sounds nothing like his usual cheerful self. "You've got balls calling me."

"Hello to you, too," I say, confused. "What's gotten into you today?"

"Don't play dumb," Chester says with an icy undertone to his voice. "I asked my daughter how she ended up submitting to you and she told me *everything*."

Uh-oh. I think I know where—

"You held her at gun point?" Chester grits out. "Shot at her?"

Strictly speaking, I played Russian Roulette with her, and she started the hostilities, but I don't think saying so would make it sound better.

"I didn't put bullets into that gun, I swear," I say instead. "I was just—"

"You kicked her when she was on the ground! Then had your bodyguard hold her at gunpoint yet again."

When he puts it like that, I kind of feel bad—especially in light of what I later learned about their tragic family situation. In my defense, the teenager said something nasty about Rose right after my friend was murdered, so I wasn't myself when I reacted so violently.

Still, I'm not sure such an excuse would stand up in court, let alone appease an upset parent.

"You're *very* lucky to have Nero's protection," Chester says in a tone that sends a chill down my spine. "But even with that, if you hurt my baby ever again, you're dead."

"I'm sorry. I really didn't mean to—"

Chester hangs up on me before I can finish.

I resist the urge to call back and remind him that he still owes me some probability manipulation lessons. Something tells me that might not be wise—not unless I want an unlucky brick falling on my head.

I just hope Chester really *is* afraid of Nero and thus won't cause me trouble—or increase the chance I get into trouble.

Unless he already did, and that's why I have to deal with Eric and company.

Well, no matter the cause of my current predicament, I need to find another way to be invisible.

Something I can do myself.

And that's when it hits me.

I *do* know another way.

A seer way.

I can do what the bannik had done when he helped me escape the banya where Baba Yaga wanted to breed us like cattle. He'd used his powers to learn where everyone will be at given points in time, then told me how to leave without being seen.

It's not quite as effective as what Chester does, but it might still work.

And if the bannik can do it, I should be able to do so as well.

Taking a calming breath, I go into Headspace.

———

IGNORING the shapes that surround me by default, I focus on the essence of Eric—or at least as close to it as I can get based on his appearance, the contents of his wallet, and what I've learned from our brief interactions. When that doesn't work, I throw in my feelings about the guy—mainly annoyance.

The latter seems to do the trick, and a large cloud of safe-seeming shapes shows up around me, with one of the shapes subtly different from the others. My guess is that they would show Eric standing in the hallway, but this standout shape might be of him doing something different. Something I can use.

Thus determined, I reach for the shape.

———

BODILESS, I watch Eric pace the hallway.

My viewpoint follows him for a few minutes, and I detect a slight irregularity in his step.

He stops by the garbage chute and sneaks a glance at the door of my apartment.

The door is closed.

Eric looks momentarily torn; then he does his teleporting trick.

Interestingly, my disembodied viewpoint joins him in this new location—which I guess makes sense since it was *him* my vision was targeting, not the hallway.

Given the rows of fancy urinals and gold plating on the sinks, this must be a men's bathroom in either an expensive hotel or a posh restaurant.

Score.

On some level, I was hoping for this when I offered him coffee—a known diuretic.

Confirming my guess, Eric walks up to the nearest urinal and starts to unzip.

Which is when the vision terminates.

———

BACK FROM HEADSPACE, I digest what I just learned.

In some hopefully near future, Eric will hear the call of his bladder and will temporarily abandon his post to drain his gecko.

That gives me a window to slip by him—likely the hardest-to-dodge sentry on my way to freedom.

Except I lack a key piece of information.

When exactly is Eric going to succumb to the needs of the mighty tinkle?

There was no clue in the vision itself, but there *is* a way I can find this out.

Walking up to the door, I take out my phone and convince myself to do the following: wait until the time feels "right," then exit and look at my phone to check the time.

When I'm on the verge of opening the door, I leap into Headspace instead.

———

IT'S a case of déjà vu. A large cloud of nearly identical shapes surrounds me, with one that slightly stands out.

I bet most of these are visions of me exiting and looking at the time right in front of Eric, but this unusual one is where I exit and he isn't there.

If I'm right, it will be proof I'm getting better at this Headspace stuff.

Pulsing with eagerness, I touch the shape in question.

———

I OPEN the door and walk out.

Yes.

Eric isn't here.

I look at the time.

The screen reads 10:31:11.

I rush to the staircase—

———

BACK IN THE APARTMENT, I look at the current time.

It's a bunch of minutes until "go time."

Oh well, I can use the time to check on some people I care about via visions.

Walking over to the couch, I set my phone alarm to 10:29 and turn on the TV as loudly as I can—which should be handy later.

The Bachelor comes on as I prepare for a jump into Headspace. And though reality TV makes focusing almost as hard as when I fight for my life, I succeed right away.

Once there, I try calling my father again.

It doesn't work.

I decide to check on Ariel next.

The Ariel-related shapes don't seem to bode anything bad, but I touch one just in case.

———

ARIEL IS SITTING on a plush couch in a soothingly illuminated room. Puffing on a vaping device, she exhales a white cloud, then swaps the gizmo for knitting needles.

A minute into her knitting, someone knocks on the door.

"Come in," Ariel says, her fingers continuing to dance around the thick threads.

To my surprise, my biological father walks in wearing a Gomorrah-chic silvery outfit that makes him look like an extra in a sci-fi movie.

Ariel stops knitting. "Grisha? What are you doing here?"

Shrugging, Rasputin points at his mouth, then his ears.

"Oh right," Ariel says. "You don't understand me."

Rasputin extends his finger in a "hold on" gesture, then takes out a small device from his pocket. In Russian, he says, "Amazing what the technology on this world can do."

The device comes to life and translates his statement into English—albeit in a robotic male voice.

"Neat," Ariel says—and the device translates that into Russian. "I think we're very close to this kind of technology on Earth as well."

"It's a marvel." Rasputin walks up to the nearby chair and carefully sits down. "We didn't get a chance to talk the other day." He smiles sheepishly. "Since we're currently stuck on the same world, I figured I'd visit."

"That's sweet of you," she says. "Unless you have a Sasha-related agenda."

He looks down at the fractal design of the rug at his feet. "Well, I *was* hoping you could tell me something about my daughter."

Ariel frowns.

"Nothing she would mind you sharing, of course. Just some trivia—like how she did in school, your favorite magic tricks of hers, what she likes to eat… anything that wouldn't be a betrayal of trust on your part."

"Hmm." Ariel puts down one of her needles and puffs on the vape again. "I'm only comfortable telling the type of stuff you'd learn from social media."

"Anything," he says.

"Wouldn't it be better if you talked to Sasha yourself?" She offers him the vape device, and he shakes his head. "I'm sure she's eager to speak with you," Ariel continues.

"I'd love that," my father says. "Unfortunately, I can't go to Earth to talk to her in person, and I've used up all my powers doing a favor for Nero."

So this is why he's not replying to my Headspace summons. Good to know he's not snubbing me—and more of a reason to escape my makeshift prison.

"A favor for Nero?" Ariel picks up the needles again. "I'm curious. How about a little quid pro quo?"

The translating machine butchers the meaning of her words, and she has to restate that she wants to exchange info about Nero for trivia about me.

"All I'm allowed to say is that Nero is about to embark on a suicide mission," Rasputin says with a sigh. "It took all my power to figure out a course of action that would give him a small chance of survival." He rubs his temples. "Even if the allies I recommended join him, the odds of success are minuscule."

Ariel's frown deepens. "I don't understand. I thought a seer could find out exactly what to do."

"What he intends is so dangerous, with so many possible ways to die, I had to look into too many futures—and thus ran out of my seer power without finding him a sure-fire path to victory," Rasputin says. "I'm still not as strong as I can be, but at least I was able to warn him of obvious dead ends."

"Literal ones," Ariel says. "Wait a sec. Is Sasha going with him on this suicide mission?" She looks ready to leap to her feet and bolt out of the door.

"No," Rasputin says forcefully. "She isn't joining. We agreed on that score."

If I had a mouth, I'd yell for Ariel to ask him more questions, but I can't, and in a moment, it doesn't matter anyway.

My vision terminates.

CHAPTER FIVE

I FIND MYSELF ON A COUCH, all calm out the window.

There's almost no doubt about it now. Nero is going after Claudia. I can't think of anything else as dangerous as a trip to the dragon world.

As if I needed *more* reason to go to Gomorrah, now I have to stop Nero from doing something that's highly likely to get him killed.

If anyone is going to kill Nero, it will be me for not taking me with him and overall acting like a jerk.

Getting up, I pace the apartment, willing the clock to move faster.

When I nearly step on the cat's tail—an offense punishable by death, based on the look Lucifur gives me—I go back to the couch.

Instead of driving myself crazy, I can at least look at Nero's future.

Closing my eyes, I summon the prerequisite focus and reach for Headspace.

———

I COMBINE Nero's essence with my urge to strangle him and get results right away.

To my huge relief, the cuboid shapes around me play a safe tune.

Good.

He's safe in *this* future.

Might as well find out what's he's up to, I decide, reaching for the nearest shape.

———

NERO AND ISIS walk into a room that looks eerily like the one Ariel was sitting in, and face *me*.

Except that can't be me. I'm bodiless, which means I'm not there. And the only times I've seen myself like this in a vision have been when I was unconscious.

Oh, and I'd never voluntarily wear that skimpy outfit, not unless I decided on a career in a brothel.

"The real Sasha looks better than that," Nero growls, crossing his arms over his chest. "Your left cheekbone is off and—"

"Impossible," the fake Sasha says in Kit's voice, then turns into herself. "You just know I'm not her, so your rose-colored glasses are off."

Nero blows out an impatient breath. "I have an important business proposition I came to discuss, but if—"

———

MY VISION CUTS OUT. What a nuisance.

I want to know what business he came to discuss with the shapeshifting Councilor.

Then again, I can guess.

Rasputin mentioned that Nero's success depends on gathering allies. If so, I can't think of a better candidate than Kit.

Eager to find out if he'll tell Kit who Claudia is, I jump back into Headspace and try to bring about the continuation of the same vision.

———

NERO, Kit, and Isis walk into a dimly lit room with futuristic-looking technology all around them.

This is either a Gomorrah version of a man cave or a spaceship.

Distant sounds of pulsing music make me think this is someplace in Nero's club, which tells me this vision is not just the wrong time but also the wrong place. This is happening outside the rehab facility and *after* Kit let herself be recruited.

"Why couldn't we just talk to her in person?" Kit asks Nero as he fiddles with the flashing lights of some device that looks like it might beam him up to the Starship Enterprise.

"If she sees you or me in person and hears the word 'favor,' she'll either run or shoot us with her powers," Nero says. "This is better for her skittish psyche. Trust me, I'm much better with people than—"

Itzel shows up in the middle of the room.

Well, not really.

It's a hologram of Itzel.

She's wearing something that looks like a lab coat, and her breathing apparatus is much sleeker than what I remember.

Wow.

That's an amazingly accurate hologram. Something like this would not be possible with Earth technology.

Oh, and I can't believe I'm seeing Itzel in a vision at all, since, being a gnome, she's resistant to my powers.

I guess it makes sense, though. It looks like only a gnome's physical presence is immune to seer visions, but not a future where Nero talks to a gnome via a hologram, phone, or Skype.

Interesting.

This can be useful if I ever have to glimpse some gnome's future. I could ask Felix to build a drone to spy on said gnome all the time and then see the future of someone looking at the drone's footage. And voila— future of a gnome.

"What do you two want?" Sounding panicked, Itzel looks back and forth between Nero and Kit. "There's no way I'm joining you on any more adventures. There isn't enough money—"

"I need you as a technical consultant," Nero says soothingly. "You're the smartest gnome I've ever met."

Instantly calming, Itzel stands straighter, a faint blush warming her face.

"Isn't she the only gnome you've ever met?" Kit mouths to Nero conspiratorially.

Ignoring it, Nero steps toward Itzel's hologram and says, "I need technology for a world where it isn't supposed to work."

"That sounds like a contradiction." Itzel's hologram steps back from him. "Can you be a little more specific?"

"Right." Nero stops his advance. "First of all, gunpowder doesn't ignite. Secondly—"

———

THE VISION ENDS on an interesting part yet again.

Well, maybe.

There's a good chance Itzel was about to geek out of control.

Either way, it was nice to see that she's okay. I'll have to visit her one of these days. I bet she'll have a heart attack when she sees me. She'll think I, too, came to recruit her for some misadventure.

In any case, it sounds like a lot of interesting things are happening, and I need to get to Gomorrah soon.

As if in reply to my thought, the alarm on my phone goes off.

Finally.

I leap to my feet and hurry to the door.

When the time is exactly 10:31:11, I open the door and sprint for the stairs.

Reaching the floor below mine, I stop running and walk softly instead.

Eric is likely back at his post by now. The TV I left blaring in my apartment should make him believe I'm still there watching it. If not, I'll get intercepted at any moment.

I creep down one floor, then another.

No one comes after me.

When I reach the second floor, I stop.

Eric mentioned guards surrounding the building, so I need a strategy.

But first, reconnaissance.

I convince myself I'm about to waltz out of the main entrance, then go into Headspace to see how that dubious plan would play out.

———

THALIA AND A GUY I don't know stare at me with varying degrees of incredulity when I exit.

I bolt in the opposite direction—but run smack into yet another guy I don't know, who grabs the back of my blazer with his sausage-like fingers.

Before I can rip out of his grasp, Thalia is already there, and so is the other guy.

It takes them a few moments to restrain me—but only because they're trying not to hurt me.

Next thing I know, I'm being carried kicking and

screaming to my apartment—

———

I'M BACK on the staircase.

Well, that went about as well as I expected. How about the back entrance? The one the building's super uses to take out the garbage?

Determining to go that way, I go into Headspace to see how it plays out.

———

A GUY in a suit smoking a cigarette is facing away from the door when I open it.

I guess this is a good start. It would be worse if he were staring right at me.

Still, I see no way to pass by without him noticing me.

If I were Jason Bourne, I'd knock this guy out with a karate chop to the back of his head, or lock his neck in a crook of my elbow until he loses consciousness. But since I'm not, I opt for a subtler spy-inspired tactic.

Taking out a deck of cards from my pocket, I toss it to the right—aiming for the garbage can.

The bang is even louder than I hoped, and when the guard looks right, I sprint left.

But I only make it two feet before a big, tobacco-smelling hand grabs my hair, nearly scalping me in the process.

"And where do you think you're going?" the guard growls and painfully grips my shoulder, no doubt leaving a mark.

———

SO THAT WAS THAT.

Not only is that guy good at his job, he's also incredibly rude.

Could I use his asshole behavior as blackmail? Given what Nero did to the orcs when I got a bruise, he would seriously mind this guy grabbing me like that.

Then again, how can I blackmail someone when the bad thing he does is in the future? Also, this guy doesn't seem smart enough to realize the consequences of his actions, and might not get the whole concept of cause and effect—which is very important for blackmail.

Oh well. At least I learned there's just one guard at that entrance, and I know where he'll face when he needs a smoke.

I use Headspace a few times in a row before I develop a plan that even the bannik might've been proud of.

First, I take out my phone and summon a cab. Next, I navigate the stairs to the basement, picking up a heavy pipe on the way. Then I make my way to the exit, stopping at the door to check the status of my ride on the app.

Just like I foresaw, the app tells me that my car is

waiting outside. I message the driver that I'm almost there and that I'm going to tip well for a quick departure.

To make sure it's time, I inhale deeply at the keyhole.

Yep. It smells like an ashtray. He's smoking as per my visions.

Squeezing the pipe so hard my knuckles turn white, I open the door.

The guard has his back to me, as he's supposed to.

Suppressing a pang of guilt and channeling Jason Bourne, I smack the back of his head with the pipe.

He drops the cigarette but is still conscious—as expected.

So I smack him twice more—that's how many strikes it took in my visions.

Someone has a *very* thick skull.

He collapses, unconscious, and I stomp on his cigarette to make sure the building doesn't burn down.

In the last of my visions, I checked the guy's vitals and he was fine, so I don't bother this time around.

So far, so good. This next part, however, is uncharted territory, as my visions didn't extend that far.

Dragging in a breath, I sprint for the cab.

As I hoped, the driver didn't see what transpired. Not that it matters because I have a sob story about an abusive relationship, just in case.

As we pull away, I pretend to drop my phone to the

floor and look for it as we drive by where Thalia and the other guards are standing.

A few blocks later, I "locate" my phone, turn on the selfie mode, and use the camera to look behind us without turning.

No pursuit.

Score.

Gomorrah, here I come.

Ariel and Rasputin are going to be psyched to see me, though I guess Nero not so much.

Then something occurs to me: Felix might resent that I didn't give him a chance to ditch work and go see Ariel.

Well, that can easily be remedied.

I dial Felix's number, but he doesn't pick up.

I text him next, but no result either.

What is it with people and radio silence today?

As I ponder that, something about Felix's unresponsiveness rubs my intuition the wrong way, and a wave of angst spreads through me.

Crap.

Is he in trouble?

Quelling my sped-up breathing, I dive into Headspace as if it were a pool of icy water.

Unsurprisingly, the shapes that stalk me here play a terrifying tune.

Prepared to see a deadly future, I reach for the worst offender.

CHAPTER SIX

I'M BODILESS—AN indicator that it's not me but someone I care about who is in danger.

A bunch of strange men stand on a gray Manhattan sidewalk. Each is wearing a *kosovorotka,* which is a white linen shirt with an off-center collar and red embroidery—traditional Russian clothing that I've learned about during my language lessons.

The oldest of the gang sports a goatee and has matching traditional pants on, as well as *lapti*—shoes that are a close relative of straw baskets.

The younger guys are less hardcore, as they have jeans and sneakers on under their kosovorotkas.

"It's here," a guy with a hawkish nose says in Russian, pointing at a large gray building.

"Are you certain?" the older guy asks. "I don't mean to offend you, of course, but—"

"It's 120 West 24th Street," the younger dude replies

and flashes his smartphone screen at everyone. "Are you ever going to trust modern technology, sir?"

According to the GPS app on the screen, they are indeed where the guy says they are.

"What do you call this?" The older guy rolls his sleeve to reveal an ancient-looking wristwatch. "The rest of what you call modern technology is just a means to become scatterbrained."

When they don't think he can see them, the rest of his crew roll their eyes. The hawk-nosed one walks into the building and everyone follows. When they get into the elevator, they press the button for the seventh floor. Once there, they walk to apartment 7J, and the older guy politely knocks.

"Do you work for Mr. Preysler?" Felix asks from behind the door. "He didn't mention anyone would be stopping by."

Of course, it's Felix who's in danger. Thinking of him was what caused my malaise.

If I had a mouth, I'd urge Felix to run, but I can't.

"Sasha, would you please?" the older guy asks, confusing me until I see he's looking expectantly at the hawk-nosed one with the phone.

So this guy's name is also Sasha? I know my name is more commonly used as an abbreviation for Alexander in Russia, but living in America, I've never encountered a male Sasha before.

My namesake solemnly nods, pulls out lockpicks from his jeans, and makes short work of the door—proving we have more in common besides our names.

"Whoever you are, I've called the police," Felix yells from behind the door. "I'm also armed—"

The door swings open and my namesake steps in, followed by the rest of the young dudes.

Felix flees, and I hear some commotion inside.

The older guy walks in leisurely and follows the trail of broken furniture.

By the time he enters the office, his allies have Felix restrained in a large computer chair, with my namesake and a weaselly guy standing menacingly to the side.

"This is most unfortunate," the older guy says in accented English and shakes his head at the countless broken monitors on the floor. Then his gaze settles on Felix's terrified expression. "There was no need for unpleasantness. We're just here to ask you a few questions, that's all."

"Who are you?" Felix asks in English, his voice shaking. Then the outfits must register, because he switches to Russian. "What are you?"

"Call me Woland," the older guy says. "That is Sasha"—he nods at my namesake—"and that's Boris." He points at the weaselly dude.

"Sure," Felix mumbles under his breath, his eyes darting from Woland to Sasha and then to Boris. "That explains everything. Thanks."

"Just give us the information we need. Please," Woland says gently. "The alternative is a world of pain."

Felix shrinks in his chair. "What do you want to know?"

"Grigori Yefimovich Rasputin," Woland says. "Please tell us where we can find him."

My roommate visibly pales. "Rasputin? You mean like the mystic from history?"

"I'd rather not play games," Woland says tiredly. "I can practically smell that *mraz'* on you." Woland gets so far into Felix's face, his goatee touches my friend's cheek. "Please tell me where he is, or I'll be forced to hand you over to Sasha and Boris."

"I'm sorry." Felix's voice quivers. "I really don't know what you're talking about."

"Be so kind and show him your power," Woland says to his younger associates.

Closing his eyes, my namesake touches Felix's exposed wrist with a look of deep concentration on his face.

"Each of us has an affinity with an organ in the body," Woland says. "Sasha's is the brain." He looks at my namesake like a proud parent. "When he masters his power completely, he'll be able to force you to say what we need. For now, though, we have to use a more indirect approach." His tone turns almost apologetic. "Though pain is a complex neurological phenomenon, Sasha found a shortcut to it by overstimulating an area called the dorsal posterior insula. The effect is a magnification of the pain experience."

He nods at Boris, who grins nastily and flicks Felix's forehead with a finger.

Felix gasps as though he was struck with a baseball bat, his nostrils flaring and his eyes watering.

He doesn't scream, but I can tell he wants to.

"Do we understand each other now?" Woland asks. "Please tell me what I'd like to know."

"I can't tell you what I don't know," Felix gasps.

Shaking his head in disappointment, Woland nods at Boris—who grins and slaps Felix across the cheek with an open palm.

This time, Felix can't suppress a scream.

Actually, it sounds like the howl of a wounded animal.

When the screaming stops, Felix's breath is ragged and uneven, like he's about to suffocate.

Woland looks at all this disapprovingly, takes out a handkerchief, and wipes away one of the rivulets of sweat pouring down Felix's face.

"Please," Woland says. "He wouldn't suffer for you if the roles were reversed."

Gasping for air, Felix somehow still manages to shake his head.

Boris looks at Woland eagerly, and the older man nods.

Turning his hand into a fist, Boris punches Felix in the nose so hard there's a sound of bone breaking.

This time, Felix doesn't even scream. Instead, his eyes roll back and his body convulses as though he's having a seizure.

Then his breathing halts.

Boris looks at his boss in confusion, then back at Felix's ashen face.

Woland walks over to Felix and checks the pulse in his neck.

"The heart has stopped," he says, glaring at Boris disapprovingly. "You were supposed to slowly escalate the pain, not send him into shock."

"Well, you're the heart expert," Boris says defensively. "Can't you do something?"

"My specialty is stopping hearts, not starting them." Woland removes his hand from Felix's throat and makes as if he's going to touch Boris with his index finger—causing Boris to pull away as though the finger were a poisonous snake. Lowering the finger like a gunslinger holstering a weapon, Woland says, "Sasha, can you spark some part of his brain to get him to snap out of this?"

My namesake's brows furrow; then he opens his eyes and shakes his head.

"Let's try to solve this as humans would," Woland says. "Lay him down there." He points at the floor.

They follow his order, and when Felix is on his back, Woland forces Boris to compress Felix's chest while my namesake blows air into Felix's lungs.

A couple of compressions—and likely broken ribs— later, Woland touches Felix's neck again and looks pleased.

"He's going to live," he says and looks at Boris with an expression that seems to imply, "And therefore, so will you."

"I'm going to take away the pain of his injuries as he

comes to," my namesake says. "Then I can remove my aid or intensify the pain to resume the interrogation."

And on that sinister note, the vision cuts out.

CHAPTER SEVEN

"WE HAVE TO CHANGE OUR DESTINATION," I yell at the driver as soon as I find myself back in the cab. I rattle out the address from the vision and desperately try to think of what I can do to prevent the nightmare I just foresaw.

To start, I call and text Felix again, but I still can't reach him. He must have his phone turned off to focus on his work.

Next, I show myself a vision of what happens if I call the police.

Sadly, Felix's fate remains unchanged—the cops simply don't get to the scene in time.

Maybe I can ask Eric and Thalia to help me?

I leap into Headspace and learn that such a future isn't great either. My guards waste time by locking me in the apartment, and by the time they get to Felix, it's too late.

Returning to Headspace, I try about a thousand

variations of the Eric-and-Thalia option in case something I might say will convince them not to lock me up.

Nope.

I never manage to find the right words.

Fine.

Time to see what happens when I get there myself.

It's two against a dozen—what could possibly go wrong?

Just as I start focusing on my next entry into Headspace, the cab jerks to a stop, giving me whiplash.

Rubbing my neck, I look up to see the cause.

Wow.

We nearly ran over a blind man—at least I assume that's why he has that special walking stick, the dark glasses, and (most tellingly) a giant canine wearing a guide-dog getup.

Before I can recover from this first shock, the door next to me opens and a woman whooshes inside with supernatural speed.

A very familiar woman.

A woman I'm not ready to face—and probably never will be.

My biological mother, Lilith.

CHAPTER EIGHT

PARALYZED, I stare at Lilith as she taps the driver on the shoulder.

The cabby looks back as Lilith's eyes turn into mirrors. Silkily, she says, "You will follow my commands and not remember anything said in this car from this moment onward. Do you understand?"

Holy cow.

Lilith found me.

As the driver robotically repeats the glamour instructions, the guide dog leads the blind guy over to the front passenger seat.

The man gets inside and feels around for the safety belt, then fumbles with the buckle until it clicks in.

I only now register the fact that he has the Cognizant Mandate aura—and so does his "dog", who is probably not a dog but a werewolf or something similar.

The creature prances over to the back and leaps in.

It looks like a Siberian husky that's been fed growth hormones until it was the size of a pony, and it smells like a dog park.

"Seriously?" Lilith looks at the beast, who looks back with intelligent blue eyes and gives the mistress of evil a doggy grin.

Rolling her eyes, Lilith scoots away from the creature and so far into my personal space that I can name her perfume—Victoria's Secret's *Sexy Little Things Noir*.

I keep staring, my brain struggling to parse what I'm seeing.

"Drive," Lilith commands the enthralled cabbie. "Go as fast as you can."

The driver floors the gas, and the car rips forward.

Crap. There goes my chance to run. Not that I could really outrun the super-vampire that is Lilith.

At least the driver is still following the GPS directions to Felix's location.

"Watch out for that yellow cab," the maybe-not-blind man shouts at the driver with a French accent, pointing to the left.

We swerve a moment before the collision, and the adrenaline clears my brain enough for me to blurt out, "You're Lilith."

It's not my most brilliant observation, but hey, at least I managed to complete a sentence and express a semi-coherent thought.

Lilith looks at me with maternal pride, then shakes her strange companion by the shoulder and says in

Russian, "You see, Michel, she really *is* a seer. Must've seen me in some vision already. How marvelous is that?"

"O ye of little faith," the man—Michel—says to her sarcastically in Russian, his French accent still noticeable. "I *told* you that your child with Rasputin would be a seer, and she is. You can be—"

"Hush, Michel. You're ruining the surprise." Turning to face me, she turns up her smile by a few gigawatts and triumphantly announces, "Sasha, I am your mommy."

CHAPTER NINE

I ALMOST EXPECT her to add, "Search your feelings, you know it to be true."

Of course, I was already pretty sure she's my mother, but hearing her admit it dispels what little doubt I still had—and makes my head spin at the same time because it doesn't explain what's happening at all.

Not even a little bit.

I force my brain to function. "What are you doing here? Who is he?" I gesture at her blind companion.

"I'm saving your life, of course," Lilith says. "According to my sources"—she glances at Michel —"you're on your way to face a group of *chorts* by yourself. They're nasty creatures—and extremely dangerous. Even to someone as powerful as I am."

Did she just say "chorts?" As in, the plural of "chort"—a demon-like creature from Russian folklore?

To this day, Russians curse using the word. There are expressions such as "thousands of chorts" (something you'd say when stubbing your foot on a coffee table) and "go to the chort" (a common response when a guy you don't like makes an indecent proposal).

If chorts are a type of Cognizant, they must be quite formidable with all that human adoration powering them.

"Rushing to face the chorts," Michel grumbles and shakes his head. "One wonders where the girl gets her impulsiveness from?"

"Hey now," Lilith says. "I think you mean where she gets her *bravery* from—and that, indeed, would be from *moi*."

I watch their exchange in disbelief. Is this really the evil vampire goddess whose world we barely escaped from? "What do you mean you're here to 'save my life?'" I blurt. "And are chorts a type of—" Glancing at the glamoured driver, I lower my voice just in case. "Are chorts like us?"

"Yes," she says. "Nasty things, can make your organs go all screwy."

"Great," I mutter. "And who or what is he?" I glance at Michel.

The man harrumphs. "Since someone rudely forgot to introduce me, allow me to do so myself." Turning around, he extends his hand slightly to my right. "They call me Nostradamus. I am a seer of some renown and—"

"Some. Right." I shake the hand, fighting a hysterical giggle. "Yeah, I might have heard that name once or twice."

"Good." He pulls his hand away. "Then you should believe me when I say I've looked into the futures where Lilith and I did *not* help you save your friend. In some, the chorts torture you to make your friend talk, and in others, they torture *him* and you spill the haricots." He shakes his head, making his sunglasses move—which allows me to see some old scars underneath. "Once they learn where Rasputin is located—and they do in almost all the futures—they kill you both to make sure you can't warn him that they're coming."

He stops talking to let the information sink in.

The idea of someone hurting Felix to make me talk is unthinkable, but now that he mentions it, that could've easily been the result of my rescue.

And, if what he says is true, being spared that fate is a huge favor.

Is that what Lilith is after? Is she trying to get on my good side?

Assuming all of this is true, of course.

I should jump into Headspace and check—

"Do not look into the future," Nostradamus says urgently, as if reading my mind. "I carefully curated the outcome I want, but if you know what happens, you're likely to alter it, and then we might—"

"Fine," I say, though now my temptation to look into the future is much stronger. "If it means we can save Felix, I won't risk messing it up."

Except, what if they're here to kidnap me? What if they have no intention of helping Felix?

Well, for starters, they'd need to change the GPS, which they didn't. Also, if they are kidnapping me, the truth will be glaringly obvious soon, so—

"Even with us there, the encounter is still risky," Lilith says, her expression turning serious. "Are you sure your little friend is worth saving? Or your father, for that matter?"

"Yes, obviously." I glare at her. "They're worth more than a hundred of you, *Mom*."

As if to punctuate my words, the driver makes a sharp right, causing the dog to whimper.

"Wow." Lilith looks at Nostradamus. "I know you said she'd say those exact words if I pushed, but wow." She makes puppy eyes at me and in the voice of a five-year-old says, "That hurts my feelings."

"Boo-hoo," I say, matching her tone. "What are you *really* doing here? And please don't say you're helping me out of your maternal instincts or trying to save Rasputin—the man you tortured and kept in your dungeon."

Her eyebrows lift. "Is that what he told you? What about my conjugal visits? What about—"

"I'm going to puke," I mutter. Then, sarcastically, I add, "But please, keep telling me how you're the best thing for Rasputin."

"Well, how about the fact that I'm the only reason the St. Petersburg Council never had a clue where to even start looking for dear Grisha?" Lilith says. "When he was in my care, he was shielded by my formidable luck. Once your boytoy Nero got him out, however, all bets were off." She touches the tattoo on her temple. "I imagine your friend's name happened to occur to one of their probability manipulators as a way to locate him, or one of their seers gleaned him as a way—"

"Unbelievable." I fold my arms across my chest. "And I mean that literally—as in, I don't believe you."

"That's your prerogative, of course," Lilith says. "But tell me, why would I need to lie?"

Our driver slams on the breaks, cutting off the long tirade I was about to unleash.

"We're here," Nostradamus says and pulls out something from his jacket. "Put these on." Turning, he offers us a pair of surgical gloves and a couple of creepy-looking rubber masks.

"Why?" I ask, not touching the stuff.

"Because chorts need skin contact in order to mess with your organs," Lilith says mockingly, putting on her gear. "You don't want that—even if the organs in question are sexual ones."

If I survive this, I may need to teach Lilith the concept of too much information.

And conscience.

She could really use some of that.

Nostradamus is still dangling the gloves and mask in the air in front of me, so I take them. And since I don't like the idea of organ failure—and don't see how wearing this stuff could benefit Lilith in some sinister way—I put it on.

The dog exits the car, walks to Nostradamus's door, and waits.

The seer gets out and grabs the guiding straps.

The pair rush toward the building, with Lilith on their tails.

I pinch myself to make sure this isn't a strange dream, then follow.

When the dog and the seer reach the elevator, Nostradamus presses the button as if he *can* see it.

"Are you visually impaired?" I can't help but ask.

"I don't have eyes, if that's what you mean," Nostradamus says. "But I can and *do* have visions of my near future all the time, which allows me to know where certain things will be and—"

"Wait," I say. "So seer visions don't require actual eyesight?"

"Not in my case," he says as the elevator opens. "Though, to be fair, I wasn't born this way, and I have no clue if a seer born blind would be able to foretell the future. I imagine it would still be possible, but I simply don't know."

As if to illustrate his point, he reaches out and presses the seventh-floor button on the first try and without feeling for it.

I sneak a peek at his scars again and wish I didn't. The last thing I want is to feel bad for Lilith's ally—which I can't help but do. Whatever happened to his eyes must've been the stuff of nightmares.

"Tartarus did that," Lilith says, following my gaze. Then she puts a reassuring hand on Nostradamus's shoulder.

"That *monstre* has a lot to answer for."

Nostradamus's face contorts into a mask of hatred that looks foreign on his features.

The dog whines, and I look away from the scars. Clearing my throat, I decide to change the subject. "And who's this big guy?" I ask, waving at the dog.

"Marius," Nostradamus says.

"Humpius," Lilith says at the same time.

The dog looks up and shows Lilith his teeth.

"And *what* is he?" I ask, studying his aura.

"Technically, a werewolf," Lilith says. "Except no one has ever seen him outside this form. Yet another victim of you-know-who—"

The elevator dings, cutting off my follow-up questions.

"Right," Lilith says. "I think I'll go in first. The rest of you just watch my back."

"Shouldn't he be in charge?" I nod at Nostradamus —who's putting on his own mask and gloves as we speak.

"No, dear. *I'm* always in charge." She winks at me. "Michel said to 'do my thing' when we get to this point, so I plan to."

Without further ado, she blurs down the corridor, and I sprint after her. I'm not about to trust her with Felix's life; after all, the woman is supposed to be vindictive. What if all this is a very elaborate ruse to hurt him?

Thankfully, catching up isn't hard. When Lilith gets to the already-opened door, she slows down and creeps forward.

Moving as quietly as I can, I follow, though my steps aren't nearly as soft as those of Lilith. She makes no sound at all—as if she's hovering just above the ground.

Come to think of it, maybe she is. She was defying gravity without any effort on her own world.

I glance back. Nostradamus is walking around a coffee table that even a sighted person could've bumped into, and Marius is clearly channeling his inner and outer wolf as he creeps forward.

"He's going to live," I hear Woland say as we near the office where everything is taking place. "And therefore, so will you."

Crap.

This means we didn't prevent Felix from getting badly hurt. They've already tortured him, then performed that rib-breaking CPR as per my vision.

Just like in that vision, the Sasha chort says, "I'm going to take away the pain of his injuries as he comes to. Then I can remove my aid or—"

Moving like the ghost of a ninja, Lilith glides into the office, and a pain-filled shriek reverberates through the apartment.

CHAPTER TEN

WOLAND—THE polite older chort with the goatee—whooshes out of the office, leaving his screaming colleagues behind.

He looks upset—at least until he spots the person in his way.

Me.

My martial arts training kicking in, I throw a punch at his face.

Instead of connecting, my fist goes through his cheek as if it were a cloud of vapor. All of Woland, in fact, suddenly looks like a cloud of vapor or a hologram.

Did he just turn incorporeal?

Fighting a swell of jealousy at this stage-worthy power, I jerk my hand away.

Woland's head re-solidifies, making his scowl more visible.

I must be stunned or confused, because I miss it

when he leaps away from me and sprints down the corridor.

Marius jumps up.

Woland dodges the werewolf's massive jaws and dives under Nostradamus's extended arm, going straight for the exit.

Before I can even think the word "chase," another chort runs out of the office.

It's Boris, the asshole who hit Felix.

Though I usually fight out of necessity, this guy I really want to hurt.

So I throw a vicious punch at his annoying face.

Instead of using Woland's trick, Boris simply dodges my strike, then hits me in the chest.

I don't even want to guess how much this would've hurt if I'd been under chort mojo, like Felix. As is, my solar plexus screams in agony as I bend over, gasping for air.

Through my watery eyes, I see Boris heading for the door—which is when Marius leaps at him, giant canine teeth bared.

Only those teeth go through a mirage of an appendage instead of Boris's forearm.

Apparently, Boris *can* do that trick when he wants to.

Must be a chort thing. No wonder Lilith said they were powerful.

Speaking of mother dearest, a new wave of sounds from the office reminds me of a slaughterhouse in hell.

Hearing the horrific screams, Boris re-solidifies his arm and leaps for the door.

Another chort escapes the office, whooshing right by me since I'm still catching my breath.

Nostradamus, who's still by the coffee table, extends his foot, tripping the bastard.

The chort goes flying—right into Marius's maw. The werewolf's teeth clamp on the throat of the chort before he knows what hit him—and more importantly, before he goes all ghostly.

With a gurgling sound, the chort tries to rip the beast away from him, but Marius's jaws are locked too tightly on the chort's neck.

Within seconds, the chort goes limp, and then his dead body turns ghostly and disappears, leaving behind nothing—not even the clothes.

I stare at the empty spot, then at Marius.

Even the blood around the werewolf's mouth is gone without a trace.

"That's chorts for you," Nostradamus says before I get a chance to ask. "They phase one last time when they die."

I finally manage to gulp in enough air and hurry into the office.

Felix is unconscious on the floor, and there are bits and pieces of chorts all around the office, especially on the shards of the broken windows.

The owners of the gore lie there with tell-tale vampire wounds on their necks, but clearly not dead—else they'd be gone.

Lilith stands over the Sasha chort in a classic vampire-drinking-blood position. Hearing my ragged breathing, she looks up and smiles a bloody smile.

"When you start drinking from them, they can't do their annoying phasing for a while," she explains, her extended vampire fangs giving her a little lisp. "That's why they fear vampires so much."

She looks down at the horrified Sasha and playfully musses his hair.

Ignoring her, I kneel next to Felix and check his vitals.

He has a heartbeat, but it's barely detectible.

I'm not a doctor, but my roommate looks bad.

Really bad.

"I can fix him for you," Lilith says, her voice back to normal. "Just say the word."

I look up, narrowing my eyes at her. "How?"

"My blood," she says. "How else?"

Oh, hell, no. Been there, done that with Ariel. "So you want to make him addicted? Is that your plan? To use Felix to—"

"Don't be silly." She walks up to the desk and picks up a blood-splattered water bottle.

Unscrewing the cap, she opens her mouth, and her right fang extends. Reaching for the tooth with her pinky, she pierces her skin, then squeezes the tiniest droplet of blood into the water bottle, screws the cap back on, and gives it a good shake.

"If he drinks just a drop of this, he'll recover and not be addicted in the slightest," she explains, handing me the bottle. "The choice is yours, of course. If you don't trust me, you can take your chances with human doctors."

"Which would lead to his death," Nostradamus says solemnly, walking in.

Sure.

I'll take their word for it.

Not.

Taking in a calming breath, I focus on Felix's fate and leap into Headspace.

———

TWO CLOUDS of shapes appear to me.

One set scary-sounding and the other not.

So far, this seems to support what Nostradamus said, but I have to know for sure.

I sprout two ethereal wisps and touch two random shapes from each of the clouds.

———

OVERFLOWING WITH GRIEF, I stare blankly at the round-faced EMT guy.

"Again, I'm so sorry," he says, looking down at Felix's cooling body. "I wish—"

———

I'M BODILESS.

Felix and Maya are sitting in the kitchen of our apartment, with him munching away on a potato salad and her looking at him worriedly.

"No, Maya," he says. "I still don't feel any urge to drink vampire blood, especially from Sasha's mother, of all people."

"It's only been a week," she says. "What if the craving starts later?"

"That's not how this works." He puts his hand on hers. "The craving starts right away or not at all. Trust me, I asked a lot—"

———

I'M BACK in the blood-splattered office, with Lilith, Nostradamus, and Marius looking at me expectantly.

"Give him the blood." I start taking off my gloves and mask. "Let's also move him out of here so he doesn't faint from seeing all this blood."

Lilith walks over to Felix and forces a droplet of the blood-infused water into his mouth.

He almost instantly looks healthier.

His broken nose begins to align back, and his breathing returns to normal.

Carefully picking him up, Lilith takes him to the bathroom and places him into the bathtub.

Then Marius and I stare at him intently while Lilith and Nostradamus take off their own gloves and masks.

Felix opens his eyes and looks around wildly before his gaze settles on me.

"Sasha," he gasps, sitting up. "What's going on?"

"Michel, can you be a dear and explain the situation to him?" Lilith says, and before I can object, she grabs my upper arm in a steely grip and leads me back into the blood-covered office.

"Nostradamus says human police are on their way." She wrinkles her nose. "We need to clean up this mess and leave before they arrive."

As if to demonstrate her point, she viciously kicks one of the wounded chorts in the head.

There's a crack of skull breaking, followed by the mushy sound of a foot decimating a brain.

Though my stomach is stronger than Felix's, I feel bile coming up.

Unsurprisingly, the chort dematerializes, as does some of the blood and gore around the office.

Leave it to my psychopathic progenitor to call *that* "clean up."

The rest of the chorts must realize their fate because they start wailing and begging for their lives.

Lilith gives them a chilling smile in response, then rips off one's head—paradoxically making the room a little bit cleaner still.

"That one is yours." She nods at the Sasha chort. "He caused Felix all that pain, so I suggest you return the favor."

"I was just following orders," the chort gasps out. "I—"

I'll never know how he was going to try to talk his way out of this situation because Lilith kneels next to him, pries open his mouth, and rips out his tongue.

It's official.

I just threw up in my mouth.

The rest of the chorts gasp in horror, and my namesake's eyes roll back as he starts twitching like he's being electrocuted.

"I know what you're thinking." Looking at me, Lilith lifts the tongue and swallows the blood dripping from it with relish. "How is he going to eat ice cream now?"

I stare at her blankly, then look at the sorry torturer at my feet.

"Go on," Lilith says. "Finish him."

My heartbeat accelerates as Rasputin's memory swirls through my head. I witnessed it thanks to our Headspace conversation, and in it, he'd had a vision of a future where a child version of me was murdering people.

Obviously, it was mommy dearest who was making that version of me do that, and now I wonder why.

Was she trying to make me more like herself? Or toughening me up in this macabre way?

Whatever Lilith's reasons in Rasputin's vision, this is similar. In fact, *this* might be why she's helping me in the first place. Except I don't see how she benefits from turning me into a cold-blooded killer. Maybe it's some sort of psychotic family legacy thing? Some doctors want their kids to grow up a doctor, and she wants hers to be a serial killer?

Too bad for her I'm in no mood to follow in *those* footsteps.

"You finish him," I say, turning to leave. "I'm going to be with Felix."

"But he hurt your little friend." She sounds genuinely confused by my lack of bloodlust. "How could you not want to rip out his liver?"

"You're right. Something must be wrong with me," I say flatly. "Maybe I should see a professional."

Trying to shut out the sounds of ripping flesh resuming behind me, I make my way to the bathroom and slam the door closed to make sure Felix doesn't hear anything.

Nostradamus and Marius intercept me by the door. "I told her you're not going to kill anybody," the seer says in a low voice. "But she hoped her luck would overrule my prediction, since sometimes it can."

"Uh-huh. Sure." I'll unpack that later. For now, I step around the seer to examine Felix—and breathe a sigh of relief. Though my friend is still sitting in the tub, he's looking much better, and all the chort blood is gone from his body—no doubt because Lilith has already massacred everyone.

"How are you?" I ask him, kneeling next to the tub.

"Fine." Felix rubs his no-longer-broken nose. "Just having trouble with all this." He nods at the giant canine and the elderly seer.

"I know," I say. "I haven't digested it either."

As if my statement were her cue, Lilith walks in—not a single drop of blood left on her stylish outfit.

"Hi there. I'm Lilith." She extends her delicate hand to Felix.

I half-expect him to kiss the hand as if he were a knight and she "Her Ladyship," but he gives it a limp shake, mumbling something that sounds like, "Pleasure to meet you."

"The police will be here in a few minutes," Nostradamus says, then looks at Felix. "Remember what I told you."

"Right. I had to help another client and wasn't here when the break-in occurred." My roommate frowns at the seer. "Are you sure that will work?"

"I've seen it," Nostradamus says. "But even if I didn't, think about it. Nothing of value has been taken. There are no bodies. No—"

"Let's just go, Felix." Rising to my feet, I extend my hand to help him get out of the tub.

He stands up shakily, then carefully steps out of the tub.

As he exits the bathroom, his gait and demeanor become more and more normal.

Lilith's blood is potent stuff.

A neighbor peeks from behind her door as we enter the corridor. Lilith captures her gaze and does her glamour thing to make the lady remember large male criminal types breaking into the apartment instead of us.

As we ride the elevator down, I look at Felix and

clear my throat. "You'll have to stay at the apartment for a while."

"Oh?" he asks. "Why is that?"

"Woland and Boris escaped," I explain. "They might get you again."

My roommate pales.

"Not just those two," Lilith says. "A few chorts jumped out of the window. If they timed their phasing properly, they could've survived the fall."

"Right," Felix says weakly. "Sounds like I'm staying home."

I pat his shoulder. "I did see you alive a week from now in a vision. And you were craving-free." I nod at Lilith.

Some color returns to Felix's face, but then he looks at Lilith—who gives him what she must consider a seductive smile. In reality, it's rather creepy.

He turns ghost white again.

Oblivious, she says excitedly, "We should all hang out before you officially become a shut-in. You know, stop by a museum, take a stroll in Central Park, visit the—"

"As much as we'd love to play tourists with you, Felix has his work and I have a prior commitment," I say, doing my best to keep the sarcasm out of my voice.

Lilith pouts. "That's a pity. I want to get to know you. How about we hang out after you're done with your errands?"

"Let me think about it," I say carefully. "For now, I need to bring Felix home."

"Fair enough." She grins at me as the elevator doors open.

Letting everyone go ahead, I use my phone to summon a cab and put two stops into the app—our apartment to drop off Felix, and JFK to finally catch up with Nero.

"I still can't believe I was attacked by chorts, of all possible creatures," Felix says once we're outside. "I've heard about them, of course, but I never expected to meet one in the flesh. Not in America, at least."

"That was a fair assumption." Nostradamus pushes his shades higher up his nose. "That lot works for the St. Petersburg Council. Woland is the head Enforcer there."

"They're Enforcers?" I instinctively turn to meet Nostradamus's gaze, but then spot the scars and realize my faux pas. "Shouldn't they be vampires?"

"Not always," he says. "There are no vampires in or around St. Petersburg. Woland and his people killed the more stubborn ones, and the rest thought it wise to move elsewhere."

Interesting. I wonder if that's why Vlad left his homeland. Then again, I'd classify him more as the stubborn kind of vampire.

"Wasn't Baba Yaga on the St. Petersburg Council?" Felix whispers, as though the deceased witch might hear him.

"Yes, she was, a long time ago," Nostradamus says. "She was one of the nice ones."

"Baba Yaga was one of the nice ones?" I look at him

for any sign of this being a bad joke. "Then what's the rest of the Council like?"

"Russia's history should give you a clue when it comes to that," Nostradamus says. "Whereas our Councils usually stay out of human affairs, such is not the case for the Moscow and St. Petersburg ones."

I blink. "Are you saying that things like the revolution, then Stalin and—"

"Yes." Nostradamus leans down and scratches Marius behind the ear. "Recently, they decided to stop meddling as much, so hopefully, things will improve with time."

"Wow," Felix says. "And *this* is who's looking for Rasputin? The St. Petersburg Council?"

"I doubt it." Nostradamus turns toward Felix. "They've probably long forgotten Rasputin's misconduct, just never called off the official execution order. That's not why Woland is doing this. It's personal for him."

"You see," Lilith chimes in excitedly, "before he met me and fell hopelessly in love, your father had a little crush on your namesake, the tsarina. This is what led to his exposure and pariah status—but, more importantly for Woland, there was the issue with the prince's alleged hemophilia." She runs her hand through her hair in a familiar fashion—the exact way I do it. "Long story short, it was Woland's daughter who'd been preventing the boy's blood from clotting— a lot of chorts have that particular power. In his effort to remove her from the royal household, Grigori had her removed more permanently from existence. He claims it was an accident, but I doubt Woland cares about such minutia."

My phone dings, informing me that our cab has arrived.

I almost don't want to leave.

I'm curious to learn more about my father's past—even if that's part of Lilith's evil plan.

And of course it is.

I can see it from the smirk on her face.

The same kind of smirk I'd have on *my* face if I had my hooks into someone.

"We better go," I tell Felix.

"Right," he says, then looks at Lilith. "Thank you."

"Yeah," I say reluctantly. "Thanks for helping me. I might've had trouble dealing with those chorts on my own."

"How about you give me a hug, and we'll call it even?" she says, grinning.

Crap.

I walked into that one.

Approaching my mother as carefully as I would a poisonous cactus, I give her a reluctant hug.

For a vampire, she's pretty warm and smells nice—and not just from Victoria's Secret's *Sexy Little Things Noir*.

I let her go and awkwardly stumble toward the cab.

"Bye, Nostradamus," Felix says. "Bye, Lilith."

"Bye, Sasha's little friend," Lilith says mockingly. "Stay safe."

Was that last bit a threat?

Marius whines like a dog. I guess that's *his* goodbye.

Before Lilith changes her mind and decides to kidnap me after all, I grab Felix's shoulder and shepherd him into the cab.

CHAPTER ELEVEN

"DUDE," Felix says as soon as the car departs.

"Dude," I reply, matching his tone.

"That was—"

"Yep," I say.

"But she—"

"I know."

Seemingly running out of things to say, we sit there, each processing the recent events.

"How about you tell me everything," Felix finally says, rubbing his temples in a circular motion.

So I tell him what little there is to tell: I was on my way to save him when Nostradamus and Lilith intercepted me. Switching to Russian so the driver doesn't hear any Cognizant stuff, I fill him in on the altercation with the chorts.

"But what does this mean?" Felix says when I'm done. "Is Lilith not as evil as we thought?"

"I wish I knew." I realize I never buckled up, so I do

so now. "The cynic in me says there was nothing maternal in that encounter. She needs me for something, and my dying as part of that rescue effort wasn't convenient for her. But of course, the more naïve part of me can't help but hope there was more to it. Maybe she has a beating heart, after all. Do vampires physically have those, by the way?"

"I think they do," he says, then waves his hand. "What about Nostradamus? What's his deal?"

"I don't have a good read on the guy," I say and wonder if Nostradamus might've already heard this very conversation in one of his visions. "Given the mess with Darian, I'm making it my policy to not trust seers too much—my father included."

"I have the same policy." He winks at me. "Barely trust even you."

"I wouldn't trust me either." I grin. "I once seriously thought my TV name would be Sasha Devious."

Felix chuckles. "Your TV magician name, or if you ended up in porn? Because it sounds more suitable for the latter. Or for stripping."

I give him a mock frown. "In your dreams. The only reason I won't smack your shoulder is your recent brush with death."

At my reminder, he pats himself all over, then shakes his head in wonder. "I can't believe I'm okay."

"Are you sure you are?"

"Yeah. It's like that time Isis healed me, but somehow even better."

I frown at him. "Don't dwell on any good feelings her healing gave you. That way lies addiction."

He grimaces. "You've got a point. I think I'm going to dive back into coding—distract myself as I recover."

"Good thinking. Play video games too, or watch TV."

Felix nods, and we ride in silence for a few moments until something occurs to me. Turning to Felix, I say, "Thank you."

"For what?" His unibrow curls in bafflement.

"For not telling Woland and co. where Rasputin is. I'm not sure if I would've been as strong as you if they were hurting me like that."

A visible shudder ripples over Felix's skin. "I think I was just too scared to talk. If there had been a round two, I'm not sure I'd—"

"I wouldn't have blamed you if you told them." I reach over and squeeze his hand. "I'm sorry you got drawn into my mess again. I'm like a curse. The worst f—"

"Oh, shut up." He rolls his eyes. "You saw what the chorts are capable of and rushed to save me—without backup or even a plan, mind you. I don't know if I would've been able to do that in your place."

"I'm sure you would've. You're braver and stronger than you think."

He starts to respond, but the car stops and I realize we're next to our building.

"Crap," I hiss, ducking down as quickly as I can.

"What are you doing?" Felix frowns at me.

"I'm not going home," I whisper-hiss from the bottom of the seat. "If Thalia and the goons see me, she might try to *make* me go."

"Hold on. If not home, where are you going?"

"I want to locate Nero. And before you ask, you're not coming with me. Not after what just happened."

"But—"

"Please go. If they see you dallying, they might get suspicious."

He looks at me, then longingly at the building.

"Dude, I'm begging you." I make my trademarked puppy eyes at him, figuring there's never been a better time to play dirty.

"Fine," he grumbles and opens the door. "But for the record, I don't like this."

"Noted. I definitely owe you one."

Felix leaves, and the cab proceeds to the second leg of our trip—the JFK airport.

I wait a few blocks before I sit up.

Crap.

We're stuck in traffic.

I peel my eyes away from the million cars and mentally replay the encounter with Lilith.

Was she genuine when she said she wanted to get to know me?

It's hard to say.

I'm not sure what I expected from my first meeting with my biological mother, but it was nothing like what happened.

Once on Gomorrah, I'm going to have to question

Rasputin in greater detail about Lilith. If it's true that he loved her at some point in the past, perhaps she's not all bad?

Or more likely, she's just *that* good of an actress... or in bed.

Shaking my head to clear it of any libido-destroying images of parental sex life, I think of Nero instead, which makes me wonder if I can still catch him on Gomorrah.

Closing my eyes, I jump into Headspace in order to find out.

———

IGNORING the default shapes in front of me, I start to focus on Nero's essence, but then I stop myself.

I don't just need *any* vision about Nero. I specifically need a near-future one—else I might see him on his quest when he's done with Gomorrah. That would be interesting in and of itself, but not my current goal.

This makes me realize I have a huge gap when it comes to my seer power.

I have no clue how to control how far into the future my visions reach.

Wow.

I can't believe I never thought of this before.

So far, my visions would show me events that ranged from a few days in the future to a few moments, but I've never had control over which.

Nor have I ever seen further than a few days into the future.

This is definitely something I'll need to ask my father about, as there has to be a way. Off the top of my head, Darian saw what I must assume is a distant possible future where he and I became lovers—a future that never came to be.

Remembering Darian casts a dark shadow on my current plans. He made a big deal about me "choosing Nero." In fact, he made it clear that this choice will cost me my life.

Could going to Gomorrah right now count as "choosing?"

As if I needed another good reason to want to see far into my own future... Unless, of course, I haven't seen far into my future for the simple reason that I don't actually have one—being dead as Darian predicted.

Well, *that* chain of thought escalated quickly.

Maybe I should do my best to see a near-future vision with Nero, then poke around my own more distant future to see if I'm alive.

"I want to see Nero a few minutes from now," I tell myself, in case I'm lucky and the trick of when the vision takes place is *this* easy.

Nothing happens.

I then think of Nero's essence in the usual way—and this works better. I get surrounded by extremely calm-seeming shapes.

All right. At least no one is getting killed in these visions.

That's a welcome change—and seems to indicate I got Nero while he's still on Gomorrah, as I'd hoped. Something tells me once he leaves, things will get more intense quickly. Otherwise, he wouldn't need powerful allies.

Excited by my success, I grab a shape and plunge into a vision.

CHAPTER TWELVE

I'M BODILESS—SO there goes my secret hope I'd see myself talking to Nero in his club, or elsewhere on Gomorrah.

Worse still, this isn't Gomorrah.

Around me is a beach surrounded by an ocean that spans to the horizon on all three sides. Above is a perfect blue sky with fluffy clouds. Deeper inland is an idyllic-looking small town that seems to have jumped straight out of ancient Greece.

Continuing the theme of ancient Greece are the mouthwateringly good-looking men frolicking on the beach. They're wearing the kind of skimpy outfits the Spartans wore in the movie *300*—with lots of powerful legs, washboard abs, and bulging pecs on display.

They also look familiar for some reason.

I then notice that they're all sporting a tan appropriate for the nice weather—all except for one guy, the one they all seem to be attacking.

He looks so pale I suspect he needs serious vitamin D supplementation.

Dodging a strike, the pale guy turns my way, and I recognize him.

It's Vlad—only I've never seen him dressed in so little clothing.

It looks good on him. Or rather, not on him.

What's also odd is that Vlad doesn't look as broody as I'd expect—no doubt thanks to the fierce concentration on his face.

Another tan guy swings a fist at Vlad's face, but the vampire jumps out of his reach, then punches the man in the gut.

The next warrior attacks Vlad, then another and another.

Hold on. How is this a vision about Nero?

Then I see him.

Nero is standing by the shore, away from the fighting, with Kit and Isis by his side.

Vlad notices them too. He barks something in an unfamiliar language, and the fierce fighters halt their attacks.

Which is when I recognize them.

Or I think I do.

The last time I checked on Vlad, he was training a group of boys to wield a sword.

If you took those boys and waited twenty years, this is probably what they would grow up to look like. But that makes no sense—unless these dudes are the fathers of the boys?

With the fight over, Vlad's face turns broody again. He walks over to Nero and looks his fellow Council members up and down. "Nero. Kit." He pointedly ignores Isis.

"Time flows much too fast here on Atlantis, so I'm going to make this as quick as I can," Nero growls. "I'm here to give you a chance to repay the favor you owe me. I'm gathering an army to reclaim my birthright. I won't sugarcoat this; the mission will be extremely dangerous. It will—"

"I'm in," Vlad says without hesitation.

"Good," Nero says. "How long do you need to get ready?"

"Hold on," Kit says and turns herself into the most fit of the warriors Vlad fought a moment ago. "Those scrumptious opponents of yours don't seem human." She turns into another one. "What are they?"

"Strongmen," Vlad says. "They claim to be descendants of Hercules himself, but I guess most of their kind do."

Wait a moment.

Ariel said she's a descendant of Hercules. Does that mean these *300* guys are the same type of Cognizant as Ariel? If so, whose bright idea was it to call them strong*men*? Shouldn't it be something like strongpeople?

"That was a good display of skill," Nero says and gives Ariel's kin an approving look.

I study them also and wonder if amazing looks are

part of the package, along with super speed and strength.

"Sometimes they're too good," Vlad says proudly and displays his hand.

Wow.

He's missing the tip of his right pinky finger. He must've lost it in a sword fight with these guys, and I guess even with all his vampire-healing ability, he couldn't regrow *that*.

The weird thing is that he's not pissed about it in the slightest.

"Impressive," Nero says, looking at what's left of the finger.

He then looks at Isis, but she shakes her head. "I can't heal his kind—nor can I regrow appendages."

Vlad drops his arm, as if he hates the idea of re-growing that finger. "I've trained this lot since they were pups," he says. "Like many of their kind, they're mercenaries, as are most others in the village. If you were to mention gold and glory, you could easily persuade them to join your—"

———

I FIND myself back in the cab, so I jump right back into Headspace.

I was right. The men Vlad was fighting/training are the same boys I saw earlier. But how? Do the so-called strongmen age faster than normal?

That doesn't seem to be the case for Ariel.

Then I recall Nero mentioning that time flows fast on that world. Is that what happened? Has it been something like twenty years for Vlad since the last time I saw him? That would explain why he seems a little healthier, less grief-stricken.

Yes, that makes sense. It might even have been his plan—escape to Atlantis to recover without anyone on Earth really noticing his absence. No doubt he did it because he takes his Enforcer duties seriously, yet was in no condition to perform them after the funeral.

In any case, if I survive "choosing Nero," I'm going to need to learn a route to this Atlantis place and take a deserved vacation during which no one would even notice that I'm gone.

Maybe I'll take Nero with me and have him dress up like Vlad and his students. I'll even—

Never mind. Right now, I need to get myself a vision of something that happens to Nero before this Vlad-gathering expedition.

Except, how?

Maybe I can ask another seer to help out?

I try to reach Rasputin.

No luck. He clearly hasn't recovered yet.

I seek the bannik next, but he isn't reachable either.

I could reach out to Nostradamus in this way, but given the company he keeps, I don't think I should.

Maybe I could make this work Peter Pan style, by wishing really hard?

So I do that. I wish to see a vision of Nero before he leaves Gomorrah. Wish it with all my being—with the same intensity as I wished for a pony for my seventh birthday.

Quickly, before the power of the wishing dissipates, I focus on Nero's essence.

Another bunch of safe-sounding vision-shapes surrounds me.

I touch one, wishing for good measure that it's the one I need.

———

I'M bodiless and not on Gomorrah again.

Either wishing isn't the way to get what I want, or it's simply impossible to catch Nero on Gomorrah because he already left it.

Like Atlantis, this world lacks any sign of modern technological advancements.

In fact, if the mud huts are anything to go by, this place is at an even earlier point of development.

Then I realize something odd about the huts.

They are immense.

Nero looks like a small kid standing next to one, as do Isis and Kit.

Vlad is with them, and so is the *300* squad, plus a number of people that look vaguely familiar. I think they might be from the New York Council, but I wouldn't bet my life on that.

Only one person isn't dwarfed by the huts, and it's a guy I've definitely seen during my encounters with the

New York Council—the being who did the Rite and whom I guessed to be a giant.

Except he's wearing what looks like riot gear—as are, in fact, many of Nero's allies.

Looks like I might've been right. Giants must exist.

Interestingly, for someone coming back to his homeland, this dude doesn't look happy to be here.

Extremely *un*happy would be a more accurate description of the expression on that massive face.

"I'm sorry, Colton," Nero says, apparently also noticing the guy's mood. "I know I'm asking a lot."

"But we're even after this?" the giant—Colton—booms. "Even if he tells you to go to hell?"

"Yes," Nero says. "Introduce me, and we're even."

Colton's enormous shoulders sag; then he inhales a breath so big I half-expect him to huff and puff and bring one of the huts down.

"Father!" he yells in a voice deep enough to drown in. "Your runt has returned."

The runt? How big are—

———

I'M BACK in the cab, reeling.

Sounds like whatever Nero is about to do, he's calling in every favor and hiring some serious help.

Also, I clearly suck at controlling the timing of my visions—Vlad was in this one, which means this was *further* in the future compared to the vision I saw right before.

Maybe I try again?

When I do, I get a vision that's further still—as Nero's crew here includes a plague (or maybe a horde) of giants.

Wearing bronze armor, they're armed to the teeth with an assortment of sharp and blunt weapons, and are indeed so big that they make Colton seem like the runt of the tribe.

He might pass for a human with an overzealous pituitary gland, but his ten-foot-plus brethren would never be able to.

The allies Nero recruits on this world look like centaurs—only their human head, arms, and torso look like those of juiced-up bodybuilders and the "horse" part is so powerfully built it resembles the body of an ox.

When the vision ends, I attempt another.

———

"WHAT'S SO special about this sorry lot?" Kit asks Nero, nodding at the malnourished-looking people toiling away in a village run by giant steam-powered machinery.

Without replying, Nero walks over to a homeless-looking man, takes out a gold coin from his pocket, and says something.

Taking off his dingy clothes, the guy walks over to a clearing and takes in a deep breath.

With a flash of light, he changes from a hobo into

something.

My first guess is a dragon, like Nero himself, but a tiny one.

But no. This thing's body design is noticeably different. The tail is longer, the paws are more lizard-like, and the head looks like it belongs on a rooster.

"A cockatrice?" Kit whispers in awed fascination. "I thought they were extinct."

"Some think the same of my kind," Nero says. "Be careful. Their gaze kills."

A cockatrice? I think I killed one in one of Felix's video games once.

It's official now.

I'm no longer getting excited about new Cognizant types. After everything I've seen, it would take invisible pink unicorns that poop rainbows to get a rise out of me.

The cockatrice changes back into a man, which must be Kit's signal to turn herself into a cockatrice—

The vision ends, and I find myself in the car again.

I scratch my head in disappointment.

No matter what I do, I can't seem to catch Nero on Gomorrah.

I guess it's time to give up on that. I clearly have no clue how to control *when* the vision happens.

Fine. At this point, I'm dying to see what Nero and his exotic army will actually do.

With a deep breath, I jump into Headspace to find out.

CHAPTER THIRTEEN

NERO IS STANDING naked on a large hill in a familiar world. The silver Grand Canyon-like mountain ridge in the distance, the alien star formations in the sky, the seven differently shaded moons, and the magnificent aurora borealis all belong to the place Nero depicted in a painting hanging in his office.

The world where he comes from.

Dragon world.

As if to prove me right, a powerful dragon roar shakes the hill Nero is standing on.

He narrows his eyes and looks into the distance.

Yep.

Two dragons are flying his way.

He looks at the hub where his army is streaming out of the gate, then back at the dragons.

"Don't you dare have fun without me," Kit yells from the bottom of the hill as she makes her clothes disappear.

"You can join me if you insist," Nero retorts. "Just watch out for dragon fire."

Kit waves dismissively, and a moment later, a giant dragon shows up where she was standing—a green beast with scales the size of dinner plates.

Taking Kit's transformation as his call to action, Nero assumes his own dragon form in a flash of energy and leaps into the air.

The roar of the distant dragons is angrier now.

Like before, there seem to be words embedded in the roar, but they're hard to make out.

Kit leaps into the air, and my viewpoint follows her and Nero as if my absent body also managed to sprout wings.

From this height, I see an army in the distance, marching in the direction of the hub. It looks to be made up of regular people, but for all I know, they could all be dragons in human form.

And speaking of dragons, the two nearby must be performing reconnaissance. Another bunch—called a flight—of dragons are hovering protectively over the army.

Nero and Kit roar, then dive toward the two spies with the speed of fighter jets.

The larger enemy dragon claws at Nero's head, but misses and pays with a limb that Nero bites clean off.

The smaller one leaps up and swoops down toward Kit, but she dodges expertly, then rakes her talons on her opponent's back—which is when I realize her talons are painted with pink nail polish.

Go Kit. I imagine it must be harder for her to fight like that compared to a naturally born dragon.

The larger dragon strikes with his tail and wraps it around Nero's wrist. Nero's snout takes on a facsimile of a smile, and he spews fire in his opponent's face.

Dragon scales, bones, and muscles melt, killing the beast instantly.

However, Nero's action must've given Kit's opponent the idea to do the same, so he inhales deep and aims.

I recall what Nero said to her about avoiding dragon breath.

Crap.

She won't have time.

Nero zooms in front of her, and the fire hits his broad back instead.

As I learned the last time I watched dragons fight, Nero is resilient to dragon breath.

Even after that blast, he looks no worse for the wear —but the same can't be said of their remaining opponent. Kit slices into his belly like a hawk ripping into a fluffy bunny.

Seconds later, Kit and Nero victoriously fly toward the hub—

———

FINDING myself back in the car, I leap into Headspace again.

I need to see how big Nero's army is, and what

happens when they meet the flight of dragons and their ground troops.

Most importantly, I need to make sure Nero is going to be okay.

———

TWO ARMIES FACE each other on a dry plateau at the foot of the hill Nero stood on earlier.

Two huge armies that bring to mind scenes from *Lord of the Rings*.

Thanks to the giants and the centaurs, I know which side is Nero's—and there's noticeably fewer of them, about one to five by my estimate.

A naked Nero and an equally nude man I don't know are standing between the two armies.

The hate radiating from them would register on a Geiger counter.

As usual, when lacking clothes, Nero looks mouthwateringly hot—an impressive feat on his part given that I don't even have a mouth right now. Relatedly, is it wrong that I want Nero to wrestle this guy? Maybe oil up first, to make—

"I don't have the authority to give you Claudia," growls the unfamiliar guy. "But even if I did, I wouldn't. My forces outnumber yours, and you're just one dragon against us all." He waves at the dragon-filled sky.

"Then you will die." Nero's face is ice cold. "Same goes for everyone else who stands between me and the usurper."

"Or I end this now," the guy says and whooshes into motion.

Nero dodges the claw-like hand that strikes at his chest. My boss either expected treachery or he's just that fast.

"I should thank you," Nero growls, his fist flying at his opponent's face. "Without you, their general, your army will be that much easier to defeat."

The glint in the general's eyes is eerily snake-like as he ducks. "And without you, yours will simply leave."

Nero's hands move too fast to track, but his opponent blocks each strike—then goes on an offensive that's also too fast to follow. I can tell, however, that he doesn't land a single strike.

A dragon roars in the distance and starts flying in the direction of the combatants. The rest of the dragons follow.

On the side of Nero's army, a dragon appears as if from nowhere—a green one who must be Kit.

Roaring, Kit launches into the air, and the rest of Nero's army takes that as their marching orders and begins to advance.

"So you planned for this," the general says almost respectfully.

"Hopefully better than you," Nero says and finally lands a powerful blow, striking the guy's jaw.

The general staggers—which is when Nero rakes a gash on his chest with his claw-like hand.

The general steps back, glows, and turns into a giant blue dragon.

Nero turns as well, roaring something that sounds suspiciously like, "Now!"

Whatever Nero's plan is, I hope it accounts for the dragons that are soon going to join the general.

A bunch of scrawny-looking soldiers in Nero's army begin to glow. With the sound of clothing ripping apart, a brood—or whatever the term is—of cockatrices shows up where the people used to be.

The strange creatures take flight, swooping over the rest of Nero's army and grabbing some of the *300* dudes into their talons.

The strongmen look different now than when Nero recruited them; they're wearing heavy armor and intricate harnesses that have clearly been designed for cockatrice claws. In their hands, they're clutching fierce-looking lances with tips that remind me of gleaming pink diamonds.

As Kit leads this makeshift air squadron, I realize she has a rider on her back.

It's Vlad.

Or put another way, Vlad is riding Kit.

I bet that was *her* idea.

The general spews fire at Nero.

As before, Nero seems undaunted by dragon breath —but it does distract him. The general uses that moment to slash at Nero's face with his tail. The strike doesn't leave a mark, but it must hurt, as Nero roars in pain.

Recovering quickly, Nero strikes with his own tail.

The general dodges the move and looks back.

The dragons are closer now, but so are Kit and the cockatrices.

Using the general's distraction to his advantage, Nero spews flame at his opponent's chest.

The general is fast and almost dodges the attack, but the tip of his tail is hit by the fire and is instantly singed.

He roars like a wounded T-rex.

His allies pick up speed, their wings flapping so hard they seem to blur.

Kit and the cockatrices match their pace, accelerating so fast I half-expect them all to lose their riders—but they don't.

Nero swipes at the general with his claw and misses.

The general tries to bite Nero's shoulder with his sword-like teeth, only to catch empty air instead.

The enemy dragons are almost within striking distance, and so are Kit and her squadron.

"Ready?" Vlad screams at Nero from Kit's back.

"Go," Nero's roar seems to reply.

Kit flies over the general, while Nero dives down.

The general starts to swoop for Nero like a falcon— which is when Vlad leaps from Kit's back, and I notice the gate sword in his hand.

As he flies through the air, Vlad activates the plasma blade, and when he passes the general's head, he swipes in a wide arc. The lightsaber-like weapon enters the dragon's skull with ease, cleaving the head into two halves.

Vlad presses the button to hide the blade and lands on Nero's back.

I realize this maneuver is inspired by something I did the last time Nero fought a dragon, and I make a mental note to tease Nero for being such a copycat. I also realize that Vlad is now riding Nero—a naked Nero at that.

That will be something else to bring up when I'm in a teasing mood.

Seeing their dead leader plummet to the ground, the other dragons freeze in the air—but the attacking brood of cockatrices only get bolder and speed up.

The strongmen dudes yell out a war cry as a screech emanates from the throats of the cockatrices—a sound that demons from hell would make if they tried to shout "cock-a-doodle-doo."

One of the larger cockatrices flies up to an enemy dragon, and a spear pierces the thick dragon hide near the shoulder.

Score! The diamond-like stuff of the spear tips must be as strong as adamantium.

The dragon roars in pain and swats at the spear, but then a dark magenta energy streams from the cockatrice's wild eyes into the wound.

The wounded dragon screeches and begins falling.

The *300* crew yell something, no doubt urging their own cockatrices to take them close to the dragons.

Then I notice Nero is flying above the dragons while Kit is diving down.

Are they doing the same trick in reverse?

They are.

Leaping from Nero's back, Vlad slays another dragon and lands on Kit.

Meanwhile, the rest of the cockatrices fly up to the stunned dragons, and spears enter flesh while magenta death stares finish the job, over and over.

Below us, the ground troops finally clash.

Colton—the smallest of the giants—swings a nine-foot claymore, chopping up a small squadron of enemy troops, and the rest of the giants do even more damage.

In the meantime, the centaurs rush at the enemy cavalry, each holding a lance taller than the spire on the Empire State building. Tumor-like muscles bulging, the leader centaur turns a dozen enemy riders into kebabs, and the rest of his squadron follows suit.

The more human-looking of Nero's allies assist the giants and the centaurs when they catch up. Isis shoots injured warriors with the healing arc of her magic, and during breaks in the action, a white-robed female dissolves the enemy soldiers with streaks of white energy that remind me of what Councilor Albina did at Rose's funeral.

It must be her, which means Nero definitely got some members of the New York Council involved.

One man turns into a giant wolf that makes Nostradamus's Marius look like a malnourished puppy. He rips into a wave of soldiers by himself, wreaking as much havoc as a dozen giants, while a guy who looks like an elf but without the signature ears goes full-on Orlando Bloom with his bow and arrows, turning dozens of soldiers into pin-cushions.

The strangest is a woman who calls animals to herself like a Disney princess, only by using arcs of energy instead of singing. Once exotic-looking birds and other creatures join her, she sends them into the enemy troops, biting and tripping them up.

But the most damage to the enemy army is done by their own dragons when they fall dead from the sky, crushing—

———

I'M BACK in the car.

My heart is hammering in my chest, and my stomach is tight with anxiety.

At first, I'm sure I'm reacting to seeing Nero in trouble, but then I realize this feeling has something to do with the chorts.

But what?

Could they be following me?

I look back. It's just heavy downtown traffic and no obvious tail that I can see.

Maybe Headspace can provide more answers?

I focus and instantly end up there, with three clouds of visions around me—two that play frightening tunes and one very mundane.

These three clouds must represent three different locations and events.

With three ethereal wisps, I reach for a representative from each cloud and spiral into the visions.

CHAPTER FOURTEEN

FOUR CHORTS ARE WALKING down a corridor in an apartment building.

A corridor that looks strangely familiar.

I don't think these four were in the room with Felix, but I'm not sure. I guess it was too much to hope that all of the chorts except Boris and Woland had perished.

A pale man in a black suit is standing next to one of the farther doors, as if guarding that apartment.

A man wearing sunglasses indoors.

When they see him, the chorts stealthily creep forward.

The guy they're approaching—a vampire, judging by those sunglasses and his paleness—doesn't react until they're about forty feet away. Then he must hear or smell something because he turns sharply. "Who goes there?"

The chorts freeze, but it's too late.

"Whoever you are, you should know you're dealing

with an Enforcer," he says evenly, staring at them. "Leave now and live."

Definitely a vampire—one of Vlad's.

Since they're busted, the chorts abandon all stealth and stand straighter, no sign of fear on their faces.

The vampire reaches into his jacket and pulls out a gun of a make I don't recognize.

A gun with a futuristic-looking silencer.

Aiming it at the chorts, he says, "I won't ask again."

"How about we let *you* walk away," says a spikey-haired chort with a thick Russian accent. "Think of it as Enforcer to Enforcer courtesy."

Without lowering the gun, the vampire reaches into his pants' pocket with his free hand and pulls out a cell phone.

"Yeah, that's not going to work," the same chort says and pulls out some weird-looking gizmo. He waves it around. "We're blocking cell reception and have cut the landlines in this building. So it's just going to be you and the four of us. Ready to stand down now?"

The vampire glances at his phone, no doubt to verify a lack of bars; then without any warning, he squeezes the trigger—producing a barely audible gunshot.

The chorts go translucent.

A bullet hole shows up in the chest of the spikey-haired one, yet there's no blood or visible pain on his face.

The vampire gapes at his still-standing opponent,

then at the bullet hole in the wall at the far end of the corridor.

Which is when I notice a large chort creeping up on the vampire from the other end of the hallway.

He must've come from the staircase to the left of the apartment, using the first four chorts as misdirection.

The vampire aims again.

The newcomer chort silently pulls out what looks like a *shashka*—a type of single-edged saber used by the Cossacks.

With an expert swing, he chops the vampire's head off.

The head drops to the floor, and the headless body follows.

"Stick him into the garbage chute for now," says the spikey-haired chort, and two of his brethren rush to execute the command.

When the clean-up is complete, the chorts regroup in front of the door where the vampire was standing.

A door I now recognize—except I hope with all my being that I'm wrong.

There are other doors like this, aren't there?

In similar-looking corridors?

It's possible.

The chorts take out black burglar masks and put them on, covering their faces.

"What time is it?" the spikey-haired leader asks a thin, wiry chort who reminds me of Boris.

"12:57," the Boris-lookalike says.

"We're cutting it close," the leader says. Gesturing at the door, he orders, "Do it now."

The thin one takes out lockpicks and goes to work. Though his technique leaves much to be desired, it gets the job done within minutes.

Please let me be wrong.

They enter.

At the sight of the countless expensive tchotchkes, I can't deny it anymore.

This is my mom's apartment—my adoptive mom's, that is.

If I had a heart in this state, it would sink through the floor.

Maybe she's not home? Maybe they're here to steal something rather than hurt her?

But of course, she *is* home. Why else was that vampire—who was no doubt working for Nero—guarding the apartment?

The sounds of TV ring out from the living room, and the chorts creep into that room.

Mom doesn't even notice them. Her gaze is glued to *The Real Housewives of New York.*

The spikey-haired chort sneaks up behind her and grabs her throat, squeezing it.

Mom's face turns ashen, and she starts flailing, a choked hiss escaping her lips instead of a shriek.

"Time?" Mom's assailant asks the thin chort.

"It's one already," the thin guy replies.

With an uncaring shrug, the spikey-haired chort squeezes harder—

———

A DIFFERENT GROUP of chorts are walking in another —this time, unfamiliar—corridor.

Based on the swipe locks on the doors and the fancy décor, I can tell this is a hotel. When I glimpse Central Park from a hallway window, I even know which hotel this is—The Plaza.

Dad's favorite place to stay when he visits New York.

Oh no. Please don't let this be what I think.

An Enforcer vampire is standing in front of one of the rooms, looking bored.

The chorts follow the script from my other vision to a T—they use themselves as misdirection until a lanky chort sneaks up behind the vamp and uses a *shashka* for another beheading.

The only difference is that instead of a garbage chute, they stash the body in an empty room.

"What's the time?" a round-faced chort asks.

"12:58," says the one who beheaded the vampire.

The round-faced chort nods and presses a key card to the lock.

The light on the device turns green.

The chort cautiously opens the door—and faces Dad, who stares at the newcomer with bulging eyes.

It's as I feared.

The chorts are killing my parents in a synchronized attack.

"I'm going to call the police!" Dad waves his phone, stumbling back.

"And how many bars do you have?" the round-faced chort asks with a Russian accent.

Dad glances at the screen and pales.

The chorts step into the room.

Dad tosses his useless cellphone at the assailants and scrambles for the landline.

The lanky blade-wielding chort dodges the projectile, then advances on Dad, as do the others.

"No dial tone?" the round-faced chort asks mockingly when Dad lifts the phone to his ear with shaking hands. "We've made sure there would be no interruptions."

He nods at the lanky chort who has the shashka.

No. Please, no.

The weapon whooshes through the air, piercing Dad's chest—

———

A NEW VISION STARTS.

I'm bodiless, in a warehouse with Woland, Boris, a couple of chorts from Felix's vision, and a few chorts I haven't seen.

They all look like they just sprinted across the entire length of New York City and are staring at a wall clock that shows 12:44.

If this is the same day, which I see no reason to

doubt, these bastards are just waiting for my parents to die.

How do I stop this cursed vision so I can actually *do* something?

Not that I actually have a clue what to do. Given my current location and the traffic, at best, I could try to reach one of my parents before 1:00, but definitely not both.

Did I tempt fate when I told Mom I'd never choose Dad over her?

Because I might have to make that awful choice, or else have them both die.

"I think it's time," Woland says when the clock moves another minute. He walks over to a small table with a bottle of water, a thick roll of duct tape, and a folded piece of paper on it.

"Is this really going to work?" Boris looks at the paper, then at his boss.

"She's a seer," Woland says and picks up the pen. "If she sees a vision of this, it will work."

"But they're not her real parents," Boris says. "Besides, she will then also see what would happen if she comes over here." He looks pointedly at the duct tape.

"Then as sad as it is, a couple of people will die in vain." Woland shrugs. "A small price to pay for a chance to get Rasputin."

"And you think he'll come to save her?" Boris rubs his temples, his weaselly face a mask of confusion. "Because he, too, can see the future?"

"That, or she'll tell us where to find him," Woland says. "Either outcome works for me."

Boris winces. "This seer shit hurts my brain."

"Not a lot there to hurt," Woland mutters under his breath and unfolds the paper. Louder, he adds, "Please, gentlemen, I need silence now."

The other chorts stop whispering among themselves as Woland clears his throat. Pointing at the paper, he says, "Dear Sasha. Please witness me signing this contract."

He stops and glances around as though looking for a ghost, then signs the paper at a dotted line. As he does that, his Mandate aura flickers, no doubt confirming the binding nature of what he just did.

I scan the contract.

If you ignore the legalese, it boils down to the following: If I, Alexandra (Sasha) Urban, arrive at the given Brooklyn address at or before 12:59 p.m., alone and without involving human or Cognizant authorities, he, Woland, solemnly pledges to call off his people and let my adoptive parents live. Furthermore, he would not hurt them ever again and would do everything in his power to make sure that no one working for him or the St. Petersburg Council would hurt them either.

Woland looks at the clock, then at the door leading into the warehouse as I process what I just learned.

Woland has devised a plan that is as evil as it is genius.

He's giving me a way to save *both* of my parents.

All I have to do is sacrifice myself.

Except I wouldn't be sacrificing myself only. The chorts hope that Rasputin would come to save me, so I'd be putting him in harm's way.

Except Rasputin doesn't have his seer mojo after helping Nero, so he won't come.

The big question is: would I tell them where Rasputin is once they begin torturing me? Then again, isn't *that* up to me? Given this contract, Woland won't be able to leverage my adoptive parents to make me talk, and I think I have a higher tolerance for pain than Felix does.

"I bet she won't come," Boris whispers under his breath and gets a glare from Woland.

When the clock turns 12:55, the vision terminates.

CHAPTER FIFTEEN

AS SOON AS I return to reality, I frantically put the Brooklyn address from the contract into my phone.

Crap.

I'll never make it in time with current traffic conditions.

I tinker with the app to see if I can do so on foot. Nope. I'd be there even later.

I look up from the phone. "Stop the car!"

The driver looks at me like I'm insane, and with good reason—because of the traffic, we're standing still already.

Without wasting time on farewells or explanations, I jump out of the car and run through the sea of vehicles until I see a ray of hope parked illegally next to the Starbucks on the other side of the road, where the traffic is moving swiftly.

It's a Vespa—a pink clone of the one I used to own.

I sprint for it and pray the owner doesn't come out in the next few seconds.

The first thing I did when I got my own Vespa was figure out how to hotwire it, so I could take measures to prevent someone else from doing so. Now I just have to hope the owner of this baby isn't a handy magician-type like me.

Nearly getting run over twice, I reach the scooter and furtively look around.

No one seems to be looking my way, so I steady my shaking hands and try the quickest Vespa-nabbing method I've devised.

If I knew I'd one day need to do this in a hurry, I would've practiced.

A few anxiety-ridden seconds later, I'm on the Vespa and maxing out the gas.

Even with all the adrenaline, I feel bad about this grand theft auto. If I survive, I'll ask Felix to help me track down the owner and make amends.

If I survive.

For everyone's sake, I better focus on that for now.

A yellow cab whooshes by as I make a sharp and very illegal U-turn onto the traffic-jammed side of the road.

Once there, I use my ride's small stature to pass by the almost-parked cars in front of me, speeding up as I go.

A minute later, I'm flying so fast that if someone were to open a door or stick a hand out the window, I'd be dead instantly, especially without a helmet.

Clutching my phone, I check it to see if I'd make my destination now and find the GPS app doesn't have an option for "scooter." If I were in a car without traffic, I'd make it—but even at this breakneck speed, I'm driving noticeably slower than a car.

If I were cycling—which is a little closer to a scooter—I'd be late.

Also, do I even *want* to make it there on time? I'm basically rushing to get myself into Woland's trap.

The problem is, my time is too limited to come up with a better way to save my parents.

Still, I ought to at least try something else.

What if I do the obvious and dial 911? I can tell one operator that I'm staying at The Plaza hotel and heard gunshots coming from Dad's room. I can then call back and tell another operator that I live at Mom's address and heard two gunshots in her apartment.

Thus determined, I jump into Headspace to see if calling the cops would change the fates of my parents.

Nope.

The police either don't make it in time or get killed by the chorts when they do.

Next, I contemplate sending the cops to Woland's address.

Again, a vision tells me that nothing changes—which isn't surprising given what the contract said about showing up alone. He must've ordered my parents' deaths once he saw the cops.

Another desperate idea occurs to me, and I dial Felix.

"Hey," he says. "How are things going?"

"Good," I lie. "Listen, can you give the phone to the good-looking guy who was guarding our door this morning?"

"You mean Eric?" Felix sounds amused.

"Yep," I pant. "Him."

"He wasn't there when I came home," Felix says.

Damn it.

Eric must be searching for me somewhere. I should've realized that. The hope was to recruit him to help with this mess. With his teleportation abilities, he could've taken Mom and Dad to safety—assuming I was able to talk him into it, that is.

"What's this about?" Felix asks.

"Going into the tunnel," I say and hiss into the phone. "Will call you back soon."

Felix doesn't call back—which means he didn't question the dodgy logic of me calling to talk to Eric right before going into the tunnel.

Or he noticed and will make fun of me later.

I sure hope he does as that would mean I have a "later."

In the distance, I see the end of the traffic. It seems the cause was an accident, where a minivan crashed into a truck.

I whoosh by the broken car parts, clutching the handles harder. There are now cars on the road, moving cars that can ram into me.

Glancing at the time on the phone, I cringe and squeeze all I can from the Vespa's four-stroke engine.

Giant-looking cars seem to zoom by me at death-on-impact speeds.

Would Woland call off his chorts if I died in a fiery crash?

No, I doubt it. Besides, how would he even learn of my demise?

It's looking like I only have one choice left.

To let Woland have me.

If only Nero were still on Earth—or Vlad, or Kit, or anyone. Almost every Cognizant I know is not available. Except maybe Chester—but he's mad at me.

Since I'm desperate, I risk my life to call Chester anyway. He doesn't pick up.

I guess there's also Lucretia, my shrink, and Pada, the cleanup guy.

Using a voice command, I call Pada first. A voicemail informs me that he's on vacation.

Great.

Not even him.

Not that I expected Pada to help in any case. Taking a side is probably bad for his job security. He only needs to wait and help Woland clean up my bloodied corpse after the torture.

I call Lucretia next, but I get a voicemail telling me she's with a client. I leave a message to call me back if she frees up soon but don't place much hope on it. She wouldn't make it from the city in time in any case. Also, the chorts didn't have trouble killing Enforcers, so what chance does a newbie vampire like Lucretia have against them?

What about the bannik, Lucretia's boyfriend? Could he assist me somehow?

Swerving into the slower lane, I focus extra hard to enter Headspace.

———

WHEN I FIND MYSELF FLOATING, I realize I've never done this while driving.

Then I spot the horrific shapes that surround me on all sides.

It doesn't take a lot of brainpower to know what these would show me—my upcoming encounter with Woland.

If I had a body, I'd pull away from the shapes as if they were covered in pus and boils. I'm afraid that if I witness that future, I might chicken out and let my parents die.

Remembering my original goal, I reach out to the bannik, but to no avail.

Well, the chance of him helping was slim, anyway.

Since I'm here, I try summoning Rasputin next—though I'm not even sure I'd tell him the situation if he answered. He doesn't answer in any case, sparing me any need to lie.

I float and ponder if I should try one more thing. Finally, I decide to go for it.

Reluctantly, I do my best to think of Nostradamus's essence.

Nothing happens.

Maybe I didn't get to know him well enough yet, or he's not in Headspace.

Or maybe he's just snubbing my summons.

Glancing at the scary shapes once more, I touch my own representation, terminating the futile Headspace session.

———

I COME BACK to my senses—and see a Honda Civic mere inches away from my front tire. It must be slowing to turn onto the upcoming ramp.

Desperately squeezing the handle bars, I veer into the middle lane without looking in the mirror.

I don't die, but my heart rate jumps sky high as a vicious honk reaches my ears.

The guy I cut off speeds up and gesticulates obscenities at me as he passes by.

That does it.

For the rest of this crazy ride, I'm going to focus on the road.

Thus determined, I empty my mind as much as I can and drive for all I'm worth until the GPS makes me turn off the highway.

Whooshing onto the exit ramp, I continue through the regular streets at the same top speed I was going on the highway.

If it weren't for my seer-boosted driving intuition, I would've died at least four times, and likely taken a few pedestrians with me. On the bright side, it's 12:54

when I park next to the warehouse that's my destination.

I sprint into the familiar room, pushing several chorts out of my way. "I'm here! Call it off. Now."

Woland's aura shimmers. I guess it recognizes the contract he signed is now officially in effect.

"Hurry, please," Woland says and raises his phone to his ear, just as Boris does the same thing.

"It's off," they both say when the other side picks up. "It worked. See you when you get here."

I gulp down some air and realize the contract said nothing about me trying to escape once I arrive here alone.

With that, I bolt for the door, but the chorts I passed earlier form an impenetrable wall in front of me.

Fine.

This place has windows. Maybe I could—

A fist connects with my chin, knocking me unconscious.

CHAPTER SIXTEEN

WAKING up to throbbing pain emanating from the lower portion of my face, I moan in complaint.

What did the cat do to me? Why?

Then I hear someone walk over, and memory floods in.

I'm not in my bed.

I've been captured by the chorts.

That moan was a huge miscalculation. It would've been much more advantageous to play dead.

"Finally, you're back," Woland says from a few feet away. "That is fortunate. I'm eager to talk to you."

Without opening my eyes, I scan my body.

Something is hanging on my neck, and my arms are trapped at my sides. If I had to guess, I'd say I'm duct-taped to a chair—which is bad. That's one of the hardest bindings to defeat.

"Please don't pretend to still be unconscious." Woland must be right in my face now, as I can smell the smoked fish on his breath. "I don't want to start our conversation by forcing you to open your eyes."

"Fine." I squint at him, then look down at the thing on my neck and find it to be a bib, like the ones they give you at seafood restaurants. How thoughtful. They don't want all the blood they plan to spill to ruin my outfit. "Before we 'talk' about anything, I wanted to check if you know who my Mentor is?"

I figure if I have to put up with Nero's bossy ass, I might as well name-drop him in case that scares these assholes.

"I know for a fact that Nero isn't around to interfere with this meeting." Woland looks me over. "How about you cooperate and make this easy on yourself?"

"Sure," I say, but instead of listening to his reply, I frantically try to come up with a strategy.

Obviously, telling them Rasputin's location is out of the question. But that doesn't mean I have to bravely refuse to talk at all and just take my torture the way spies in movies do.

What if I try something different? Like sending the chorts on a wild goose chase? I can refuse to talk at first for verisimilitude, then pretend to "break" and tell them Rasputin is somewhere very far. When they go to locate him, I'll think of a way to escape. They might be pretty mad if they learn I lied—but what are they going to do, tie me to a chair and torture me?

Something about this plan makes me uneasy, so I decide to use my powers to see what would happen if I went through with it. Now that I can't chicken out of coming to this place, visions are an option again, especially if I don't mind living through torture twice.

Of course, I *do* mind, but in this case, the benefits might outweigh the costs.

"Are you even listening to me?" Woland asks, sounding frustrated, but I ignore him and jump into Headspace.

————

AS SOON AS I find myself among the shapes, I start by trying to reach Rasputin, the bannik, and Nostradamus.

Once again, none of them reply.

Fine. Back to why I came here.

I look at the four clouds of visions in my immediate vicinity: one deadly and three neutral in comparison.

Crap.

Maybe this is enough?

I can already tell lying is a bad idea.

But no.

I must know for sure.

Reaching for a representative of each shape, I prepare for unpleasant experiences.

————

THE PAIN IS SO unbearable that I have no doubt they'll believe me if I pretend to "break" now.

I'm on the verge of genuinely breaking.

"Stop," I rasp out. "I'll tell you where he is."

"Please go ahead," Woland says soothingly.

"I don't know the exact name of the world, but dragons live there," I say through a parched throat. "There's a silver Grand Canyon-like mountain ridge near the gates." I spit up blood. "I can draw you a map."

What I don't add is that this map will take them through hellish Otherlands with hungry gnomes, radiation, poisons, giant insects, and lots more fun.

Woland sighs. "I have it on good authority that Rasputin is here, on Earth," he says. All usual politeness gone from his voice, he adds, "Lie to me one more time, and I'll stop your heart."

The chorts around me murmur as I wonder if he's bluffing.

He sure sounds sincere.

Also, whoever his good authority is, they're wrong—Rasputin isn't on Earth right now.

Crap.

This means even if I broke and told them the truth, they wouldn't believe me.

Then again, that might be a good thing.

"Now," Woland says. "Please tell me where he *really* is—"

I don't hear the rest because the vision halts in that moment, and another begins.

———

I FEEL on the verge of breaking for real again, which means I might as well fake it the second time here and now.

"Stop," I rasp through chapped lips, my voice hoarse from screaming. "This time, I really *will* tell you where he is. No more lies."

"Please go ahead," Woland says soothingly. "Just remember, lie to me again and you die."

He must be bluffing.

How is he going to find out where Rasputin is if I'm dead? I guess there's Felix, but still. He must be bluffing.

I hope he's bluffing.

"Queenstown, New Zealand." I cough up more blood. "Rasputin is staying at the Four Seasons there."

I have no idea if there's a Four Seasons there, but I sure hope so. I just named the farthest place I can think of, and the first famous hotel that popped into my head.

Woland takes out his phone and swipes a few times.

"You mean the Four Seasons Motel on Stanley Street?" he asks.

"Right," I say. "Room 7."

A motel? It must not be *that* Four Seasons, but hey, I'll take any lucky breaks I can get.

"Thank you," he says. "You can relax now."

Turning away from me, he says to Boris and a few other chorts, "Stay and watch her. The rest of us will go deal with Rasputin."

———

THE WAREHOUSE DOOR OPENS, and a furious-looking Woland rushes in, the rest of the chorts on his tail.

What the hell? They were gone for much too short a time to go to New Zealand and back.

Then I get it.

They must've cheated and used the Otherlands as a shortcut—like Ariel and I did when we went to Vegas.

Looks like I'm going to find out if Woland was bluffing.

I swallow audibly, and he advances on me.

"I told you what would happen if you lied to me again." Grabbing my aching chin, Woland forces me to meet his gaze.

Crap. Judging by the murder in his eyes, he *wasn't* bluffing.

"Wait," I say frantically. "I can tell you where he is. For real."

"No." Woland's face is stone hard. "You've wasted enough of my time."

And with that, foul energy spreads from his hand into my chin and throughout my body.

"Stop!" I want to yell, but I can't get the word out because my breath is too ragged. I'm shaking and sweating, waves of nausea hitting me, one after another. It feels like a tower of elephants has perched on my chest, and my left arm goes numb as horrific pain explodes in my torso.

My head spins sickeningly, black spots dancing in front of my vision, and with one last choked gasp, I die.

———

I FIND myself in the same warehouse, but bodiless.

The reason for the body loss is clear. That's my freshly dead corpse in the chair.

The visions showed me where the path of lying leads, and this is the finale.

"It's poetic justice," Woland says to the dead me and removes his hand from her chin. "Rasputin took my daughter, and now I have taken his." He straightens, looking lost in thought until Boris clears his throat.

"Yes?" Woland looks at his minion.

"What now?" Boris asks. "Should we—"

———

I RETURN to the reality of the chair and look around in confusion.

"Help her focus," Woland says to Boris.

Grinning, Boris walks over and smacks my cheek with the back of his hand.

The pain is sharp and stinging, but at least it's not amplified by the recently departed Sasha-chort the way it was for Felix.

Then again, maybe Felix was in a better position. When they could amplify the pain, they could get away with less damage to the victim's body.

Before I can think more cheerful thoughts such as that one, Boris hits me in the stomach.

Air rushes out of my lungs as my solar plexus shrieks in pain for the second time today. And it's again Boris's fault.

Gasping, I try to go into Headspace but find it almost impossible to concentrate.

Who knew reaching the needed state of focus is so much harder when you're in debilitating pain?

Boris smacks my other cheek.

I want to scream, but I still don't have enough air to do so.

There's a strong taste of copper in my mouth, and tears stream down my cheeks.

"Enough," Woland says just as I expect to get hit again.

For a few blissful minutes, I'm left alone, so I use the reprieve to regain my breath.

When I refocus on Woland again, he looks at me pityingly. "This doesn't need to get so unpleasant," he reminds me. "It's just a matter of time before you tell us what we need to know. Why don't you just do it now before the damage is permanent?"

"Please." I cough. "What is it that you want to know from me? I'll tell you anything you want."

He looks confused. Then he asks hopefully, "Where is Rasputin?"

"Who?" I say, figuring if I can't send them on a wild goose chase, I can at least feign ignorance for a bit.

Woland sighs and gestures at Boris.

Boris punches me in the nose this time.

I see white stars, and the pain almost makes me pass out.

Almost, but unfortunately not quite.

Woland waits until I can talk again, then says, "I have it on good authority that Rasputin *is* your father, and you know where he is." All usual politeness gone from his voice, he adds, "Lie to me one more time, and I'll stop your heart."

The chorts around us murmur nervously.

Crap.

I didn't realize he'd count *that* as a lie. This might be a case of the future liking certain patterns.

I'm only down to a single lie before he gives me the heart attack I experienced in my vision.

Also, who is this authority he keeps talking about?

"I'll ask again," Woland says. "Where is he?"

"*Idi k chortu*," I say—a Russian curse I chose because it references his kind.

Woland shakes his head in disappointment. "Did you know that sayings like that are why my kind is so powerful?" he says. "It makes it so that some Russians still believe in us to this day."

Instead of a reply, I give him my best death glare.

"Fine," he says and looks at Boris. "Use your power on her this time."

Boris grins wider than before and grabs my neck in a chokehold.

Only instead of squeezing, he does something, and

an energy like the one in my vision spreads through my body.

A sharp pain blooms in the upper left side of my abdomen.

What the hell?

What just happened?

"Boris just killed your spleen," Woland says.

I stare at him uncomprehendingly, my insides painfully churning.

"The spleen is responsible for filtering antibody-coated bacteria," Woland says, clearly misunderstanding my look. "It also reprocesses old red blood cells and recycles the iron in your hemoglobin."

The power of thought finally comes back to me. "No." My voice shakes. "You can't do that."

"We can and we did," Woland says. "There's someone in this room who can do the same thing to every single one of your organs. As long as you refuse to talk, you're going to lose them one by one."

The horror I feel is indescribable.

I just lost my spleen.

Though I'm still fuzzy on its function, I think I'm now going to be more prone to certain infections. Not that the exact effects matter. The very idea of losing an organ like that is beyond creepy.

I think I'd rather they keep beating me—which is probably why they opted for this.

"You ready?" Woland nods at a blond chort who steps forward. "Your tonsils are next."

Fighting the mother of all panic, I try to focus on Headspace.

I'm in too much pain to concentrate, but I have to. This might be my last chance, as the pain will only get worse from here.

I suck in a breath and focus again.

Then again.

Finally, it works.

CHAPTER SEVENTEEN

I'VE NEVER WELCOMED the bodiless existence of Headspace as much as I do now.

Maybe I can now think of something—though my thoughts boil down to one simple mantra.

I don't want to lose any more organs.

I really don't.

But I also can't tell them where Rasputin is.

I'd rather live without a spleen and tonsils.

Ignoring the shapes around me, I float until I calm down to mere panic levels, and then I reach out to Rasputin.

He doesn't answer, which is probably for the best.

I'm so freaked out right now that I'd be tempted to tell him what's happening. And then he might want to sacrifice himself for my sake.

I float some more and do my best to calm down further. Then I try reaching out to the bannik again.

It doesn't work.

Just for completeness, I try to think of Nostradamus's essence one more time. He seems perceptive, so I add that to my summons. Troubled as well—no doubt thanks to his loss of sight. For good measure, I even add my desperate need to talk to *someone* into the mix.

To my shock, an entity shows up in Headspace next to me.

A being that radiates power and curiosity.

Spotting me, he reaches toward me.

With great eagerness, I reach back—and fall into the joining.

———

I'M WALKING down the street, a tiny palm held firmly in my much bigger hand.

Well, not *my* hand. This is Nostradamus's memory, so the bigger hand is his.

This is a memory from a time before he lost his sight—and he's enjoying looking at the greenery all around. He especially enjoys watching his beloved son.

"Can we go to the bakery and get a pastry?" the boy says in French—which I understand, as I'm inside Nostradamus's head.

Nostradamus grins. "What do you foresee I'd say in reply? Do you think I'll agree or not?"

The love he feels for his son is overwhelming.

It almost makes me scared to have my own kids one

day—loving someone this much just seems against the rules.

"Does everything need to be a lesson?" the kid sing-songs. "It's Sunday. I just want—"

———

ANOTHER MEMORY BEGINS, and this time, Nostradamus is standing in total darkness that is his new existence.

He's not brooding about losing his eyes, however. It's the loss of his family—which had been murdered by Tartarus—that weighs on him.

Cold rain pelts his head as he reaches out and feels for the small gravestone.

When he finds it, he reads the inscription in braille.

It's his son's grave.

An empty grave.

The actual corpses are on another world—a world Tartarus decimated.

"I'll make that monster pay for what he did to you," Nostradamus promises grimly. "He won't get away with it, I swear. I'll—"

———

AS HAPPENS every time the memory part of the joining is over, I find myself in complete emptiness with a synapse-hologram of Nostradamus floating in front of me.

He's attached to the uncanny shape-entity that is his Headspace representation, and his glasses are missing—which gives me a look at the scarred mess that used to be his eyes.

"Sasha," he says calmly. "This is a pleasant surprise."

"How do you know it's me?" I ask, still staring at his injuries.

"When in this place, I can see just fine," he says. "Or more accurately, it's not eyes that one needs to see in this place—nor is it ears you hear with."

"Right." I float down a foot. "As much as I'd love to discuss metaphysics, right now I urgently need your help. I can't risk one of us running out of seer mojo before I tell you what's going on."

"Of course." His accent sounds thicker as he floats down to my level. "Talk."

Rattling out information as swiftly as I can, I explain what happened, finishing with, "I was hoping you and Lilith could help like you did earlier today. I know it's a lot to ask, but—"

"I'm in, but I can't speak for Lilith," he says. "I'm assuming she'll want to help her daughter, though."

"Great. When do you think you can be here?"

His forehead creases in concern.

"We're on another world," he says. "It may take a while to get to you."

"Crap." I float down about five feet. "I'm not sure I have enough organs to wait a while."

"You'll have to think of a way to stall them," he says. "Now, let's terminate this conversation so both of us retain as much of our seer powers as we can. I have a feeling we'll need them."

"You're right," I say and float toward my Headspace representation.

"Be brave," Nostradamus says as he does the same.

We both touch ourselves—in a non-dirty way, of course—and the joining terminates.

———

I'M BACK in my chair with hope in my heart.

Hope that evaporates as a chort walks closer to me and touches the back of my hand.

"Last chance for your tonsils," Woland says.

Cringing, I shake my head.

The energy enters my body again, and my throat spasms as though I've gotten the worst case of strep in the history of medicine.

I gag, and tears stream down my face.

It's hard to believe I just lost my tonsils. Again, I have only a vague idea of their purpose, but I believe I will now have an increased chance of throat infections.

"Ready to cooperate?" Woland looks at me and nods at a short chort to his left. "Your gallbladder is next."

"Screw you," I try to say, but thanks to my swollen throat, it comes out more like a hiss.

The round-faced chort walks up to me and touches my wrist.

This time, the pain is in my upper right abdomen.

Brutal, pulsing pain.

Realizing that I'm screaming my lungs out, I do my best to calm down, but it's hard, knowing that I won't store bile in my gallbladder anymore.

Speaking of bile, there's plenty in my throat.

Woland catches my gaze. "Please talk. We're running out of non-vital organs."

I swallow a fresh surge of bile. "He's my father," I manage to croak out. "I can't give him up."

"A father you never knew existed," Woland points out.

Battling a wave of nausea, I shake my head.

"Fine." Woland nods at a thin chort on his left. "Which kidney do you want to keep for now—left or right?"

I grit my teeth and do my best not to show my horror.

"Left one it is," Woland says and nods to his minion.

The guy walks over and does his thing.

This pain is the worst one yet. I shake as if in the grip of a seizure and pray for unconsciousness—but it doesn't come. Instead, there's just never-ending agony. Radiating from my stomach, it pulses through every nerve ending in my body until I feel like I will throw up.

I don't—barely—but I'm so drained by the effort I'm barely able to keep my head up by the time the worst of the shaking stops.

"Are you done with this resistance nonsense?" Woland asks.

Battling through the agony, I stiffen my neck and pointedly press my lips together.

Sighing, Woland gestures to the spikey-haired chort who killed my adoptive mom in my vision.

The bastard steps forward.

"You can live without the thyroid gland," Woland says pedantically. "But you'd have to take hormone replacement pills for the rest of your life."

I try to spit at him, but my throat is too swollen and mouth too dry.

"So be it," Woland says.

The spikey-haired asshole walks up to me and touches my hand.

An energy spike later, the agony in my throat seems to spread farther down my neck.

I break out in a cold sweat. I feel on the verge of losing my mind—or breaking down and telling them what they want to know.

But no.

I can't.

"What else is unessential?" Woland looks at the lanky chort who stabbed Dad with a shashka in my vision.

"Well, women *can* live just fine without ovaries." He nods at the round-faced chort who was also at Dad's hotel.

A chill spreads through my whole body. Just minutes ago, in Nostradamus's memories, I wondered if I'd want to have a child, but that was just a spur-of-the-moment thought. In reality, I very much want to have the option to have kids, and to have that taken away is—

"I think it's also possible to survive without the pancreas," the round-faced guy says, nodding at a skeletal-looking chort in the crowd.

"She'd need insulin very soon, and we don't have any," Woland says, studying me. "No, I think the ovaries are a great target. There are two of them, so Sasha can have two chances before irreversible consequences."

"Please!" I choke out. "Don't."

"Then tell me what I want to know," he says soothingly. "This stops whenever you want it to stop."

I tug at my bindings, but to no avail.

"Make it the right one," Woland tells the round-faced chort.

The guy walks up to me and touches my cheek. "Just tell him what he wants to know," he whispers. "You will anyway."

When I don't reply, he shrugs and sends his vile energy into my body.

It feels as though all the cramps I've ever had in my life condense into a single moment, and the cold sweat trickling down my back turns into a river. At the same time, I feel like I've been thrown in a sauna, where someone has turned up the heat to human-barbecue levels.

My stomach heaves, and my vision darkens, but somehow, I remain conscious—and agonizingly aware of the pain.

Forget fertility. I'm ready to tell them anything just to stop this.

A desperate idea pops into my swimming head, and I struggle to go into Headspace to see how it would pan out. But no matter how hard I try, the cramps from hell make it impossible.

I try again.

Nope.

Headspace and pain are refusing to play well together.

Fine then. Maybe I risk my idea without checking it via a vision?

"You have two seconds before you go sterile," Woland says from somewhere.

No.

Not that.

"Stop," I moan. "I'll tell you where he is."

The sweaty palm of the round-faced chort is removed from my hand.

"Please go ahead," Woland says soothingly. "Just remember, lie to me again and you die."

That's right.

This will be the second time—and I know he's not bluffing.

"New Zealand," I squeeze out as I did in my vision. "He's staying at the Four Seasons Motel in Queenstown."

The rest of our interactions proceed as in my vision. He checks to make sure a place called Four

Seasons exists in that part of the world; then he takes a bunch of chorts and leaves.

Dragging in air through my painfully swollen throat, I sag in the chair.

My big gamble is that Nostradamus and Lilith come before I get caught in this lie.

My crappy choices were to risk my life or lose my other ovary and who knows what else.

"Do you want to play some chess?" Boris asks another chort and takes out a tiny box from his pocket.

"We have to watch her," the chort replies.

"Not necessarily," Boris says, then smiles nastily at me and cracks his knuckles.

"Wait," I croak as he makes a fist, but he ignores me and smashes it into the right side of my already-swollen face.

Something—probably my cheekbone—cracks, and my consciousness drops away.

———

I COME to my senses in a symphony of pain.

My whole body is in agony, and my face feels like it's been through a meat grinder.

There is a bright side, though.

Thanks to the pain, I know where I am—so I don't show anyone that I'm back to the land of the conscious.

I just breathe shallowly and hope the agony subsides.

Only it doesn't.

In fact, it's so bad I'm unable to reach Headspace no matter how many times I try.

After I stew in misery for what feels like hours, I hear the door opening.

Hoping with everything I've got that it's Lilith and Nostradamus, I crack my lids a sliver. The irony of this doesn't escape me. If someone had told me this morning I'd be this eager to see Lilith, of all people, I'd laugh in their face.

When I see who came in, all hope deserts me.

I gravely miscalculated.

It's not Lilith and Nostradamus.

It's Woland—and he looks furious, just like he did in my vision.

And like in that vision, he's about to kill me.

He'll stop my heart, and that'll be that.

As if in rebellion over what's about to happen, my heart hammers wildly against my ribcage.

"I told you what would happen if you lied to me again." Just like in my vision, Woland grabs my aching chin and forces me to look into his eyes.

This is it.

"Wait," I say frantically. "I can explain."

"No." Woland's face is like stone. "You've wasted enough of my time."

CHAPTER EIGHTEEN

BEFORE WOLAND CAN SEND his heart-killing energy
into me, the warehouse ceiling explodes.

Woland's eyes widen as a shard of cement flies right
at his wrist.

He goes transparent and leaps back, and the shard
lands exactly where he was standing.

Everyone looks up.

It's Lilith.

She's floating down from the hole in the ceiling like
a dandelion seed on a breeze.

Looks like she can defy gravity here on Earth as
well—for a Cognizant-only audience, in any case.

First to recover his wits, Woland rushes for the exit.
Boris races after his boss, as does the spikey-haired
chort and a few others.

The rest of the chorts stare at Lilith as if transfixed
—and maybe they are. Maybe they see her godlike

visage, or maybe she's using some other power on them—it's hard for me to tell.

Reaching his destination, Woland puts his shoulder to the door and runs outside at the same time as Lilith gestures toward the hypnotized chorts that remain.

With a flash of red energy, small punctures appear on everyone's necks—including Boris's, who's by the door.

"Yes," Lilith coos creepily. Then she makes a new gesture, and a tiny stream of blood extends from each of the wounds, flying straight into her mouth in a gravity- and logic-defying feat.

The chorts seem to come out of their stupor, gaping at Lilith in horror.

I can't blame them.

They must be thinking the same thing I am: she can feed on her victims remotely?

Looking fatigued, Lilith lowers her arms, and the blood stops flowing.

The chorts keep staring.

Lilith lands on the ground and loudly swooshes the liquid in her mouth.

"Complex." She grins like a shark. "Velvety with floral tones. And the best part is, no more phasing for you."

Tearing his eyes away from her, Boris leaps for the door but immediately stumbles back.

With a loud growl, Marius-the-werewolf rips into Boris's right thigh.

Screaming in pain, the chort falls and tries to punch

the werewolf—only to get his arm decimated. He moves to kick, but that just delivers his other leg into Marius's jaws.

Seeing the werewolf busy, the spikey-haired chort sprints for the exit—which is when Nostradamus shows up as if from nowhere, and slices at the chort's throat with a curved dagger.

The chort evaporates. Permanently.

Apparently deciding that Nostradamus might be an easy target, four other chorts face the blind seer head on.

As if he can see them, Nostradamus strikes with his dagger, his movements swift and precisely calculated—like those of a special forces soldier or a well-programmed robot.

He must be using his power to help him fight like that.

Quickly dispatching his attackers, Nostradamus kills more chorts to reach me. He then stands by with his dagger ready—no doubt to prevent the remaining chorts from using me as a hostage.

Meanwhile, Lilith grins in excitement as she reaches for the largest chort she can find. A blur of motion, and she's holding the chort's head with his ripped-out spine attached.

The surrounding chorts whiten.

Grinning wider, she floats off the ground and swoops down, aiming for the chort who killed my gallbladder.

Almost playfully, she punches him from midair—

causing the guy to fly ten feet and slam into the cement wall with such force that his body literally explodes.

The rest of the chorts stampede away from her, but anyone who goes for the exit meets Marius's jaws.

I'm too lightheaded to follow the rest of the fight, only registering bits and pieces of what happens.

Lilith lands, grabs the guy who stole my tonsils, and kicks him in the groin. He flies almost to the broken ceiling, then crash-lands and dissipates.

Nostradamus dodges a swipe from the lanky, shashka-wielding chort, then buries a knife in the chort's belly.

Lilith rips the leg off the round-faced ovary expert and flies around, clubbing other chorts to death with it.

Marius growls and disembowels the kidney expert.

Lilith sinks her fangs into the gallbladder guy and drinks him dry in one giant gulp—then burps exaggeratedly.

My vision starts to blur at that point, which is a blessing, as Lilith's killings get even more creative.

Nightmares-for-years kind of creative.

Eventually, the only chorts alive are Boris with his ripped-to-shreds body parts and a few others, who are too wounded to move.

This is when Nostradamus frees my hands and feet, then takes off the blood-splattered bib from my neck and tosses it on the floor. I can't get up, though, partly because I'm in too much pain, and partly because the lack of blood circulation gave all my limbs enough pins and needles to make an army of porcupines.

Lilith goes over to the small table that managed to survive the battle and picks up the bottle of water.

Walking toward me, she pricks her finger and squeezes the tiniest droplet of her blood into the bottle.

Stopping next to my chair, she gives the water a good shake and examines my face. "You poor dear." She presses the bottle to my lips. "Drink this, and you'll be good as new."

Since Felix didn't seem to get hooked on this—and because I'd do anything to stop the pain—I greedily gulp a big sip of the blood water.

An almost orgasmic relief whooshes through my body. It's like eating after starvation or drinking after being dehydrated to a husk.

The bones in my face are the first to heal, but the rest of my pains disappear also, as do nausea, lightheadedness, and the pins-and-needles feeling in my limbs.

Wow.

Felix was right. This is Isis-level healing, if not better.

Though I don't think I'm addicted, I can see why a more direct blood-tasting might be a problem.

"Thank you," I say, marveling at how my voice is completely back to normal. Turning toward Nostradamus and Marius, I thank them as well.

"Of course," Lilith says. "We're family. I'm sure you'd help me if I needed it."

Hmmm. Would I, though? What do I reply to that? This is really awkward.

"Does your blood heal internal organs?" I ask, deciding to switch to a much more important topic.

"Of course," Lilith says with more than a tinge of pride.

"Even if it's chort damage? Because they killed my spleen and a bunch of other things."

"I don't see why not," Lilith says and looks at Nostradamus, who shrugs. "But since I've never tested it, we should probably take you to a human hospital to check."

"Great idea," I say and stand up with ease. Gleefully, I take a few steps on my newly steady legs.

The recovery is amazing.

"Before we go, we have to finish *them*." Lilith nods at the still-moaning Boris and his surviving crew. "Which one do you want?"

For a few moments, I actually consider it.

I'd like nothing better than to walk over to Boris and bash his stupid head in with a blunt object—or kick one of his injuries and say something cold, like, "Payback is a bitch, bitch."

Thankfully, my rational side kicks in, and I remember Rasputin's visions of little me turning into a killing machine. Lilith clearly has some weird agenda when it comes to this, and I'm not about to go along with it.

I'm not going to let her turn me into a monster.

Unless, of course, I already am a monster.

I certainly have the genetics for it.

But no. Sure, I've killed enemies in the heat of

battle, but I've never murder-tortured anyone, and I'm not about to start.

"Still squeamish," Lilith tells Nostradamus disappointedly. "Oh, well. Her loss is my gain."

With that, she prances over to a wounded chort and snaps his neck.

"Sure, let's call it 'squeamish,'" I mutter, looking away as she finishes another one.

"But this is the one who hurt you the most, right?" She points the toe of her shoe at Boris. "I think he also hurt your little friend."

"That's him." I can't help rubbing my chin and cheek—the completely healed parts of my face that Boris damaged.

"Yet you don't want to finish him?" She looks genuinely puzzled.

"Maybe another time," I say as politely as I can. "You can do the honors right now."

"Oh, I will," she says menacingly. "I think he needs a lesson in etiquette."

She kneels next to Boris and casually rips his ear off.

He screams.

She forces some blood-water from the bottle into his mouth, and his injuries begin to knit. As soon as they're gone, she creates new ones.

I look away again.

Lilith starts to do something new to Boris—something that sounds like she's making hamburgers from scratch… without any kitchen appliances.

Boris screams like a banshee, and keeps screaming until I plug my ears to keep my sanity.

Muffled, the screaming continues for a very, very long time.

When it stops, I turn and see that Boris's body has already disintegrated, like those of the rest of his kind.

"I know," Lilith says, looking at the empty spot. "I had to make this quick so we can take you to the hospital."

That was quick? How long would she have tortured the guy if she had more time?

Maybe she didn't lie when she said she'd treated Rasputin well. Compared to what she can do, those beatings from the guards were kindness itself.

Slowly shaking his head, Nostradamus grabs hold of Marius and heads for the exit.

I wait for Lilith to go next, then follow them.

A sleek Ferrari is waiting outside. Marius and Nostradamus get in the back, while Lilith jumps behind the wheel.

Great. Let the psychotic one drive. Why not?

I gingerly get inside and buckle up.

At least if we crash, I can always lick some of Mommy's blood to feel better.

Wait a second, is that addiction talking?

Grinning, Lilith floors the gas pedal.

The regular streets zoom by at NASCAR speeds, and when we reach the highway, Lilith manages to speed up more. I squeeze the bottom of my seat and check that my seatbelt is fastened as she brings us to the brink of one accident after another.

She must be using her luck powers again. This is similar to what Chester did when he drove the other day—but on steroids and in need of antipsychotic drugs.

"Did Woland escape?" I ask Nostradamus—mostly to think of something besides the impending car explosion.

"I have no idea," Nostradamus says, fluffing Marius's fur. "Did you see him leave?"

Marius growls.

"Then why didn't you kill him?" Lilith asks—and to my horror, she looks at Marius instead of at the road.

Marius growls again.

"You're right," Nostradamus says. "Sasha's safety *was* the priority."

Are they pranking me, or do these growls actually mean something?

"Woland lost all of his people," Lilith says, this time looking at me instead of the road. "He's probably tucking his tail and running all the way to St. Petersburg." Returning her gaze to the road, she adds, "No doubt he's going to get demoted for getting all the Enforcers killed."

Marius growls one more time.

"No." Nostradamus scratches Marius's fluffy ear. "You can't hunt him down. Without Lilith around, chorts are extremely hard to kill."

I'm on the verge of asking some questions when we

violently screech onto a ramp—and almost right into a building labeled "NYU Lutheran Medical Center."

Marius gets funny looks from the medical personnel when we enter the lobby—at least until Lilith uses glamour on everyone. She also makes them admit me as quickly as possible, and I'm soon rushed inside and subjected to every scan known to science.

"Her organs are perfectly fine," the doctor tells Lilith, his voice sounding robotic due to the glamour. "In fact, she's in as perfect health as I've ever seen. It's extraordinary."

I exhale a breath I didn't realize I'd been holding. I was worried about my organs—especially the ovary and the kidney.

As it turns out, I feel very attached to them.

Lilith beams at me proudly. "My blood is extraordinary." Turning back to the doctor, she asks, "What about my drink?"

"Right." The doctor hands her a blood bag. "Type O, as you commanded."

Lilith takes the bag from him and slurps on it like a poor-mannered kindergartener.

Just as she's almost done with this one bag, a nurse runs over and hands her another one.

"What if they get a patient who'll need that for a transfusion?" I ask as I get up to leave.

"Would you rather I get the blood from one of those very convenient receptacles?" Lilith smiles predatorily and waves at a cute little girl down the hall from us.

"No," I say quickly. "I'm sure they have plenty of blood in the bank. You enjoy yourself."

We walk in silence as more medical staff bring Lilith bag after bag—Lilith because she's slurping away and me because I decide to keep my commentary to a minimum lest I get people killed.

Once outside, I check my phone.

Still nothing from Nero, but I do have a voicemail and two texts from Lucretia, asking why I called before and whether I'm okay.

I'm on a different planet from okay, I text back. *Maybe a different galaxy.*

She writes back instantly:

Want to meet up? I'm leaving the banya to go back to the city in a few minutes.

"Sexting your boyfriend?" Lilith asks, noticing my phone. "You might want to pay him a visit. They say my blood makes—"

"Please do not finish that thought," I say and jump into the car, still thinking of what to reply to Lucretia.

"—sex much better," Lilith says with relish, joining me in the Ferrari.

Pretending not to have heard, Nostradamus pets Marius's fur, and the werewolf growls contentedly.

"So," Lilith says. "What now?"

That's a great question.

It's been hours since I had my visions about Nero, and I bet there's zero chance I can catch him on Gomorrah at this point.

Do I still want to go there to talk to Rasputin and

Ariel? I guess I do, but that's not a priority—not when Nero is in trouble.

Should I go to the dragon world to help Nero with those epic battles? Assuming I didn't miss them, that is.

He'd be pissed if I showed up—which is a bonus. But what about my current companions? Should I bring them along? Lilith certainly could be useful in a fight and might consider all the bloodshed a good mother-daughter bonding experience.

No, wait.

Asking Lilith to save my life in a moment of desperation is one thing; asking her to help out my boss/Mentor/crush is quite another.

Actually, it's a moot point anyway. When Nero attacked her on her world, she mentioned she had a contract with the dragon king, by which she was supposed to stay out of his world if he stayed out of hers. The very same dragon king whose wish to marry Claudia was the catalyst for Nero's warmongering. Which reminds me of the million-dollar question: who is Cl—

"Are you all right?" Lilith asks. "Was your brain scan clean?"

Despite her mocking tone, she seems genuinely concerned for me, at least for a fraction of a second.

But no. I must've imagined that concern.

Maybe scanning my brain more thoroughly is a good idea.

"I'm just shaken up," I tell her honestly. "I know you wanted to hang out around New York, but I'd really like to see my therapist." I wave my phone. "By sheer coincidence, she's also in Brooklyn right now, so I'd love to meet her."

"If that's what you need, then I'm sure her proximity isn't a coincidence," Lilith says smugly. "I want you to be well, and my luck powers undoubtedly brought this about."

"Great, thank you—and your powers," I say. "Let me see where she wants to meet."

Lucretia and I text back and forth and settle on an Uzbek food restaurant where Felix and I once had lunch with his parents.

I explain our destination to Lilith, and make sure to also explain that there's no rush to get there.

Starting the car, Lilith smirks, then floors the gas pedal anyway.

As we barrel down the street, her driving feels extra reckless—probably because I'm not busy worrying about my organs this time.

"I have to say, I don't often meet other seers," Nostradamus says over the roar of the engine. "Especially ones as powerful as you."

"Me neither." I gladly peel my eyes from the road to look back at him. "It's frustrating. Learning to wield my powers has been a headache."

"That's a shame." He clears his throat. "You know, I like teaching that sort of thing. If there's something specific you ever want to learn, just ask me."

I'm so excited I almost forget about Lilith's *The Fast and the Furious* audition.

Nostradamus himself is volunteering to teach me how to use seer powers.

Christmas has officially come early.

Unless he has some agenda, of course—which isn't out of the question given the company he keeps.

Still, as far as evil shenanigans go, answering my questions is probably my favorite kind.

"How do you target a specific time in a vision?" I ask, remembering my most recent Headspace-related dilemma.

"Ah." He mindlessly runs his hand over Marius's fur. "You're talking about an extremely advanced technique. Choosing a specific time in the future is costly in terms of seer power—and it's also pretty difficult to explain."

"Oh?" I say disappointedly.

"Well, let me try." He looks thoughtful. "Okay, so at the core, what you need is to focus on the essence of time," he says, pronouncing "essence" in a French manner.

"Essence?"

"That's right."

"So a little bit like you would with a specific person, but with time?" I say.

"Yes, very good. Only it's harder to do with an abstract concept such as time."

"Harder?" Lilith looks back. "What is the essence of a second? Or an hour? Or a day?"

Though I wish she'd focus on the road, she has a

point—"essence of a second" is a pretty nebulous concept.

"Right." Nostradamus takes on a professorial tone. "Time perception is key to this—which makes the skill very personal. You have to get at the core of what the time slice in question feels like to you. How it passes. What it means. Things like a seer's age and state of being play an important role. For example, a child will perceive a month as a very long time, yet for an ancient like me, a month is a triviality. It's the little blip before I must get a new haircut." He runs his hands through his messy locks.

"I think I understand," Lilith says.

"You have to also consider your emotional state," Nostradamus continues. "When you're having fun, time flows faster, but when you're waiting for a letter from a lover to arrive, time can slow to a crawl."

A paper letter? He *is* ancient.

"So," I say. "If I want to know your future in a day's time, I'll need to dwell on your essence and the essence of the idea of a day?"

"Put crudely, yes," he says. "Just bear in mind that the day in question will be purely from *your* perspective, not mine."

"Huh?" Lilith furrows her perfect brows. "Isn't a day twenty-four hours for everyone?"

"Not if the vision target is in the Otherlands," Nostradamus says. "Or, hypothetically, if they're flying at the speed of light."

"Relativity," I say uncertainly.

"Exactly," he confirms.

"Okay," I say. "Let's pretend I'm on Atlantis—a world where time goes so fast that a day here is ten years there."

"Right," he says.

"And let's also assume you targeted my future in a day for you."

"Sure," he says.

"So, if I understand you correctly, you'd actually see my future in ten years from my point of view, but a day from yours, right?"

"You're close," he says. "What you say is almost true, but would get much more complicated if I decided to go visit you on Atlantis."

"My head hurts," Lilith says. "I'm glad we're almost there. Remind me never to be in a car with two seers again."

"I think I get it," I say, ignoring her. "I probably need to experiment with this to really understand."

"That's an excellent idea," Nostradamus says. "Why don't you try it now?"

Why don't I indeed?

I've been itching to check up on Nero, and now I can do that and test out my new skill—assuming I can get it to work.

Evening out my breath, I leap into Headspace.

CHAPTER NINETEEN

NO SCARY SHAPES surround me this time, which means Lilith's driving isn't going to kill us.

Hopefully.

Getting right to my task, I focus on Nero's essence—something I can do in my sleep.

Probably better in my sleep given all the wet dreams he gives me.

Now for the hard part—the essence of the concept of a day.

Usually—back when no one was trying to kill me every five minutes—a day, at least a weekday, was a rather boring and slow-moving chain of events in my life. Okay, maybe not all of it. The morning routine would fly by, but the ride on my Vespa would feel longer sometimes—probably because I had to pay attention to the road. Research for Nero would usually drag, then the trip home would mimic the ride to work, and my evening routine would be fast also—

especially if I did something fun, like read a magic book.

Today, though, my day has been *very* different. With all the torture and losing consciousness repeatedly, it's felt more like a month.

A new set of shapes shows up around me.

Hopefully, this is my meditations on the concept of a day bearing fruit.

Choosing one, I grab it with my ethereal wisp and fall in.

———

NERO IS STANDING in a tent surrounded by a group of people who look to be generals in his army. They include an underwear-model-hot guy of the strongmen variety, a giant, a massive centaur, and a thin man who must be the cockatrice leader.

To the side stand Colton (the smallest giant), Vlad, Isis, Kit, and other Cognizant from Earth.

They're all staring at a beautifully hand-drawn map on the floor.

"Just one more battle and a day's journey before we finally face the usurper," Nero says. "Like the last time, our goal is not to just defeat them, but to also spread the word of my return throughout the continent." He gestures at the enormous landmass that's the centerpiece of the map—a supercontinent that reminds me of Gondwana, which was South America, Africa, Antarctica, Australia, the Indian

Subcontinent, and Arabia smooshed together. "To that end, any humans who lay down their arms today are not to be killed. I will talk to them just like the last time and unveil the usurper." His fist flexes at his side.

So this place also has humans—and they must be the bulk of the ground troops. I guess that would have to be the case if the dragons want to retain their powers on this world. Sounds like the humans let dragons rule the world—and are aware of royal bloodlines on top of that.

"Yes, sir, no killing humans after they surrender," Kit says in a mocking tone, then turns into Winston Churchill for some reason. In her own voice, she asks, "What if some dragons surrender this time?"

"I will personally decide the fate of dragons," Nero says, his expression darkening and his limbal rings expanding.

Everyone looks down at the map—or anywhere but Nero's face—and I can't blame them for that. Nero looks kind of scary—and to me, quite hot.

Tearing my gaze away from him, I scan the map.

All the landmarks are in a strange, barely readable form of Cyrillic, but I can make out some of the names. Easier to follow is the red line. It starts at a place marked by circular symbols and labeled "Ворота"—which is Russian for "Gates." From there, the line loops around a giant mountain ridge drawn with silver paint, and continues in an s-shape to a city marked as—if I read it right—Godiva.

No one comments about the delicious-sounding destination. Their expressions are grim.

"Listen," Nero says, his face smoothing out. "You all fought hard. You all fought well." He gives everyone an approving once-over. "Those who did it to repay a favor"—he looks at the members of the Council when he says this—"should know that not only will we be even after this, I will owe each and every one of you a great debt."

Everyone except Kit looks dumbfounded—even the usually calm Vlad. It's hard to tell if they find it frightening that Nero will owe them a favor, or it's just a boon they didn't expect in a million years.

"Those of you who are fighting for glory, riches, and power"—he looks at the generals—"the humans you faced in battle will tell legends of you for many millennia. You'll be known as dragon slayers. No matter where you are, your powers will grow from this worship." He turns to the strongman guy. "The battles we're about to face will overshadow what happened earlier. They will be something you'll tell your grandchildren's children about." He looks at the cockatrice leader. "The riches you are about to gain are beyond your wildest imaginings, and your biggest problem will be how to transport your obscene wealth."

As I listen to Nero's rousing speech, I can't help but envy my boss and mentor for his oratory skills. When he talks at Wall Street conferences, he's good. Here, though, he's outstanding. I bet if he put his mind to it, he could become Alexander the Great of the Otherlands.

Concluding the spiel with something that reminds me of the "they may take our lives" speech in *Braveheart*, Nero adjourns the meeting, and everyone leaves the tent with a bounce in their steps.

Everyone except Kit.

She walks over to Nero and turns herself into Rasputin. In his voice, she says, "This is the last battle we're guaranteed to win, isn't it?"

"The last one he foresaw, yes." Nero's face turns inscrutable. "Rasputin ran out of power before he could see how the battle at Godiva would play out, so I would understand if you want to leave after this. I'd still owe—"

"Leave?" Kit turns back into herself and winks at him mischievously. "The next battle is when things are really going to get fun."

"I hope you realize that just because a seer saw me win today, it doesn't mean *you* survive. Or anyone else for that matter." Nero walks toward the tent exit. "So if uncertainty makes things more fun for you, today should also be a blast."

"I didn't think of that," Kit says and grins even wider.

As they step out of the tent together, I wonder if Kit has replaced her addiction to sex with a similar craving for violence. They do go together for some people.

In the next moment, however, I catch a glimpse of

the outside, and the sight takes my nonexistent breath away.

We're in a Manhattan-sized clearing of a gargantuan forest that's mostly made up of pine-like trees with needles that are not just green, but also purple and pink.

The ground under everyone's feet is covered by some similarly colored fungal-like growths that remind me of snakes (or giant worms) but made out of a coral reef-like material. The longest of these tentacle things pull away when someone steps anywhere near them, while the budding growths usually fail to do so and simply crunch under feet and hooves.

On the two sides of the clearing, at the very edge of the forest, are the two armies.

The human portion of the enemy army is nearly three times that of the one in my earlier vision—and the number of dragons is about double.

On Nero's side, there are noticeably fewer forces.

They took serious losses in the last battle.

I'd estimate there are now twenty enemy soldiers to one of Nero's—and the ratio of dragons to Nero, Kit, and the cockatrices is even worse.

Did Rasputin lie when he predicted Nero would win this battle? Also, even if they do win by some miracle, will there be enough of them left to help Nero when he gets to Godiva?

On the plus side, the size disparity doesn't seem to affect Nero's army morale in the least. In fact, the newly psyched generals giddily rush to their respective troops and attempt to do for their soldiers what Nero did for them in the tent.

On his end, Nero starts taking off his clothes, and his abs, along with other parts, steal my attention from the rest of the goings on.

If he had more females in his army, this bit would be pretty motivational.

Before I find a way to drool without a mouth, Nero turns into a dragon, flies to a nearby hill, and roars incessantly.

A large enemy dragon roars in a similar fashion and flies to join Nero.

This must be a parley chat, like the last time.

When they assume human form and start speaking, I see that I'm right.

The newcomer demands Nero leave or else.

Nero demands Claudia or else.

Just like the last time, the guy says he doesn't have the authority to give Nero Claudia, and that someone with an army as puny as his doesn't get to make demands.

Unlike the other guy, at least this dragon doesn't break the spirit of the parley by attacking. Instead, he says grimly, "I'll meet you on the battlefield."

"It's your funeral," Nero retorts before turning back into his dragon form and returning to his army.

With the parley done, the enemy forces mobilize and begin to advance, but Nero's army doesn't move as he rejoins their ranks and turns back into his human form. Tensely, they stand by the forest edge, readying themselves for something.

If I didn't know better, I'd think them scared to attack.

Not that they could be blamed if that were the case —the enemy horde looks even more formidable now that they're advancing on Nero's army with fierce determination on what seems like millions of faces.

The enemy dragons roar and fly slightly ahead of their ground support. When they're about midway through the clearing, Nero yells, "Now!"

With a hoorah, Nero's allies rush forward.

Seeing this, the enemy dragons speed up and start breathing their Napalm-like fire—scorching the ground where Nero's troops are headed as a pretty effective psychological deterrent to the attack.

Nero shouts some new command, and a small squadron of giants walks out of the cover of the pine forest.

Interesting.

I thought they'd been killed in the last battle, but seems like they were just hiding out.

Their enormous muscles bulging, the giants carry minivan-sized wooden contraptions. Steam-powered and as creaky as a wooden rollercoaster, the machines look like distant cousins of harpoon guns, only made for, well, giants. Out of each mouth of the weapon, familiar-looking spears stick out—the ones with those diamond/adamantium tips that can pierce dragon hide.

Ah, yes. These weapons must be Itzel's design. After

my vision cut out, she must've figured out a way to make *something* work on this technologically challenged world, and Nero had his troops build the machines on the way to this battle.

The dragon squad also notice the problem, and their limbal rings expand—only it's too late at this point.

"Fire!" Nero roars.

The giants aim and pull on ropes sticking out of their weapons.

The guns boom, and a cloud of spears torpedoes forward, blocking the sun as they fly in the air.

I'm glad I don't have ears right now because the roar of injured dragons is so loud it would cause permanent damage.

Looking like pin cushions, the dragons try to scatter, but the giants reload and fire again, then toss the contraptions aside and rush forward, rejoining the rest of the army.

The spears reach their already-wounded targets, and the new roar is just as deafening as the last.

As if waiting for this, the cockatrices turn into their lizard forms and take flight, but without the strongmen this time—which is not good for the enemy ground troops because said strongmen are leading the army instead.

Also not good for the enemy troops is Vlad's new role in the fight. Instead of riding on Kit or Nero's back, the vampire is running shoulder to shoulder with his former students, the lethal gate sword in his hand.

The battle cries intensify as Nero's army clashes into the enemy forces, cutting through them like a hot spoon through ice cream.

Though they're still horrifically outnumbered, Nero's allies' sheer ferocity gives me hope.

As the strongmen and the giants decimate enemy troops using their superior strength, the strongmen look to be enjoying themselves. They must like ground battle more than being carried by cockatrices. There's almost creepy excitement on their faces as they make mincemeat of the enemy forces.

Still, the strongmen have nothing on Vlad, who's death personified for the enemy soldiers. Each swing of his deadly blade takes two, three, or four lives at a time, while not even the most skilled soldiers can so much as land a blow on him. Like an army unto himself, he cuts through the enemies, leaving his allies far behind. As he goes, he spills so much blood that a decent amount ends up dripping into his mouth—and when it does, he greedily swallows it, his fangs fully extended.

Nero's other allies get busy as well. Councilor Albina incinerates whole squadrons with her power, and the maybe-elf guy shoots enough arrows to stand in for a hundred regular archers. At the same time, the cockatrices hunt wounded dragons in the sky, using their deathly gazes to finish them off, and the centaurs decimate the enemy cavalry, their lances butchering everything in their path.

With a roar, Nero and Kit take to the skies. She

joins the cockatrices, but Nero flies over the enemy army.

Arms shaking with fear, the enemy archers shoot at him, but their arrows don't even scratch his scales.

Roaring his disdain, Nero spews fire at the back of the enemy troops—melting people and their armor into puddles and demoralizing an already-shaken army.

Meanwhile, Kit leaves the cockatrices and flies for an enemy dragon that's not currently surrounded by anyone.

A large green dragon with at least a dozen spears stuck in his body.

"You're not even a true dragon," the roar of her opponent seems to say as he breathes fire at her.

Kit dives below the flames, then swats at him with her claws.

That is a mistake, though. The green dragon dodges her swipe, and before she can recover, he rakes his claws through Kit's shoulder.

Kit roars in pain.

Seeing an opportunity, a wounded red dragon joins Kit's enemy.

Oh no.

If I had a mouth—and a loudspeaker—I'd tell the cockatrices or Nero to go help, but I don't and they're too busy fighting their own battles to notice.

Seemingly undaunted by the fight on two fronts, Kit uses her tail to swipe at the red newcomer just as she bites the green dragon's scaly wrist.

Her opponent roars so loudly that some of the cockatrices—and more importantly, Nero—look that way and see Kit in trouble.

A lot of trouble, as the green dragon rips into Kit's other shoulder with his unbitten claw.

Nero and the others rush to help Kit, but they're too late.

Using the distraction his green ally has created, the red dragon slams Kit's head with his tail, over and over, leaving her stunned. Then he performs an aerial maneuver that ends with those giant claws raking deep gashes in Kit's back.

Letting go of the green dragon's wrist, Kit plummets toward the ground in a spiral, like a shot-down airplane.

With a heart-wrenching splat, she lands on top of a small squadron of enemy soldiers, crushing them to death, and lies there unmoving.

CHAPTER TWENTY

NO.

This can't be.

Kit can't be hurt or worse.

I refuse to accept it.

Despite what Nero said earlier, I can't believe Rasputin would call something "a victory" if it involves a friend of mine dying.

The enormous werewolf and Colton, the small giant, join the other troops in an effort to keep the enemy soldiers away from Kit's body. Vlad starts to make his way back to her also, but he's too far to do any good anytime soon.

Then Kit-the-dragon seems to disappear. I panic for a second, but then I see she just turned back into her usual shape.

Is that a good or a bad sign?

She still has the wounds she received as a dragon, and is still lying there without any sign of life.

A squadron of cockatrices direct their deadly stares at the wounds of the green dragon who hurt Kit, while Nero roars viciously and blows a mighty fire breath that incinerates the red dragon on the spot.

Done with vengeance, Nero dives down like a falcon.

Reaching the ground, he turns back into his human form and grabs Kit in that signature bridal carry he's practiced on me.

"Hold on," he says soothingly to her, then blurs into a too-fast-to-track run in the direction of the tent.

His army parts for Nero like the Red Sea did for Moses.

After their leader passes through their ranks, everyone begins to fight even more viciously.

Supporting the ground troops, the cockatrices attack the remaining dragons with greater fury, their death glares crisscrossing the sky like lasers at some surreal concert.

Approaching the tent with Kit in tow, Nero shouts, "Phase two!"

Smirks appear on the faces of Nero's allies as a new surprise comes out of the forest.

It's an army of human soldiers that look eerily like the bad guys—same armor and everything—but they're led by the strongmen and are looking angrily at what's left of the wounded dragons in the sky.

Looks like some soldiers not only laid down their arms after the last battle but actually switched sides.

I bet Nero's truth-telling came in handy that day.

He would've made sure they had no other agenda before letting them join his forces.

Seeing yet another turn for the worse, the enemy dragons farthest from the action begin to flee.

Nero enters the tent and faces Isis.

Oh yeah. I didn't see *her* on the battlefield.

Was she hiding out here? Why?

"You think it worked?" Isis asks.

"Heal her," Nero says instead of answering and gently lays Kit on the map. "No time to talk."

Nodding, Isis shoots Kit with her energy, and Kit's grievous wounds start mending immediately.

I wish I could jump up and down in glee.

Kit is going to be fine—especially if her disturbing moans of pleasure are anything to go by.

"Now sell it." Isis nods at the tent entrance. "Be wrath."

Nero nods gravely and storms out of the tent, an expression of grief on his face.

Huh?

What's that about?

With no time to ponder the mystery further, I observe as Nero turns into his dragon form and roars something that sounds suspiciously like, "You will pay for that."

What few enemy dragons remain in the sky literally tuck their tails between their legs and fly away.

Instead of giving the dragons chase, the cockatrices swoop down to use their gazes and claws on enemy troops.

Nero doesn't chase anyone either. Instead, he trims the enemy ground troops with his breath.

Yet no matter how many losses they take, there are still too many human soldiers remaining.

Realizing this too, Nero roars something, and the woman who controlled the animals the last time steps out of the forest, followed by a whole army of creatures with sharp claws and even sharper teeth. With a gesture, the woman sends her critters at the enemy army, then touches the snake-like coral stuff on the ground and concentrates.

All of a sudden, the tentacle-like things stop avoiding enemy soldiers and begin to grab them by the ankles instead—which gives Nero's army yet another huge advantage.

The human army takes unimaginable losses, and the tide of battle begins to turn—but just barely.

"Phase three!" Nero roars, and human soldiers appear from all sides of the clearing—surrounding the enemy army.

"Surrender!" the giants shout through their massive throats.

"Surrender!" Vlad and the strongmen yell as they deliver deadly blows.

"Surrender!" Nero's dragon roar also seems to say, right before he spews hellfire yet again.

"Surrender!" the centaurs growl.

"Surrender!" the human part of the army screams. "Join the true heir of our world."

And it seems to work.

One by one, the enemy soldiers lower their weapons and kneel on the ground with their hands behind their heads—

———

I'M BACK in the real world, and it takes me a few moments to reorient myself. I'm in a car with Nostradamus and Lilith, on the way to see Lucretia—and all this adrenaline in my blood is thanks to Lilith's driving.

I must say, seeing Nero win that battle was awesome. But what worries me now is that it was the last "safe" battle as far as Rasputin's visions go. What if—

"So did your little seer test succeed?" Lilith asks when she sees me open my eyes—doing so by looking at me instead of the intersection she flies through, nearly killing a nice old lady and a poodle.

"I think so," I say, mostly to get her looking back at errant pedestrians. "Then again, I didn't see any proof that the events I saw in my vision will transpire exactly a day from this moment."

"You managed to target a day into the future?" Nostradamus whistles. "Most seers only have enough power to work with seconds when they first try this out."

Great. That would've been useful to know *before* I did the test.

Oh well. Let's just hope I didn't use up too much of

my seer mojo with that day-away targeted vision. There's still plenty I'd like to foresee, starting with Nero's final battle.

Before I can return to Headspace, we take a nauseatingly sharp turn onto Brighton Beach. Storefronts begin flashing before my eyes. Though I can read the Russian names now, they pass by too quickly for me to actually register them.

Two seconds and ten gray hairs later, the Ferrari screeches to a rubber-burning halt.

Amazed to be alive, I unbuckle my safety belt.

"Thank you, Nostradamus." I turn around to look at him. "You too, Marius." I smile at the shaggy beast. "And especially you." I look at Lilith, who's grinning like the Grinch.

Opening the passenger door, I stumble out of the car on unsteady legs.

Lilith exits as well.

"Maybe I forgot to mention, but this meeting is with my therapist," I tell her. "So it's private. That means you can't join us."

"Oh." Lilith pouts. "But I'd like to spend more time with you."

"How about sometime in the future?" With my best poker face, I extend my hand. "Why don't we exchange numbers so we can set something up in a few days?"

She eagerly pulls out her shiny new iPhone, unlocks it, and places it on my upturned palm.

As I take the device, scores of mentalism effects swirl through my head—all that involve one devious underlying secret: snooping around someone's phone. I'd often used that method during my restaurant gig. Only there, I'd pretended to need to use the person's calculator app, or to see some picture they took that "really represents them" or an image of their pet so "I can guess its name."

Just as I would during a performance, I look bored and uninterested as I stealthily navigate to the recent calls with rehearsed proficiency. Once I arrive there, I memorize the few numbers I see. Sadly, not a single one has a name listed next to it. It doesn't matter, though. Felix should now be in a better position to figure out whom Lilith called in that vision I had earlier. Also, if we're lucky, he might find out what was actually said.

Dirty work done, I exit the recent calls with a practiced set of moves and bring up the contacts app. Turning the screen so Lilith can actually see it—and later swear she never took her eyes off it—I demonstratively click the "new contact" button and fill out my info, then place a call to myself.

Handing her phone back, I wait for mine to ring, then add Lilith as a contact, all the while suppressing another satisfied smile.

Now I can also give Felix *her* number to work with.

"Anything you'd like me to put as your last name?" I ask Lilith before clicking "save contact." "Is it Rasputina —the feminine variation of my dad's last name?"

"No," she says. "Though Grisha and I did have a ceremony, I wasn't officially divorced from my previous husband." Feigning shame, she clutches her nonexistent pearls. "You were illegitimate, I'm afraid. What a scandal."

"I doubt I could care less if I try," I say, then start typing "the evil one" instead of a last name.

"How about you put down Rossi?" Lilith says. "That was my late husband's name. Now *there* was a man who knew what I wanted—often before I did." She wiggles her eyebrows lasciviously.

Eww. She *really* needs that TMI lesson.

Wait a sec.

Why does the last name Rossi sound so familiar?

"Sasha!" Lucretia's usually calm voice is anything but. "What are you doing talking to *her*?"

I turn and see Lucretia standing outside the restaurant, her blue eyes practically jumping out of their sockets.

Then it hits me.

Except it can't be.

But that *is* where I heard that name before.

I turn back to Lilith, then look at my friend and therapist, then once more at the evil one.

Yep.

If people at work think Lucretia and I look alike, they haven't compared her pale facial features to those of Lilith.

Now that I'm looking for it, the resemblance is uncanny.

And, of course, Lucretia's last name *is* Rossi.

A name she must've gotten from her father—a father who no doubt was an empath, like his daughter.

Lilith also looks at Lucretia, then back at me, and a wicked smile splits her face. "I thought this was a lunch with your therapist," she says. "You said nothing about this being a family reunion."

CHAPTER TWENTY-ONE

"YOU'RE MY SISTER?" I gape at Lucretia. "Why didn't you tell me?"

Lucretia is staring at me like I've just sprouted horns. "You're her daughter too? Wait, no, you can't be. You were born on this world and she left it a hundred —" She stops talking, no doubt recalling the story of how my birth certificate is from a century ago.

Turning to Lilith, she regards her with undisguised contempt. "So you spawned more of us to abandon? How many siblings do I have at this point?"

"Siblings?" I say, stunned. "Plural?"

"We better go, dear," Nostradamus says to Lilith from the car. "Something important just came up."

"Saved by the seer," Lilith says and heaves a dramatic sigh. "You enjoy your gossip," she tells me as she walks around the front of the car to the driver's seat. "And keep in mind Lucretia was the one who introduced the whole concept of 'blame the mother' into the field of psychology on this world. Her bias against me is as unfair as it is strong." She waves a beauty pageant goodbye, then slides into the driver's seat and speeds away.

Lucretia continues staring at me. "How is this possible?" she asks unsteadily. "How do you even know her? Why is she back?"

Numbly, I shake my head. "You're my sister? A half-sister?"

"Looks like it." Lucretia studies me as if seeing me for the first time. "Well," she says after a pause. "I think this calls for at least a hug."

Hesitantly, I step toward her and hug her slim frame. Her hair smells like tranquil mossy woods, and my head spins as I attempt to make sense of my tumultuous emotions.

Underneath the shock, there's a peculiar lightness, mixed with growing excitement. This, here, is how I always fantasied about reuniting with my birth family.

It's so different from when I met Rasputin, the father who abandoned me to save me, and it's certainly nothing like my encounters with volatile Lilith.

This joyful reunion is what I always hoped for—and it definitely helps that I liked Lucretia before I knew we were family.

Liked and respected her.

In fact, if I put together a list of people to whom I'd want to be related, she'd be very high on it.

I squeeze her tighter.

After what feels like a few minutes, we gently pull apart and grin like stoned loons.

"Let's feed you," she says and nods at the restaurant. "You're starving."

How did she—oh right, she can feel my hunger with her empath powers.

I hope she also sensed the joy I felt at this revelation.

We walk in and take a seat.

"Sorry," I say to her when the waiter hands us two menus. "I just realized I asked you to a restaurant, but you can't eat anything."

She raises her eyebrows. "I *can* eat." When the waiter leaves to get us water, she whispers, "I just don't need to—like with sleep."

"So vampires can eat and sleep?" I open the menu. "Vlad made me think otherwise."

"Just because you can hypothetically do a thing doesn't mean you'd want to when you don't have to." She looks inside the menu and wrinkles her nose. "The pleasure of eating human food dulls in comparison to the ecstasy of feeding the way we do." She looks up and glances around, making sure we're not being overheard. "Sleep too doesn't provide any rest for us after the transition—just a chance to dream, a dubious reward for wasting eight hours lying in one place like a log."

I shake my head, trying to imagine what it would be like not to want to eat or sleep. In this very moment, I'd give a hundred dollars for a nap and double that for a nice meal.

Hopefully, though, I won't have to. The prices in this place look reasonable.

Then something strikes me. "Wait a minute," I say. "How am I able to speak to you about all the Cognizant stuff? You lost your Mandate aura when you turned, so I should be forbidden from speaking to you, right?"

She smiles. "The Mandate is actually subtle enough to account for this sort of thing. Its main objective is to keep us from revealing Cognizant secrets to the uninitiated. Since I already know everything, you can speak to me freely."

The waiter comes back, and I impress Lucretia by ordering everything in Russian.

Speaking English, she orders the *tushpera* soup, claiming for the waiter's benefit that she isn't very hungry today.

"All right, spill it," she says when he leaves. "How do you know Lilith, and more importantly, why is she back on this world?"

"Oh yeah. I guess we didn't get a chance to talk after my last adventure," I say and launch into the story about gnome-powered spacesuits, a trip through the deadly Otherlands, and my biological father's rescue. The part I pointedly gloss over is that Nero is a dragon, since it's not my secret to reveal, and I also keep quiet about what happened between us in that hotel room because, well, oversharing.

"She came to get revenge on Nero, but learned about me," I say toward the end. "Then she saved my life twice today, but as to why she's here, I have no clue."

"She saved you?" Lucretia furrows her brows. "That doesn't seem like her. The woman has no shred of maternal instincts."

The waiter brings our soups and the *lepyoshka* bread, so we temporarily stop speaking.

"What was it like growing up with her?" I ask when we have privacy again.

"I wouldn't know," Lucretia says bitterly. "My father raised me pretty much on his own. She just showed up from time to time to, and I quote, 'have the best orgasms of her life.'"

Damn. Lilith's TMI thing seems to go *way* back.

I blow on a spoonful of my *lagmon* soup and look at Lucretia. The irony of our usual therapist and patient role reversal isn't lost on me.

"Being an empath can sometimes be a curse," my newfound sister says as she mindlessly stirs her soup. "When my dad was alive, I could feel his joy when he spoke with me. But when Lilith deigned to show up, there was a black hole where warm feelings should be. The only thing I'd ever felt from her is an occasional sense of disappointment. I suspect Lilith has always seen me as an annoying side effect of having that mind-blowing sex with my father." I'm not sure Lucretia realizes it, but she's bending her spoon with her tight grip. "To Lilith, I'm like an STD that talks, nothing more." She lets go of the spoon, looking almost

Vlad-broody, and I wonder if it would be inappropriate to give her another hug or two.

Seeing how she doesn't do it in her capacity as a therapist, I don't either, but I do cover her hand with mine and squeeze it reassuringly.

"Sorry about that." She shakes her head, her usual composure returning as she pulls her hand away and gives me a small smile. "As you can tell, this is a sensitive topic."

"Of course," I say softly. "But are you sure she's all bad?" Realizing I sound pathetically naïve, I add, "I mean, she didn't have to save me today, but she did. In a psychotic way, sure, but I'd be dead if it weren't for Lilith—and Rasputin would've likely been killed as well."

"I don't know," Lucretia says, her blue gaze hardening. "I long ago accepted the truth—that my mother is a monster—and now I can't get disappointed."

I make the mistake of putting a spoonful of soup into my mouth, and the rich flavor of noodles and spicy meat overrules everything else for the next few moments.

"She may see more of herself in you," Lucretia says, bringing a spoonful of soup to her own lips, only to cringe in distaste. Putting the spoon down, she says, "Maybe seeing those similarities woke up something maternal in her? I mean, even drekavac mothers love their horrific spawn."

"Wait, are you saying I'm like her?" I nearly choke

on my soup from indignation. "The person you see as a monster?"

"I don't mean it that way." She stirs the soup again. "The two of you do share a certain deviousness, but you've always channeled yours into positive outlets, like your illusions, which makes all the difference in the world."

I rip off a large chunk of bread, stuff it in my mouth, and think about this as I chew.

Rasputin also said I have some things in common with Lilith. And it must be true because his comments helped me figure out Lilith's essence and see a vision of her.

So that begs the question: Could I be a murdering psychopath under the right circumstances?

Is that why she was trying to get me to finish those chorts—and the scores of innocents in the alternate history Rasputin prevented?

Is she like Dr. Evil, seeking her Mini-Me?

"I'm sorry," Lucretia says. "I didn't mean to make you feel all that. I'm the worst sister and an even worse therapist."

I swallow a mouthful of noodles so fast I nearly choke on them. "You're an amazing therapist and an awesome sister," I say when I can talk. "Speaking of sisters, you said something about more siblings earlier. What did you mean by that? Do I have some other sisters or brothers?"

"Umm." She looks into her cooling soup bowl. "There's just one person that I know of. Someone our lovely mother had with yet another man. But that sibling is someone who might not appreciate me telling you their identity just like that. I'm sorry."

"Oh, come on," I say, wondering if it's too soon to take back my "awesome sister" comment from seconds ago. "You're really not going to tell me anything?"

"How about I talk to our joint sibling?" she says soothingly. "I'm sure they'll want to discuss this with you once I do."

"I guess," I say, and suppress the urge to add, "Or I can ask Lilith instead of you." Taking a deep breath as Lucretia herself had taught me, I tell her, "I really want to know who it is. My whole life has been full of questions about my biological heritage, and now you're giving me one more mystery to dwell on."

"I'll do my absolute best to make sure this gets resolved quickly," Lucretia says, then stops talking because the waiter brings out the rest of my food.

As he takes our soup bowls away, Lucretia takes out her phone and sends someone a text.

"I just asked for a meeting," she says once the waiter is out of earshot. "I'll keep you posted."

It takes all my willpower not to snatch the phone from her hands and check whom she just texted.

On second thought, maybe I can ask Felix to track this text along with the calls from Lilith. After all, we know Lucretia's number and—

"Don't do whatever you just thought about doing," Lucretia says. "Please. As a favor to me."

"Fine," I snap and attack my *plov*.

"You're upset with me," Lucretia says, watching me clean my plate in sullen silence.

"Wouldn't you be?" I chase the food with water.

"When you meet this person, I think you'll understand," she says.

I freeze, blood draining from my face. "It's not Nero, is it?"

"No." She grins knowingly. "You and Nero aren't related. Given how you both feel, it would be pretty disturbing if you were."

"You think?" I say sarcastically, not even bothering to address the whole "how you feel" comment.

Of course, Nero and I are not related. She texted this mystery sibling, and Nero isn't reachable by text right now. Also, Lilith didn't act like she knew Nero when they fought on her world—and she would hopefully know her son.

"All right," I say magnanimously. "I'm not upset with you. Not that much, anyway."

"Good," Lucretia says. "But the check for this meal is on me."

"Fine. But you're also going to tell me things about yourself. Private things you'd only tell a sister."

"Always looking for an angle." She smiles like Mona Lisa. "Well, since you insist, there *is* something exciting going on in my life that I haven't told anyone. Wasn't even planning on telling anyone, but it looks like I owe you something of this magnitude." She pauses, as if hesitant to go on.

"Wow. You do have something juicy to share." I

spear a piece of lamb with my fork. "Out with it. I won't leave you alone until you tell me."

"Okay." She looks around as if she's about to share the US nuclear codes. "It's about Yaroslav," she says conspiratorially, then stops talking again.

Her secret has to do with her relationship with the bannik? I shift to the edge of my seat and chew carefully, worried I'll spook her.

"He and I, we're trying," she finally says. "Please keep this between us."

Trying?

When I parse her meaning, I nearly choke on a half-chewed piece of lamb. Recovering, I examine her face for any signs of joking but find none. "You're trying to have a baby?"

"He's been using his power to find a future where we succeed," she whispers. "It took a lot of his seer power, to the point that he's been completely drained for days, but he believes he's found the right time and place for us to be intimate that will lead to the result we want."

Drained for days? Okay, then. Seems like oversharing runs in our family.

Still, I'm glad Lucretia told me this. I once suspected she might be my mother and asked her if she had kids. She hinted that she'd had a human lover at some point, and that they never managed to conceive. Reading between the lines, I got the impression that she really wanted to have a child.

On a more selfish note, I'd love to have a little niece

or nephew. And given how gorgeous the bannik is—not to mention, Lucretia herself—this baby will probably be super cute.

"I guess this confirms it," I muse out loud. "A vampire *can* get preggers. I mean I figured as much since Lilith had me, but—"

"It just makes it less likely," Lucretia says. "Hence Yaroslav's hard work."

I burst out laughing.

"Anyway," she says, pretending she didn't understand the double entendre. "Before you ask, any Cognizant type—including a bannik—is compatible in that way."

"I wasn't going to ask that. I'm more interested in these visions Yaroslav must be having over and over. Must indeed be such 'hard work.'" I wiggle my eyebrows. "No wonder he ran out of his seer juice. No, wait, seer juice sounds dirty in this context. Seer mojo? Nope, still dirty."

I learn yet another fact about vampire physiology.

They can totally blush.

"You're just using humor to change an uncomfortable subject," Lucretia says and gives me a meaningful look. "Let me repeat my earlier point: any Cognizant, even Nero's type, can—"

"I think I want dessert," I say loudly enough for the waiter to hear.

The waiter walks over, and Lucretia rolls her eyes at me behind his back.

Does she actually know what Nero is? It seems like she does.

Though I'm already full to the point of bursting, I order a green tea and one piece of baklava.

"Do you have any idea when your efforts will bear fruit?" I ask Lucretia when the waiter leaves.

"Changing the subject again." She cocks her head. "You know, I could tell you skipped something important when you told me about your most recent adventures. Something that happened in a hotel perhaps?"

Damn her shrink/empath abilities. She must've picked up on my earlier omission. Unless—

"Did Nero say something to you?" I ask, leaning forward.

"If he did, it would be protected by doctor-patient confidentiality," she says. Then a grin appears on her face. "And now you've pretty much confirmed my suspicions."

The waiter brings the dessert, and I debate if I want to tell her what happened.

"Fine," I say when he leaves. "Here goes."

I tell her how Nero and I kissed, repeatedly, and how on that day, he did more to me but didn't risk me doing anything for him.

"I think it's not just about his fear of losing control and hurting you—which is a valid concern," she says thoughtfully, further confirming that she knows about his dragon nature. "But I can't discuss this with you in any more detail because he's a patient."

"He's talked to you about this?" I grip my scalding-hot teacup.

"I'm sorry. I can't confirm or deny."

"Oh, come on. What did he say? Remember, you owe me after the sibling mystery."

Lucretia's phone dings.

"Oh, shoot," she says, looking down at it. "I have a patient emergency I have to run to."

"Sure. And I'm a ballerina."

"I swear I have to go." Lucretia rummages through her purse, takes out her wallet, and puts a hundred-dollar bill on the table. "Please don't be mad."

"You make that difficult," I say, stuffing the baklava into my mouth.

"I'll make it up to you, I promise," she says, then kisses me on the bulging-from-the-dessert cheek and sprints for the door.

Maybe there really is an emergency?

I finish chewing, and as I sip my tea, I realize that all this sibling stuff has distracted me from something pretty urgent that also has to do with Nero—the future battle at Godiva.

Well, no time like the present to find out about the future.

I put down my cup and focus on getting into Headspace.

Once I'm floating among vision-shapes, I debate if I should utilize my new ability to target a specific timeframe or not. If I do, I could target two days into the future—one because my last vision was already a day from today, and one more day because Nero said that's when they will be at Godiva... though he meant a day for him, which might not equate to a day for me thanks to seer relativity.

No, given that I'm liable to screw it up, and since Nostradamus said targeting takes up too much power, I'd rather save the practice for later. I've been using so much juice today I'm bound to run out soon.

In any case, if a non-targeted vision doesn't get me what I want, I can always expend the power at that point.

I prepare to envision Nero's essence, but some intuition tells me to target Kit instead.

She did get hurt in the last battle, so it would be a good idea to check on her anyway, my intuition aside.

When I bring Kit to mind, a number of shapes show up.

Dire-looking shapes.

Crap.

I reach out to one of them and hope with all my being that I'm not about to see Kit die.

CHAPTER TWENTY-TWO

SIMILAR TO HOW my previous vision began, Nero is standing in a tent surrounded by his generals. Colton, Vlad, Isis, and other Cognizant from Earth are here as well, along with two groups of people I've never seen before.

One group is dressed just like the humans who switched sides during the last two battles. I assume they're the commanding officers in charge of those troops. The second group is the more interesting one.

They all have limbal rings that behave like Nero's —which makes me strongly suspect that they're dragons.

"This is it," Nero says to the dragon group. "If you want to withdraw your support, this is your last chance. Once you're seen in the sky wing to wing with me, your fate becomes my fate."

"I'll stand with you, the true heir of the Gorinych dynasty," says a tall man with a hawkish nose. "And I doubt anyone else here made their decision so lightly as to quit at the last moment."

"Indeed," says a strikingly beautiful blond female dragon. "You've seen the state of the empire with your own eyes. You've seen the mismanagement that is Yudo's so-called rule."

"Call him only 'the usurper' in my presence," Nero growls. "And yes, I have seen the poverty and degradation of dragon and human alike. My father is no doubt choking on his own fire in the afterlife."

The dragons nod grimly.

"Even before your arrival, whispers about the usurper's right to power turned into outright conspiracies," a thin dragon with ocean-green eyes says. "He probably thinks he can add legitimacy to his reign by marrying Claudia, but for the oldest of us, it just makes him look weak and insecure."

Nero's face is so angry I half-expect him to turn into a dragon and breathe fire. All the non-dragons in the tent—even the giants—take a step back.

"Until the marriage announcement, we didn't even know she was alive," says the oldest-looking dragon. "Now many of us elders wonder why he kept her all this time. Why not kill her or marry her long ago? Why not—"

"The coward kept her as a hostage," Nero growls. "He knew I might return one day, and she'd be the only thing stopping me from leveling Godiva outright."

"That, or he might've foreseen the need to mix his blood with that of the royal line one day," says the hawk-nosed guy. "He's always been rather good at figuring out ways to save his hide."

"No matter what his reason for keeping her, this marriage looks like an act of desperation to us," says the female. "He's even less worthy of power now, as far as I'm concerned."

"My concern is for Claudia once Yudo's—I mean the usurper's—back is against the wall," says an athletic-looking dragon who hasn't spoken until now. "Unless you think he's going to trade her life for his?"

"The usurper will not live until tomorrow." Nero's limbal rings expand to fill his eyes. "Let me worry about Claudia. Your job is on the battlefield outside this tent."

The dragons nod solemnly, their limbal rings in varying levels of excitement.

"Listen to me, everyone," Nero says, his deep voice carrying through the tent. "We've seen the usurper's crimes. We've defeated his lackeys. We've grown stronger and made alliances." He looks meaningfully at his new human and dragon friends. "Today we finish this. Legends will be told about the battle at Godiva." His gaze shifts to the strongmen. "Songs will be sung about each and every one of you." To the cockatrice delegation, he says, "It doesn't get any bigger or grander than this," and then looks up at the giants.

He continues his moving speech for a few more minutes until everyone in the tent looks ready to rip the enemies apart with their teeth.

Nodding in satisfaction at the ferocity on every

face, Nero strides out of the tent, and his properly motivated allies stampede after him.

Outside the tent, I see another silver mountain ridge, this one in the shape of a half-moon.

The mountains are not just tall, they seem to leap into outer space. I bet even the smallest one is higher than Mount Everest on Earth, or maybe even Olympus Mons on Mars. Though the sky is cloudless, there's no sign of the mountain peaks. It's as though the tectonic plates of this world conspired to create a landscape that would make even creatures as large as dragons feel small and insignificant as they gaze up at it.

Inside the half-moon stands a castle—though at first glance, it also looks like a mountain. It's both tall and wide enough to be one. Made from chrome-tinted obsidian, the structure looks like it was melted out of the tallest mountain by a million dragons breathing fire together—and, for all I know, maybe that's how it was originally formed.

The castle is the perfect place for a seat of imperial power—with those astronomical mountains around, the mouth of the half-moon is the only place one can enter Godiva by ground or air, making a sneak attack all but impossible.

And Nero is clearly expected here. Every inch of the rocky ground around the castle is filled with enemy troops.

Archers, cavalry, and foot soldiers are all armed to the teeth and wear armor of much better quality than that of the prior armies Nero fought.

More importantly, these people look very determined to fight to the last man. I doubt the surrender trick will work on them.

Crap.

What makes this worse is that Rasputin didn't tell Nero how this particular battle will end. It's possible that the odds against Nero's guys are proportional to the disparity in the army headcounts—fifty to one or something along those lines.

The sky above the troops looks even more intimidating, with every cubic foot teeming with enemy dragons of different colors, shapes, and sizes.

There's no way Nero's army can handle so many dragons—even with the help of the dragons from the tent.

"No parley this time?" Councilor Albina asks as she looks up worriedly at the sky.

Nero's nostrils flare. "The usurper isn't even on the battlefield. It was too much to hope he'd face me alone."

"What about that one?" Albina points at a dragon who looks twice as big as the rest.

"Zmey is strong but not very intelligent," Nero says, looking up with a narrowed stare. "I doubt the usurper ordered him to parley."

"Okay. Then when do we start?" Albina says and arcs white energy between her palms.

"On my signal," Nero says and strides over to where a few squadrons of soldiers are mingling with the dragons from the tent. All but two of the dragons—the athletic and the hawk-nosed one—are naked, and most of the troops behind them are in their birthday suits as well.

Interesting.

These troops are either nudists or dragons in human form who don't want to ruin their armor when they turn—and if it's the latter, the disparity between the armies won't be as bad as I feared.

"Turn," Nero says to one naked group, and they transform into particularly large dragons, then crouch as close to the ground as they can.

Yep.

Definitely dragons.

That evens things out a bit—that is, if thirty enemy dragons to one of Nero's can be considered better odds.

Nero then gestures at nearby giants, who are carrying Itzel's steam-powered harpoon weapons. They lumber over and place the devices on the dragons' backs, then use thick ropes to secure them.

A bunch of cockatrices in human form climb up onto the dragons and perch behind each of the weapons, grabbing onto the rope triggers.

"Now you all," Nero says to the naked peeps standing behind the female dragon from the tent. Despite the tense situation, I'm glad to see that Nero's gaze slides past her perfectly shaped body, seemingly oblivious to its charms.

She and her people turn into dragons in a flash, and the rest of the cockatrice warriors get on their backs, armed with diamond-tipped spears.

Nero nods at the older-looking dragon next. The elder turns, and his naked troops do as well.

I expect the athletic-looking dragon to disrobe and turn next, but he and his troops—who are actually clad in armor—grab more spears and climb onto the backs of the older dragon's squadron without changing shape.

Either the athletic one's soldiers aren't dragons, or this is a tactic to hide the number of dragons on Nero's side.

My bet is on the latter—at least if my boss is running this battle the way he usually runs his portfolios.

"Pozoj," Nero says to the hawk-nosed dragon from the tent. "You will make sure that no one, especially the usurper, leaves the battlefield."

Pozoj nods solemnly, then issues orders.

As he speaks, it occurs to me that Godiva's strong defensive position will be a double-edged sword for the usurper if he tries to escape.

If I could chime in, I'd ask Nero if he wouldn't be better off using Pozoj in the air battle to come. The usurper's escape seems less important to me, but I guess I'm not driven by a vendetta.

Done talking with fellow dragons, Nero walks around the rest of his army and instructs troop leaders on what to do. At some point, he must deem them ready because he turns into his dragon self and roars what sounds eerily like, "Attack!"

The ground shaking under their feet, the giants

march toward the castle as the centaurs head for their usual target—the enemy cavalry. At the same time, Councilor Albina shoots her white energy at the nearest enemy squadron, dissolving them on the spot.

At the head of the human troops, the strongmen rush forward in a bloodthirsty rampage, quickly setting a Guinness World Record of kills per second, and east of them, the werewolf guy turns into his giant form and starts ripping enemies to shreds.

On the western side is Vlad. This time, he's holding a sword so big that it must've come from one of the giants. To Vlad's left is Isis, armed with just a shield and a short sword, and to Vlad's right is Colton, the small giant from the Council. Behind them is the elf-like guy, who's shooting arrows with the speed of a semi-automatic rifle.

Also with Vlad are a few cockatrice warriors—who must not like riding dragons as much as their brethren do. They're armed with the same diamond-tipped spears, which enter enemy armor as if it were aluminum foil.

At the very back of Nero's ground troops is the lady who can control animals—and she's a miniature army herself, thanks to the zoo of critters under her command.

Minutes into the battle, I start to feel hopeful. Though outnumbered, Nero's side seems to have saved up all their stamina and ferocity for today.

With every muscle twitch, each strongman dude

kills or maims an enemy soldier, and they show no sign of waning enthusiasm.

The giants also look energized as they decimate thousands of soldiers with lethal arcs of their massive swords—and anyone they merely wound gets stomped to death under their giant feet.

As before, the centaurs make short work of the cavalry and are soon using their lances and hooves on the dispirited ground troops that are unlucky enough to fall in their path.

Colton and the elf fight just as hard, and Isis heals everyone around her when they get so much as a papercut.

Still, when it comes to the ground battle, no one's killing spree compares to that of Vlad's. Each swing of his giant sword seems to fell whole regiments, and the blood he spills leaves a macabre abstractionist work of art for the dragons in the sky to stare at.

Except that the dragons are too busy fighting to look down.

The enemy's formidable air forces are in a carefully arranged formation reminiscent of what army planes do during an air show. At the head of the formation is the behemoth of a dragon that Nero called Zmey. Smart or not, he's huge and terrifying, and his malevolent gaze never strays from a single target.

Nero.

"Now!" Nero's roar seems to say, and his allies roar in reply—a frightening dragon version of a war cry.

Nero dives down, and Zmey leaves his formation to follow.

The large dragons that have Itzel's weapons on their backs clump together and fly to the right wing of the enemy formation. The dragons with cockatrice riders on their backs follow suit.

The enemy dragons who escaped from the prior battle must've warned their comrades about the danger of Itzel's weapons because everyone within reach of the steam-powered guns breaks the pretty formation. Some of them dive under where they think the guns will shoot, some fly up, and some dart to the side—smashing into their brethren.

Like a set of dominos, the formation dissolves into an uncoordinated mess—which is when the gun-wielding squad changes course and aims at the center of the escaping foes.

The guns boom, piercing a few hundred shrieking and roaring dragons with spears, while the cockatrice warriors jump off their dragons' backs, turn into their flying forms, and point their death stares into the freshly made wounds.

Amidst the pandemonium, a large group of enemy dragons flies to attack what they must think is an easier target—"humans" that are wielding spears on dragons' backs. Except these humans are dragons and are able to toss the spears with supernatural strength and speed, piercing dragonhide with ease.

Spears gone, the "human" riders jump down from their brethren and turn into their dragon forms, their transformations ripping their armor apart as they go to town on their wounded opponents.

Meanwhile, Nero dives under Zmey's enormous stream of dragon fire, then stops mid-air and readies himself for a fight.

If I could, I'd tell Nero to reconsider this. I'd remind him that the outcome of this battle wasn't guaranteed by Rasputin—and that Zmey is just too big to fight fairly dragon to dragon like this, even for someone as powerful as Nero.

Seeing Nero face him, Zmey roars so loudly that the castle and the mountains vibrate in the distance.

Nero zooms forward with blurring speed, then performs an aerobatic loop where he whooshes over Zmey's body and swoops under the beast.

With a vicious swipe, he leaves a gash on Zmey's underbelly.

The giant dragon roars in pain and swats under his body with his Eiffel Tower-sized tail, hitting Nero on the head.

My boss reels back, stunned, and Zmey reorients his body and swipes at Nero's head with his claws.

Nero reacts in time to avoid getting gouged, but the back of Zmey's bulldozer-like claw still scrapes across his snout.

Growling in pain, Nero lashes out at Zmey's face. The large dragon tries to dodge, but Nero's claw enters his opponent's ginormous eye with a nauseating squelch.

Zmey's roar makes the air around him shimmer as

if it got superheated. The beast swats at Nero with his tail again, which Nero dodges; then, with speed born of pain and desperation, he rakes at Nero's chest with his talons.

To my horror, a wound opens in Nero's stomach. An ugly, six-foot-long gash that starts spurting blood like a fountain.

Nero roars in pain.

Unable to believe what passes for my senses in this vision-nonexistence, I pray that the wound isn't as bad as it looks.

Except reality cares nothing about my denial. Clutching his gushing wound like a hero in a tragedy, Nero plummets down in a deadly spiral.

CHAPTER TWENTY-THREE

SOMETHING about the way Nero is falling reminds me of another vision, the one in which Kit was spiraling down like an airplane with disabled engines.

Zmey growls and swoops down after his dying enemy.

My nonexistent blood turns to ice.

He's either going to rip Nero to shreds, or Nero will hit the ground at full speed. Either way, he'll die—and in the second scenario, he'll also squish Vlad, Isis, and the rest of the people below.

I desperately will Nero to recover and fight Zmey, but he keeps falling.

And falling.

Until he's about twenty feet from the ground, that is.

At that point, Nero turns back into human shape.

A human shape that is *not* Nero, however.

What?

Though Zmey's snout is lizard-like, there's no doubt the expression on it is that of confusion when he sees a woman where a man should be.

And that's when it clicks for me.

No wonder the spiraling-down reminded me of what happened to Kit.

This *is* Kit. Or, more accurately, the person I thought of as Nero in this vision was Kit all along.

Recovering from his confusion, Zmey dives to snatch Kit from the air—which is when the cockatrice warriors around Vlad launch their spears at him, piercing his scales in multiple locations.

At almost the same time, the cockatrice warriors turn into their scaly forms and Isis shoots Kit with a stream of healing energy six inches thick.

The wound on Kit's chest disappears instantly, and Kit opens her eyes, grinning as the cockatrices turn their death stares on Zmey's ruined eye and the spear wounds.

Then Kit disappears again, and I see the number of Zmeys double.

With a final roar, the original Zmey goes limp—and Kit uses her new massive claws to snatch the body from the air and toss it at the enemy troops, crushing them under the enormous corpse.

Winking her huge eye at Isis and the rest, Zmey-Kit flies up to rejoin the air fight.

I'M BACK in the restaurant, dizzy from what I just foresaw.

I feel like I've witnessed another magician's effect—and was fooled by it, which is rare.

All that time, I was actually observing Kit, not Nero—which makes sense, now that I'm thinking about it. I targeted Kit, yet I didn't see her anywhere until that reveal at the end.

With a pang of guilt, I recall that going into the vision, I was expecting something bad to happen to Kit. Yet once inside the vision, I was too busy observing the battle and worrying about Nero to even think of Kit. What's worse is that Kit did nearly die.

But why the switch?

Was all that a ploy to defeat Zmey?

This does explain something strange that happened in the last vision: the part where Isis told Nero to "sell it" and how Nero then acted as though Kit was killed. Was that all part of this ploy? Did Nero, Isis, and Kit hope to make the retreating enemy dragons think Kit was out of the picture? If so, why? Was this Zmey guy worth such an intricate plan?

Then it hits me.

This wasn't about Zmey. It was a way for Nero to pretend to be in the Godiva battle while really doing something else.

As I ponder the mystery of why Nero would miss the most important battle of his campaign, my seer intuition blares an alarm.

Picking up my tea, I take a big gulp, then slam the cup down and leap back into Headspace.

Focusing on Nero's essence, I examine the dreadful-sounding shapes that appear around me.

Yep.

There's little doubt about it.

Something truly terrible is going to happen to Nero or someone else I care about.

I touch a shape and prepare for the worst.

———

NERO and two other men are walking at the foot of the Godiva mountain range dressed in black outfits that are just a hood away from ninja costumes. Instead of katanas, though, Nero is armed with the gate sword, and his companions are carrying broadswords.

If their eyes are anything to go by, the companions are dragons, and they look enough alike for me to suspect them of being brothers.

The taller of the two takes the lead as Nero and the shorter one follow more carefully, with Nero looking around the barren, rocky terrain as if searching for something specific.

The Godiva half-moon entrance is far in the distance from this location, and it must be the same day as the battle because I can see the tail end of Nero's troops arriving on the scene.

"Hold on," Nero says, studying three giant boulders

intently. "Step aside," he then tells the taller of his companions and points at a perfectly smooth and ordinary rocky surface under the guy's feet.

Shrugging, the taller man walks over and stands behind Nero, who uses his finger to draw a Cyrillic letter "zhe" on the smooth section of the smaller of the boulders.

Nothing seems to happen for a few moments, and Nero's companions exchange worried glances.

Then, with a screech, the ground where the taller guy stood slides away, revealing what must be a secret tunnel.

"Follow me," Nero says and climbs into the hole.

Once everyone is inside, the hole closes ominously behind them.

Nero's companions glance at the exit with concern, but my boss is already striding deeper into the tunnel that's illuminated by glowworm-like luminescent critters that are creepy-crawling on the slimy ceiling and walls.

The two dragons hurry to catch up with him, and once they do, Nero speeds up his pace. Eventually, the tunnel gets more winding, and they're forced to slow down.

"Remember, once in the castle, we won't be able to turn," the taller dragon says to the shorter. "The wards—"

"I didn't grow up in a cave," the shorter one growls angrily, then turns to Nero. "Is it true the members of the imperial family are the only dragons who can still turn, despite the wards?"

"Old wives' tale, unfortunately," Nero says. "If she *could* turn, Claudia would've freed herself long ago."

"Right," the shorter dragon says. "I still can't believe she's alive." He glances at Nero. "I can't believe either of you is alive, to be honest."

"The usurper was highly motivated to keep my escape a secret." Nero squeezes his sword handle so hard I half-expect it to break.

"It won't stay a secret for much longer," the taller dragon says. "After today, even the worst shut-ins will know that you're back."

The shorter guy nods approvingly, then looks at Nero and says, "Is it true that even you didn't know she lived?"

"I saw her get stabbed and then lie unmoving in a pool of blood," Nero growls, his limbal rings overtaking his eyes. "I assumed." His jaw clenches, and he walks silently for a few steps.

"Your mistake might be for the best," the short dragon says. "Because you ran, you survived. You grew strong, and now you're back. If you'd stayed with her, you'd be—"

Nero blurs into motion and has the dragon gripped by his throat and dangling off the floor before anyone can say "temper tantrum."

"Sir," the taller dragon says soothingly, placing a careful hand on Nero's shoulder. "He didn't mean it that way."

"I didn't," the short one chokes out. "I'm sorry."

Nero looks at his hand as though it developed a mind of its own, then releases the guy and stalks down the tunnel.

"What have I told you about your tongue?" the tall dragon hisses at his comrade. "You always say the—"

"Let him be," Nero growls without turning. "Your brother had a point. I just can't stand the thought of Claudia living in a cage while I was biding my time on another world, oblivious to her suffering."

If I had ears that could perk up, they would at this point. I still don't know what Claudia is to Nero, and this is the most I've heard on the subject since I first learned of her existence.

"Even as a small child, she loved her freedom above all else," Nero continues, picking up his pace. "She found this tunnel on her own—then used it to run away from the castle and get lost in the forest." A distant smile touches the corners of his eyes. "It took the royal guards a week to locate her that time—and she was only four years old. And it only got worse from there."

So Nero knew Claudia as a small child. That's a strong argument against my biggest concern: that she's his wife or some other kind of romantic interest. Unless, of course, she was a princess he was betrothed to as a child—such things might be normal for an imperial dragon family.

"Will you even recognize her when you meet?" the

taller dragon asks carefully. "She was still so young when—"

"I will," Nero growls. "My heart will recognize her, no matter what."

If he last saw her when she was young, she can't be his wife, can she?

At least I hope not.

"Besides," Nero adds. "Claudia has a port wine stain on her face—a kind of birthmark." He touches his left cheek. "It's shaped like a cloud and is visible whether she's in or out of her dragon form."

"That's helpful to know," the short dragon says. "If we split up and look in cells that—"

"No splitting up," his taller brother says. "The usurper is too clever to leave the castle unattended, which means we'll need to fight our way in."

"Speaking of guards." Nero lowers his voice to a whisper. "We might be within hearing range of the ones guarding the castle entrance."

With this, all three men fall silent and start moving more stealthily, their steps inaudible.

They walk for quite some time—Nero must've meant dragon hearing when he was talking about that range— but finally, they reach a rusty metal door that could give the thickest bank vault entrance a run for its money.

Nero locates a smooth surface next to the door and draws the same symbol as on the tunnel entrance.

Everyone stands expectantly for a few moments, but nothing happens.

Maybe the opening mechanism died? Or is it magic?

Undaunted, Nero activates his gate sword and pierces the door, the shimmering plasma cutting through the thick metal like scissors through paper.

He cuts out a hole large enough for the tall dragon to enter, then pulls the chunk out and softly places it on the ground.

Behind the door is a brick wall.

Someone must've blocked the entrance during a remodeling.

Nero's sword cuts through the stone with equal ease. Then he kicks in the cutout, revealing a room with ten armed guards.

The guards stare at the intruders with varying degrees of shock—that is, until Nero blurs forward and slashes them all into bits before they can even draw their swords.

The tall dragon steps after Nero and examines the massacre. "Maybe we *can* split up—the two of us can go one way, and you can go the other."

"Not yet," Nero says and walks through the basement-like room they find themselves in.

"We're in," he says, examining the silver-tinted obsidian walls. "Unless he moved it, the prison should be close."

The next room looks like a wine cellar—and Nero and his companions make short work of the guards inside.

They walk through a corridor with high ceilings next, then enter a giant room full of various torture paraphernalia that looks extra sturdy compared to what I've seen in museums. I guess that's what you need when dealing with dragons.

"This room was used for battle training before the usurper perverted it," Nero whispers disapprovingly.

"There've been rumors about what happens to the usurper's enemies here." The short dragon seems to pale as he looks around. "I thought them an exaggeration until now."

"He really *is* a bastard," his taller brother says matter-of-factly. "Now, which way?" He looks at the two available doors—one very large and one regular-sized.

"This way." Nero walks around an open device that looks like a sarcophagus with short swords sticking up from inside—a type of iron maiden, I'm guessing—and heads for the smaller door.

From there, they enter another long corridor, and Nero strides to the very end, then slices off the lock on the door with his sword.

The next room is spacious, like an empty dance hall.

Seven guards are standing around a heavy-duty metal cage in the middle of the room.

Three of them leap at Nero while the rest attack his allies.

Nero dodges the strike of the first attacker, then slices him into two even pieces with his sword.

When Nero strikes at the next one, the man tries to parry, but the gate sword's shimmering material goes right through his metal weapon, cleaving it cleanly into two. Then, continuing the trajectory, Nero's sword slices through the guard's flesh and bones.

The last guard tries to back away from Nero, but doesn't make it more than a couple of steps before my boss slices off his head.

Nero's companions aren't as swift at killing, but they're holding their own with the guards.

Leaving them to it, Nero turns toward the cage.

There's a woman inside.

Dressed in a plain dress, she has long reddish-brown hair, a pretty face, and—most tellingly—a birthmark in the shape of a cloud on her cheek.

Despite the situation, she doesn't look panicked, all her attention trained on Nero's face.

With a grunt, Nero's taller companion kills his last guard—then teams up with his brother to get the last one.

"Claudia," Nero says, stepping toward the cage.

Her unshakeable calm seems to crack. "Nero?" she asks raggedly. "Is that really you?"

"Step away," Nero orders, and when she backs deeper into the cage, he slices through the cage bars with his sword, making a large hole.

Then he steps inside.

"It *is* you," Claudia gasps. With tears streaming down her cheeks, she leaps at Nero and envelops him in a hug just as his companions finish the last guard.

"You came for me. I knew you would come for me. I just—"

"We need to get you out of this place," Nero says gruffly, pulling away. "It's not safe here."

"Of course," she says. "How did you even—"

"We'll talk later." Nero turns toward the hole in the cage. "I'll take you outside, then come back and kill the usurper."

She solemnly bobs her head, then follows Nero out of the cage, where his companions are already waiting —and staring at her with fascination.

Carefully stepping over detached body parts, she approaches one of the dead guard's remains, viciously kicks his torso, and picks up his sword.

"You won't need that," Nero says.

"Better safe than sorry." She takes a practice swing, then stabs it in the air. Lowering the blade, she says, "Lead the way."

Nero heads into the corridor they came from, and everyone follows.

When they enter the torture room again, Claudia looks extremely nervous.

Did Yudo—the usurper—bring her here at some point in the past? What kind of a monster would do that to someone he plans to marry? Unless it was some sort of BDSM thing for him, à la Christian Grey's Red Room of Pain.

As Nero is walking by the open maw of the iron maiden, the larger set of doors bursts open, and a whole squadron of guards rushes in, followed by a tall man with the physique of Arnold Schwarzenegger in his prime.

Is that Yudo—a.k.a. the usurper?

The intricate armor and the gold crown he's wearing seem to imply that, as does the arrogant set of his harsh features.

"Nero, get her out. We got this," the shorter of Nero's companions says, readying his sword.

The taller dragon stands shoulder to shoulder with his brother, and they wait for the guards to reach them. Then they start swinging their swords with preternatural speed.

They kill four guards right away, but that still doesn't make me optimistic about their chances. There're just too many opponents for the two of them to handle.

In the meantime, Nero grabs Claudia by her upper arm and blurs into motion, getting her to the door that leads to the tunnel in less than a second.

"Go, and I'll meet you after I'm done here," Nero growls. Without waiting for her reply, he turns to face the usurper and his soldiers, his glare so supercharged with hatred I half-expect cockatrice-like mojo to shoot out of his eyes.

"You know how I figured you'd come down here and put yourself in my power?" the usurper asks in a voice deep enough to sing death metal.

Ignoring the question, Nero blurs into super speed once again, and before anyone can track him, he reaches his allies. Two slices of Nero's sword later, four guards are dead. Another flurry of sword swipes from Nero—and six more guards join the rest in the afterlife.

"I'll tell you anyway." Standing behind his guards, the usurper unsheathes a monster broadsword and checks the blade for sharpness. "I asked myself what your late father would've done in your stead, and that's exactly what you did."

His face a mask of rage, Nero wields his sword impossibly faster, cutting through the guards coming at him like a scythe through fresh grass.

But there are still too many soldiers between Nero and the usurper.

With the sound of sword clanking against sword, the short dragon parries a strike from a guard a head taller than him, then stabs another but gets a fist to the face from the third.

Using his momentary confusion, the guard follows his hit with a sword stab, and his blade enters the short dragon's chest.

Clutching his wound, he falls to his knees—and another guard finishes him off.

Roaring in rage and grief, the taller dragon attacks the man who just killed his brother with even greater ferocity. Within a second, he slays him, then kills the guards to his left.

"Focus on Nero," the usurper orders the remaining guards, and all but the ones fighting the taller dragon rush to obey.

Blurring like Nero, Yudo moves in the direction of Nero's ally.

Being so close to his worst enemy, Nero turns into a berserker. He cuts apart the guard to his left, then punches through the chest of another with his fist and rips out a third guard's throat with his teeth.

Meanwhile, the usurper swings his sword viciously, killing his own guard in order to slice a deep gash in the tall dragon's back.

The wounded dragon ignores the pain and continues fighting the last of the guards. He strikes him down at the same time as the usurper delivers his own lethal blow.

Blood gurgling in his throat, the tall dragon falls on the floor next to his slain brother and stops moving.

Nero growls with fury and seems to move even faster as his sword takes life after life. Within moments, every guard around him is in pieces.

"Looks like it's just us," the usurper says and steps toward Nero over the bloody remains on the floor.

Except he's wrong.

It's not just the two of them.

Though Nero doesn't realize it, Claudia didn't leave the room when he told her to do so.

Instead, she's creeping toward the combatants, clearly itching to use her sword to help Nero—except she's more likely to get herself killed than to help.

"This is it for you." Gripping his sword tighter, Nero takes a menacing step toward the usurper, the cold smile on his face reminding me of a cat toying with a bug.

As if to make Nero's advance even more

frightening, a mighty dragon roars outside the castle in Kit's perfect imitation of Nero's vocalizations. It seems to say, "Attack!"

Claudia swings her sword.

To my horror, instead of striking Yudo, her blade slices Nero's right forearm to the bone.

Stupid woman. Why didn't she leave when Nero told her to?

Nero grunts from the pain, and the gate sword slips out of his grip, hitting the floor with a clank.

At the same exact time, the usurper slices at Nero's head—a strike that my boss dodges but just barely.

"I told you to go," Nero growls at Claudia without turning, then sidesteps another strike from Yudo. "I had him exactly where I wanted him."

Claudia doesn't look the least bit ashamed. Instead, with cold determination in her gaze, she thrusts her sword forward—burying it right between Nero's shoulder blades.

Wait. She's doing this on purpose?

Nero roars in pain and looks back at Claudia uncomprehendingly.

His lips seem to soundlessly mouth a single word.

"Why?"

Not meeting Nero's pain-filled gaze, Claudia nods at the usurper, and the asshole smiles nastily, then swings his sword at Nero's exposed neck.

With a sound of tearing flesh and broken bone, Nero's head separates from his body and drops to the floor.

In a macabre moment of surrealness, the head rolls, only to stop next to the iron maiden, the eyes staring up at Claudia as if still looking for an explanation.

Claudia rips the sword out of Nero's back and faces the usurper. "So? How did I do?"

CHAPTER TWENTY-FOUR

I'M BACK in the restaurant, the Uzbek delicacies I've consumed sitting like frozen cement in my stomach as a single horrific thought circles through my mind.

Nero is going to die.

I leap to my wobbly feet, snatch my phone out of my blazer pocket with a shaking hand, and summon myself a ride.

Nero is going to be betrayed by Claudia, the woman he's fighting so hard to save.

Luckily, there are a ton of car services nearby, so one arrives before I sprint on foot to JFK. Jumping in, I bribe the driver to hurry.

If traffic permits, we'll get to the airport in twenty minutes.

My plan is simplicity itself. I'm going to find Nero and warn him—and the sooner I catch up with him, the better.

The question is whether I'll make it in time.

I know that a day from my perspective is when the second battle is going to happen—assuming I mastered the technique of targeting a specific time. But I'm going to that world, which, according to Nostradamus, makes timekeeping more complicated. I also recall Nero saying that Godiva is a day's journey from where the second battle happens—but that's from Nero perspective in that world. Oh, and did Nero mean twenty-four hours, or marching during the day and then sleeping during the night, which would be more like twelve hours? Also, now that I'm thinking about this, when I was focusing on the essence of a day, I didn't picture sleeping as part of it. Does that mean I got myself twelve hours as a target instead of a full day?

To avoid going insane, I put worries about time out of my mind. As far as what I need to do, it changes nothing. I'm simply going to chase after Nero as quickly as possible and pray that I make it.

With the plan decided on, I do my best to recall the map of the continent on the dragon world, especially the line that represented the route to Godiva.

Then my phone rings.

It's Felix.

After a moment's hesitation, I pick up.

"Hey, Sasha," he says. "Do you still want to talk to this Eric guy? He just came by and asked if you showed up. I said no, but I can still catch him."

I bring the phone closer to my ear and ponder the idea of involving Eric. Would the teleporter join me to go help Nero, which would be a great help indeed, or would he try to keep me here on Earth?

My bet is on the latter.

Still, since I could use the help, I convince myself I'll talk to Eric, then go into Headspace to take a look at the consequences.

A cloud of shapes that looks pretty uniform surrounds me there, but since this is an important choice, I sprout multiple ethereal wisps and touch them all.

It's not good.

In every single future where I talk to Eric, I end up locked in the apartment again. In most of the visions, he doesn't believe my story about Nero in trouble—even when I ask him reasonable things like "why would I come to you myself and make up such a story?" He thinks I just stubbornly want to join Nero on his quest and the story is to make him do my bidding. Even in the visions where he claims to believe me, Eric locks me up anyway.

"No," I tell Felix when I'm back from Headspace. "I don't need to talk to Eric anymore."

"You know," Felix says. "Something else just occurred to me about our last conversation. Why did you call right before you went into the tunnel? You knew you'd lose reception."

I snort. "It took you *this* long to figure that out?"

"Yeah, well, you so rarely do something illogical that I didn't realize you suddenly did it."

"Whatever," I say. "I'm totally allowed to do something illogical after the day I just had."

I then bring Felix up to speed—mostly verbally but also by texting when I get to the parts that the Mandate would not want the human cab driver to overhear.

"Don't go," Felix says when I get to the end. "Remember how dangerous the path to the dragon world was? Where are you even going to find another spacesuit?"

"I'll take the much safer path Rasputin showed us," I say. "The one we took on the way back."

"And then what? What can you do against dragons?"

"I don't need to do anything. I just need to warn Nero about Claudia, and he can do all the doing himself."

"Fine. Then I'm coming with you."

"I don't have time to wait for you to get to JFK." I look at the traffic-free highway in front of the cab. "I'm about ten minutes away from there."

"You're going to walk into a literal warzone, and you expect me to let you go alone?"

He has a point.

Could I ask Lucretia for help?

No, that's a bad idea. Not only do I not want to put my newfound sister in danger, but she has the same problem as Felix—she's in Manhattan with a client, too far to get to JFK quickly.

Maybe Lilith then? No, she's too volatile—and I have too many unanswered questions regarding her motives.

"Look, just wait for me," Felix continues, and I interrupt him with a question.

"Did you get anywhere with Lilith's phone calls?"

"Don't try to change the subject."

"It's related. I'm debating asking *her* for help."

"In that case, no. I need more to go on than what you told me."

"Okay," I say and text him Lilith's phone number, as well as the numbers she called. "Does that help?"

"Yes, probably," Felix says. "But I won't be able to find out anything before you have to decide whether to take Lilith with you or not."

"Still, if you want to be helpful, please work on *that*."

"Sasha, I'm not letting you—"

"Oh no," I say. "I'm going into another tunnel."

"There's no tunnel between—"

I hiss into the phone and hang up on him.

When he calls back, I let the call go to voicemail, then repeat this a few more times until he stops calling.

Really mature, his text says. *You're making a bad choice right now.*

I ignore the rest of Felix's tirade because the word "choice" makes me uneasy.

Darian claimed to have foreseen that I would pay with my life if I chose Nero, and Nero's truth-telling abilities confirmed this in my vision.

Does me rushing to warn Nero count as "choosing him?" Or did I make the choice as soon as I started having feelings for my bossy Mentor?

Not liking where that train of thought is leading, I let myself ponder something a little safer.

Why will Claudia betray Nero?

To answer that, it would really help if I knew what exactly their relationship is.

Until that betrayal, I would've placed my money on her being his sister, or some other close family member. Then again, that could've been wishful thinking, since the other option is that she's his child bride or something along those lines.

Now, though, I don't know if the sister option tracks. I mean, who'd betray her own flesh and blood like that? I just learned about Lucretia being my sister, and I'm not bringing her on this misadventure—and, obviously, nothing would drive me to kill her.

If she's his bride, though, it would make a little bit more sense. After all, when a person is mysteriously murdered, the first suspect is the spouse.

Is it possible then?

Was that a draconian way of getting a divorce?

It still seems a little dubious—with her being Yugo's prisoner and Nero waging world war to save her and all.

Unless she has Stockholm syndrome? Maybe Claudia fell for her captor over the years, and is now a masochist to his sadist. Maybe the marriage thing appeals to her. For all I know, it could've been her idea to get hitched in the first place.

Alternatively, maybe this is pure ambition. Maybe

she *is* Nero's sister, but wants to rule the dragon world herself rather than having her brother do it.

Wait a sec. Is Nero planning to rule the dragon world?

I always assumed Nero would save Claudia and come back, but that's not a given.

The cab screeches to a stop, bringing me out of my contemplations.

I get out and run for the secret door to the hub. After I enter the tunnels and make a few turns, a deep dread assaults me—a feeling I've come to associate with my seer intuition.

Oh no.

Not this crap again.

In my rush to get here, the one thing I didn't think to do was check to see if I actually make it to the gate— or to Nero's location.

Now, though, I have no choice.

With effort, I focus and leap into Headspace just as I turn the corner.

There, I get the confirmation I desperately hoped I wouldn't get.

The shapes around me play a terrifying tune.

I reach for the nearest one, knowing it most likely shows my demise.

CHAPTER TWENTY-FIVE

I'M STANDING in a corridor under JFK, looking wide-eyed at Woland—the leader of the recently departed chorts.

"I thought you ran back to St. Petersburg," I say and back up a step.

"I'm going there soon." Advancing on me, he pulls out a syringe. "As are you, assuming you want to live."

I stare at him, my brain having trouble working with all the adrenaline sloshing around my skull.

"I'm going to give you two choices," Woland says. "Get on your knees and put your hands behind your head so I can inject you with this tranquilizer"—he waves the syringe in the air—"or I'll stop your heart right here and now."

I take another step back.

He tsk-tsks. "Last chance. I'm not bluffing."

Great. My choices are fight him so I can rush to

save Nero, or get put under to wake up in Russia where fun tortures await.

Doesn't sound like much of a choice.

I'm obviously going with the Nero option.

As I think this, though, a sinking feeling comes over me.

Is this officially the moment Darian was always going on about?

As I learned earlier, Woland doesn't bluff. He *will* stop my heart if I don't let him prick me with that needle.

"On the count of three," Woland says. "One."

I straighten my back.

"Two."

I look at Woland defiantly.

"Three."

Balling my hands into fists, I prepare to make use of all the skills Thalia and Nero have drilled into me.

Woland pockets the syringe. "This will be poetic justice," he says. "Rasputin took my daughter, and I will take his." He stands there, looking into the distance, and I take that as my cue to leap forward and throw a punch at his face.

My fist smacks his jaw, snapping him out of his daydream-like state, and he snarls at me.

I execute another punch—aiming for his jaw once more in the hopes of knocking him out.

Except he does the chort-phasing thing, and my fist whooshes futilely through his head.

Before I can regain my balance, he grabs my wrist, and I feel foul energy spread from his touch.

"No, wait!" I want to yell, but I can't get the words out because my breathing is too ragged.

Then, like in a recurring nightmare, my left arm goes numb, and a horrible pain explodes in my torso—one that feels like a tower of elephants just perched on my chest.

My head spins, my lungs refuse to draw in air, and then the world fades as I die.

BACK IN THE TUNNEL, I slow my running pace. The last thing I want is to stumble onto Woland before I figure out a way to avoid the fate I just foresaw.

Clenching my teeth, I do my best to focus.

After that vision, I find it difficult, but after a massive mental effort, I find myself back in Headspace.

This time, I'm surrounded by a set of clouds, each with hundreds of shapes all playing the same deadly tunes.

I think I know the reason for multiple clouds—each of them represents a different course of action I might take.

If I'm right, I need to view them all, so I don't miss the one where I avoid a Woland-induced heart attack.

The problem is, reaching for all these visions might use up my power—especially considering how much I already used it today.

I need to work out a way to give myself some options but keep some seer mojo for later.

What if I just sample one vision from each of the clouds as a compromise?

Do I have enough power for *that*?

If it weren't for the targeted-time vision training with Nostradamus, I'd be sure about my reserves, but as is, I have to rely on hope.

So here goes nothing. Spawning an ethereal wisp per each cloud, I reach out and touch the shapes that my intuition deems most useful.

———

I'M STANDING in a corridor under JFK—a slightly different corridor this time. Woland is facing me again, but I'm not wide-eyed and confused this time.

Without further ado, I rush him—and as soon as I'm close enough, I throw a punch at his nose.

He phases, and my fist whooshes futilely through his head, throwing me off-balance.

He grabs my wrist, and I feel his foul energy spread through me until my left arm goes numb.

The horrible pain follows, then lightheadedness and death.

———

THE NEXT VISION is nearly identical to the last—down to the new corridor. The only difference is that I kick

Woland in the balls instead of punching him in the face.

He phases before I can do any damage, though—and I stumble, which gives him a chance to grab my hand again. Then the heart attack follows.

———

I'M in the cursed corridor staring at Woland for a fraction of a second. Then I spin around and sprint as if shooting for Olympic gold.

My heart is hammering in my chest, and my breathing is like that of a dog on a hot day, yet I hear ever-nearing footsteps behind me.

The stupid chort is supernaturally fast.

Before I even get the chance to turn the corner, a hand grabs the back of my blazer.

Desperate, I wriggle out of it, but Woland's fingers grab my neck.

"Wait," I start to say, but he shoots me with his heart-stopping energy, and—perhaps due to the exertion of the sprint—the heart attack kills me even faster.

———

"FINE," I say when I'm faced with Woland. "You can stab me with your stupid syringe."

I get on my knees and put my hands behind my head.

Woland is the one who looks confused this time, but he quickly recovers. Taking out his syringe, he walks toward me.

When he's a leaping distance away, I pounce—but my kneeling position leaves me at a huge disadvantage.

Woland's foot smacks into my face—and I pass out.

———

THIS TIME, I give up again, and actually let Woland inject me.

What follows is what I'd expect. A vision with me outside my body begins, and I watch as Woland picks up the drugged Sasha and starts carrying her away.

———

VARIATIONS of the prior visions follow, and I'm defeated in every single one.

———

I'M BACK in the real world, turning the corner.

I stop.

If I go farther, I risk facing Woland, and I still need to work out a strategy to use on him.

Evening out my breathing, I gather the focus I need to get into Headspace.

Except the familiar state eludes me.

Oh, come on.

Not now.

I further steady my breath and try again.

Nope. It's like hitting a cement wall with my head.

Even though I know what's going on, I make a dozen attempts before I call it.

I've used up the last of my seer juice.

Now I'll have to face Woland for real but without the use of my powers—and somehow avoid the fate that befell me in all the previous visions.

Or die, as Darian foresaw.

CHAPTER TWENTY-SIX

WHAT CAN I do that I haven't tried already?

What new elements can I introduce?

Nothing I have on me—like the deck of cards—would be of much help. At best, I can confuse him momentarily, but that won't be enough—especially since this is my one and only chance at this.

What I really need is a weapon, preferably a gun.

What makes this extra frustrating is that my gun isn't even far away from here. Itzel made me leave it in the lab down here before we departed to save Rasputin. However, the lab is the last turn in the tunnels before the hub, so I'll run into Woland before I can get there.

But wait. Maybe there's some other way I can get a gun.

I *am* in an airport—which means TSA agents all over the place. Do they carry guns?

I take out my phone to check and, to my disappointment, learn that it's not the case. However, there have to be cops here too. The unarmed TSA agents must be able to call someone if they need a weapon, right?

Maybe I can use my pickpocketing skills to nab a gun from a cop. Seems impossible, but not more impossible than fighting Woland empty-handed.

Of course, even with a gun, Woland might be tough to deal with. If he phases when I shoot him, the bullet would go right through him.

I'd have to shoot him when he's not expecting it—and I think I have a distraction in mind.

Feeling hopeful, I turn on my heels and run back toward the airport.

A small voice in the back of my mind wonders what I'll do in the very likely event where I fail to steal a gun from a trained professional. Could I get to Gomorrah from another airport? Or maybe I should involve Lilith after all, since all *she* needs to make Woland vulnerable is to drink a little of his blood.

The problem with all these ideas is that they would take time that Nero might not have.

I'm wasting time gun-hunting as is.

When I turn the next corner, something about the corridor makes me uneasy.

It must be in my head, though. All these corridors are so alike.

I stop anyway, and with a sinking feeling, I see Woland turn the next corner and come face to face with me.

Damn it.

All this time, I assumed Woland was waiting for me on my way *to* the hub. It didn't occur to me he was actually *behind* me.

But it makes sense. My visions showed me what happens after he uses his super speed to catch up with me. I bet the thing that happened right before my visions was me turning to hear who was following me.

"Woland," I say with fake calmness, desperate to give myself time to think of something that I haven't already tried. "Fancy meeting you here."

He brings out his syringe. "Sorry, no time to chitchat," he says. "I'm going to give you two choices—"

Since I never tried charging him mid-sentence before, I do so now. Then, instead of punching or kicking—which didn't work in my visions—I headbutt him instead.

My forehead smashes into a bony part of his face, though it's hard to say exactly where because of all the white stars exploding in my vision.

Ears ringing, I throw a punch where I hope Woland's jaw is.

If Thalia saw this, she'd approve. There's an audible crack when my knuckles connect with what is definitely a jaw.

My knuckles scream in agony, and Woland curses in Russian.

Crap. He's not knocked out.

I kick him in the balls almost instinctively before I realize I tried that in my vision.

He phases, and I lose balance.

Woland catches my wrist.

No.

This also happened in my visions.

It's what always preceded my end.

I rip my hand away, but it's too late.

The foul energy is already spreading into me.

"This can't be happening," I want to yell, but I can't get the words out because my breathing is too ragged.

When the all-too-familiar symptoms begin, I can't deny it any longer.

This is the end.

My left arm goes numb, and horrible pain blooms in my torso. Dreadful lightheadedness follows, and for the last time, the world fades as I die.

CHAPTER TWENTY-SEVEN

SOMEHOW, my consciousness comes back to me.

How weird.

I was so sure I had died, I would've bet my life on it.

But then what is this? Did I mistake a vision for real life?

No. If that had been a vision, I'd be bodiless and looking down at myself right now, but I have a body. It just so happens that my body is simply lying here on the floor, completely unfeeling—pretty dead-like.

Then, for no reason I can see, my heart starts pumping again.

As blood starts circulating through my body, the worst feeling of pins and needles accompanies it.

If my mouth worked, I'd be screaming in pain, but since it's on vacation, I examine myself for an explanation of what's happening.

Maybe this is the afterlife?

Though it doesn't seem to fit anything I've heard

about, perhaps we Cognizant get our own version and it looks like this?

But no. If anything, this feels more like a resurrection.

As the pins and needles reach my ear, my hearing returns, and I hear Woland say, "It's poetic justice—"

I don't hear the rest of this familiar monologue.

My body completes its recovery, and as it does, a single feeling overrides everything else.

No, not a feeling. This is more like an emotion. Actually, even that's not right. It's a desperate need, a compulsion—a desire to rule all other desires.

After another moment of agony, I put a label on it.

Thirst.

Yet to call this "thirst" would be like calling those enormous Godiva mountains "little speed bumps."

It's a thirst like nothing I've ever felt. A craving to drink that I'd do anything to satisfy. A compulsion that makes me forget everything else—even my name.

"—took my daughter, and now I—"

My lids snap open of their own accord, and time seems to slow as my eyes zoom in on the source of the air vibrations—a vein pulsing on a neck a couple of feet away from my mouth.

The vein pulls me to itself like the strongest magnet —especially if said magnet were made from heroin and chocolate chip cookies.

"—have taken his," my prey says as I leap, and sink my extended fangs into that sweet, sweet flesh.

As soon as I swallow my first gulp of this elixir of

the gods, the thirst eases and my thoughts begin to make sense again.

For example, I understand that Woland's gurgling scream is totally justified under the circumstances. It's what one does when fangs rip into one's throat, especially when the owner of the fangs starts to greedily suck the blood.

Two gulps later, the horrific thirst is almost a distant memory, and I realize how pleasurable this experience is. It's like having an orgasm, a yum-gasm (for lack of a better term), a thirst-quench-gasm, a shoegasm, and every other gasm combined into one.

A part of me knows I can stop now—as far as my needs are concerned, I'm done.

But my memories are back, and I know that I won't stop.

Woland was going to kill me—did kill me—and now he's going to pay. That I'm going to enjoy his death like I've never enjoyed anything else in my life is just icing on this very disturbing cake.

If Lilith saw me now, she'd swell with pride.

Eventually, the blood flow ceases.

Disappointed, I pull away and wipe my mouth as my fangs retreat back into my gums.

There's no more thirst, nor any other distractions, to prevent me from realizing what happened.

Darian wasn't lying. My choices really did lead to my death—but it wasn't the end.

Seems like I did inherit a power from Lilith after all.

I *was* a pre-vamp—and now, I'm a vampire.

CHAPTER TWENTY-EIGHT

MOVING ON AUTOPILOT, I snatch the syringe from Woland's exsanguinated corpse and pocket it right before he poofs out of existence, like the other chorts did.

Great. I won't need to call Pada to get rid of this body. That'll save me a small fortune.

Wait a minute. Why am I thinking about money when I've just turned into a freaking vampire?

Probably because money worries are easier to wrap my head around, I decide—then realize I have something much more important to focus on.

Nero.

I have to get to him, quickly.

I start running toward the hub, and as I do, I look at my hands.

They're paler than usual—and I've always been pretty pale to start with, which, of course, is a common feature for pre-vamps and what they turn into.

Oh, and I can see my hands much better than usual—as odd as that sounds.

Turning the corner, I roll up my sleeve and check out my Queen of Hearts tattoo.

Wow.

This reminds me of when Felix convinced us to re-watch our favorite movies in ultra-high definition. The reds of the tattoo are sharper and somehow redder, and the image itself is crystal clear—as though I'm looking at it through a magnifying glass.

No one told me vampires had enhanced vision.

This is so cool.

I sniff the air to see if my olfactory senses are sharper too.

Now that I'm paying attention, I *can* detect nuances to the smells around me. For example, my blazer could certainly use a good washing.

Holy Dracula.

I'm a vampire.

I'm not going to age or die. Well, unless I get myself killed, which I'm really good at.

On the bright side, I'm now much harder to kill.

I try to shove aside these contemplations so I can focus solely on getting to Nero, but everything reminds me about my new situation. Like the running itself. It's incredible. I'm moving faster than I ever have, yet my breathing is impressively even.

Zooming through the next corridor, I try to go into Headspace—in the hopes that turning into a vampire reset my seer gas tank.

Nope.

I'm still out of juice—that is, if I still have my seer abilities at all.

Are there seer vampires? Is that a thing?

Before I can get too scared, I recall that Lucretia kept her empath abilities and relax.

I'm probably going to regain my seer mojo in a day or so.

Assuming I live that long.

Then more questions pop into my mind.

Am I going to become a monster, eating people left and right?

No, I decide after a moment. Lucretia and Vlad are pretty civilized, so why not me?

Still, I'm not entirely sure how vampires are regarded in the vampire community, if there's any stigma that goes along with drinking. Specifically, I can't help wondering if Nero will still like me like this.

I certainly hope so. Looks-wise at least, I'm going to be set for the rest of my un-life—and I believe he likes my looks.

Of course, if I'd known I'd be stuck like this forever, I'd have hit the gym harder over the past year. And would've gone on a diet. I would've then enjoyed eternity with washboard abs.

Oh, well. At least I whitened my teeth a few months back. My fangs will look nice and healthy as I sink them into my victims' necks.

Turning the corner, I see the path that leads to the lab and decide to take a little detour.

The lab looks just like before, with Itzel's books and instruments sprawled all over the place.

My gun is also where I left it, so I grab it and stash it in my waistband.

Though gunpowder is unlikely to work on the technologically backward dragon world, the weapon might come in handy during my trip there.

Fighting the temptation to test my vampire-senses-boosted aim, I sprint to the hub room.

The mirror-like floor there lets me take a look at myself.

Like my hands, my face is a bit paler than usual, but I otherwise look the same.

Except for when I will my fangs to come out. Because they do, and make me look ready for Halloween.

If I were allowed to show this to people, it would make an amazing "illusion." Speaking of that, I could also glamour people and sell that as hypnosis, except it would be so much better than what mentalists usually do on stage.

Assuming I can figure out how to glamour someone.

I imagine that, to start, I'd need to make my eyes turn into mirrors.

My vision feels funny, and I look down again.

Double wow.

My eyes *are* mirrors, just from me wishing for them to be that way.

Great. I'll try to glamour someone as soon as an

opportunity arises.

For now, I turn my eyes back to normal and face the gate leading to Gomorrah.

Which is when Eric, Thalia, and Felix poof into existence right between me and my goal.

CHAPTER TWENTY-NINE

"DUDE," I say to Felix when I find my tongue. "What are you doing here?"

"I'm sorry," he says. "I didn't want you to die, so I spoke to Eric and he—"

"You little traitor," I hiss at him, then pivot toward Eric. "You're too late, by the way. I already died." I expand my fangs and smile. "Luckily, it turns out I was a pre-vamp after all."

Thalia glances worriedly at Eric, while Felix gapes at me.

"Wow. Is that a magic trick?" He sounds appropriately awestruck. "If so, it's your best one yet."

"No." Eric examines me with a frown. "She's missing her Mandate Aura, like all newly turned vampires do."

Oh yeah. That happened to Lucretia also. And—speaking of auras—now that I lack mine, I can't see theirs anymore. I guess you need the Mandate aura in order to see one.

"But you said you weren't a pre-vamp," Felix says, his unibrow wiggling in confusion. "You saw yourself die in visions and didn't turn."

"Maybe I didn't watch my dead body long enough," I say with a lisp, thanks to the fangs.

"No, I doubt that," Felix says. "I've heard it said that some pre-vamps don't turn when they die unless they first drink blood from a powerful vampire—and you drank Lilith's blood today. I bet that's what did it."

"Oh yeah, I heard something like that from Lucretia," I say with a lisp, then hide my fangs. "That would mean mommy dearest saved my life yet again. In a manner of speaking, anyway."

"Yeah," Felix says sarcastically. "That woman's a saint."

"How about the two of you finish your conversation at the apartment?" Eric suggests, his frown deepening.

"What?" I glare at him. "Did you just seriously suggest I go to the apartment? Didn't Felix tell you that Nero is going to die without my help? His own—"

"Nero is already going to be furious about me letting you lose your pre-vamp life," Eric says. "If you also die the final death, so will I."

"You don't get it. *He* will die if I don't go."

"I gave my word," the teleporter says, his jaw tightening. "He knew the risks before he left, but he still forbade me from letting you get yourself killed."

Crap. We've had a version of this conversation

before—in a vision where I tried to see what would happen if I asked Eric for help.

Nothing worked that time—but that was when I was trying to be nice.

"I'm not going home." I put my hands on my hips. "And before you even think about it—I'm no longer that easy to handle."

Just as in my visions, a look of stubborn determination settles on Eric's face.

"Are you okay with this insanity?" I ask Thalia. "Are you going to help him?"

Thalia looks at me, then at Eric, then shakes her head.

"See," I tell Eric. "Thalia isn't with you, nor is Felix."

"Hey," Felix objects. "I didn't say that. I don't think you should—"

Not listening to the rest, I turn my eyes into mirrors, stare at Felix, and in a honey-laced voice say, "You will not interfere with me going."

"I will not interfere with you going," Felix says in that robotic tone glamour-controlled people use.

Damn.

I can't believe that just worked.

Felix must be extra vulnerable to glamour. That, or it's a side-effect of the vampire blood he drank earlier today. I remember something like that happened to Ariel.

Emboldened by the success, I turn my glamour gaze on Eric. "You will not interfere with me going either."

His eyes narrow. "Your vampire mind tricks won't work on me."

I look at Felix to see if he noticed how close that was to a quote from his least favorite *Star Wars* episode, but my roommate is still under my glamour.

"Move out of my way, or Thalia and Felix will hold you down as I leave," I tell Eric.

Instead of a reply, Eric grabs Felix and Thalia by their shoulders and disappears.

Great. I thought he might do that. Now for my plan A—reaching the gate before he comes back.

I sprint forward as fast as I can, but also set everything up for a plan B, in case Eric's teleportation is too fast.

I'm only halfway to my destination before Eric is in my path again—alone this time.

My hand moving gunslinger-fast, I raise the gun I recovered from the lab.

"Let me go or I'll shoot you." I stop, aiming the gun. "Or better yet, come with me and actually be useful for a change."

Eric disappears again, then reappears next to me and grabs the gun. Before I can even blink, he disappears with the gun.

Crap. At least I got to see him in action, which might come in handy.

In the next moment, Eric reappears next to the Gomorrah gate and tosses the gun inside it.

All right. If plan B doesn't work, Nero is screwed.

I pull out a knife and say, "If you come anywhere near me, I'll stab you."

Eric disappears again.

I start a chopping motion with my knife before he reappears.

He shows up just outside my knife's reach and extends his hand to grab my wrist.

Only his fingers close on empty air because—his teleportation aside—I'm now faster than he is.

The knife continues its arc, and lands on the wrist of my left hand.

With a fountain of blood, my hand falls off and hits the floor.

Eric stares at it in shock, and I can see the thoughts on his face.

First realization: Vampires can't regrow appendages.

Second: Nero is going to be murderous.

CHAPTER THIRTY

USING Eric's shock to my advantage, I stab him with Woland's syringe.

Eric tries to jerk away, but I push the plunger before he gets the chance.

"I didn't actually lose that arm," I tell him as I watch his eyes glaze over. "See?" I kick the fake hand and detach the special apparatus in my blazer that I finally got the chance to use.

He still looks shocked—or the drug is kicking in.

To ease his mind, I pull out my unharmed hand from its hiding spot in the left sleeve and show it to him. "Don't feel bad," I say. "You're not the first person defeated by my illusions."

Eric's eyes roll back in his head, and he drops to the floor.

I check his pulse and find it steady, which makes sense. The dose in this syringe was meant for me—a smaller person.

Tossing the special prop knife on the floor, I run into the gate that leads to Gomorrah.

Stepping out on the other side, I look for the gun, but of course, it's not there.

Itzel mentioned this feature of the gates. They don't let objects through without a Cognizant attached to them.

Oh well. The gun wasn't going to work on the dragon world anyway.

Ignoring the gorgeous Gomorrah skyline, I step into the gate that leads to the world where the hub looks like the one at JFK. Then, from there, a gate takes me into a world with rings like Saturn's.

A turquoise gate later, I end up on the world with two suns. Around me is an island surrounded by a never-ending ocean, with millions of birds making such a ruckus, I'm happy to escape into the next gate.

I come out in a hub that's another airport. This is the long leg of my journey. On this world, I have to travel from its equivalent of Newark airport to JFK. And, on top of that, suffer pretty gloomy scenery.

I dash through the secret corridors and come out in the airport proper—which is where I see the bodies.

Wow, I forgot how depressing this is.

The people look like dehydrated mummies and are everywhere. It's clear that one moment they stood in line to pass security, then something sucked all life out of them.

No, not something.

Tartarus.

An uber-powerful Cognizant who—if I understand it right—can feed on whole worlds.

Jumping over bodies when I have to, I sprint out of this world's Newark airport equivalent, trying to think of the best way to proceed from here.

The last time, we took a boat, but I don't know if I can operate one by myself, or whether it'll still be waiting for me on this side. Given my new vampire speed and stamina, it makes more sense to take a bridge and run the entire way.

Sprinting out of the airport, I enter the car cemetery that is the I-95N highway and run it like an obstacle course.

The husks of whole families stare at me sightlessly from inside the cars, but I do my best not to pay attention to them.

Channeling Forrest Gump, I just run and run—and when I get to the bridge, I run faster until I'm in this world's equivalent of Manhattan.

It's official.

Vampires have incredible stamina.

All this marathon-worthy running has made me about as tired as going up a steep flight of stairs.

Unfortunately, I still have many hours to go.

When I get to downtown, I can't help but recall the last time I was here. We slept over in a hotel, and things got heated between me and Nero.

The X-rated images flip through my mind, and I feel an extra burst of motivation to save my boss.

His tongue skills alone are worth the trouble.

Pushing aside lascivious thoughts, I run into the tunnel, and when I exit on the Brooklyn side, I feel a pang of thirst.

Not the mind-blanking need that was there when I turned, but more like a parched sensation after a salty meal—or a desire to nap after a day in the sun.

Considering how long I've been running at full speed, a little thirst is pretty reasonable.

Which reminds me: I don't need to either eat or sleep anymore—a strange concept.

If I survive, I'll try sleeping and eating anyway, just to see what it's like for a vampire.

Continuing to run, I try to forget about the thirst. I don't have time to raid a blood bank, or figure out how to hunt the most dangerous game in this desolate world.

I'm on Belt Parkway, about an hour's sprint from my destination, when a familiar motley crew of degenerates blocks my path.

Their faces are covered in burns and tattoos, and one of them is wearing a necklace of dried human ears.

We came across them—or a group just like them— on the last trip, only they were scavenging New Jersey at the time.

When they see me, they almost salivate from excitement, and hey, it's pretty feasible they want to literally eat me.

With a chilling war cry, they raise their clubs and charge at me.

CHAPTER THIRTY-ONE

I TAKE the stance Thalia taught me, and when the first man tries to club me, I dodge with vampire speed, then grab his wrist and break it as though it were made from cardboard.

Before the club drops to the ground, I catch it and use it to whack the head of the next attacker.

The club cracks in two—and the guy's skull does as well.

"I'll give the rest of you one chance to leave," I say and show them my now-extended fangs.

The last time, it took Nero's dragon form to scare them off, so I guess I shouldn't get offended that they don't seem as impressed with my display.

When the next two idiots leap at me, I punch one in the chest—causing him to fly some ten feet back—and grab the other by the neck.

To my shock, I'm able to lift the guy off the ground and toss him at the next two attackers like a frisbee.

But the idiots still keep coming.

How tasty do I look?

"I don't have time for this," I say and ready my eyes for glamour. "Leave now, or I'm going to use you as Bloody Marys."

The ear collector who's leading the attack grunts something, and they keep on coming.

Fine, then. They're asking for it.

Catching their gazes, I say in a seductive voice, "Stop."

They halt in their tracks.

Clearly, whatever mental illness made them immune to Tartarus didn't give them resistance to vampire glamour.

"You could've left." I walk over to the one with the dried ears. "Now a promise is a promise."

Leaning in, I bite his neck.

It's crazy how the guy smells worse than a dead skunk's dirty socks, yet I find him more appetizing than an ice cream sundae.

As I take a dainty sip of his blood, I have to suppress a moan of pleasure—because that would be weird.

Doing my best not to think of the kind of diseases that might be swimming in his blood, I take another sip.

My earlier thirst is gone.

Great.

Just to be a woman of my word, though, I drink a little from each of the glamoured assholes.

Then I also drink from the knocked-out ones, just

for the sake of fair play. They wouldn't want to be the only ones to wake up without a hickey from hell, would they?

Realizing I'm wasting time, I leave the snacks alone and resume my run—now with an extra spring in my step.

When I get to the JFK airport clone, I speed up to the point where the dead husks are a blur in the periphery of my vision.

Swiftly reaching the secret door, I whoosh to the hub, realizing as I run that I managed to get here in a third of the time it took us to cover this distance before.

Inside the hub, I jump into my target gate and proceed from there, taking gate after gate until I get to a world that that looks like Mars.

Looking around, I do my best to recall which gate we took the last time we were here.

Crap.

I should've written it down.

I do *not* want to get lost in the Otherlands.

Taking a guess, I jump into a gate and end up in a familiar dusty world with too many moons.

Phew.

Not lost anymore.

I think.

Hopefully.

After going through a few more gates, I reach another world where I'm not sure where to go, but then a pink gate looks vaguely familiar, so I enter it and end up in a world-sized forest.

Yes.

This is where Nero yelled at me for risking my life to save his.

And here I am doing it again. Oops.

If I'm right, the gate over to the right should take me to a snowy world.

And it does. I step into a frozen wasteland with white penguin-like birds.

Great.

The next world is also familiar. I recall wading through this crystal-clear shallow water.

Next, I go through a red gate into a world with too many stars, then a purple gate that leads me into a cavern where we bandaged Nero's wounds.

Which means the green gate to my right should be the one that leads into the dragon world.

I step in and come out on the world with a silver Grand Canyon-like mountain ridge—just as depicted in Nero's office painting.

Finally.

Dragon world.

From here, I just need to follow the map I saw in my vision until I reach Godiva.

I launch into a run—and as I go, I quickly realize I don't actually need the map after all.

Nero's army left an obvious trail behind them— ashes from campfires, decimated grass, garbage, and even a few dead bodies of enemies they must've come across.

After some hours of non-stop sprinting, I reach the scorched battlefield from my first vision.

Oh, wow.

The smell of dead bodies is so bad I can almost see it shimmering the air. Carrion-feeding birds and animals are feasting on dead dragon and human flesh, and I deeply regret having seen any of it.

Even for Nero, I can't bring myself to go directly through this mess, so I speed up and run around it.

The second battlefield is not as bad as the first, thanks to the fact that many dragons fled the fight and human soldiers switched sides.

According to Nero's words in my vision, Godiva is a day's journey from here.

But that's for an army.

I'm bound to be faster.

Not wanting to waste time going around the battlefield, I run through it, doing my best not to step on the dead. Jumping over bodies slows my usually brisk pace, as does holding my breath, trying not to inhale the noxious fumes.

Finally, I leave the battlefield far behind me and speed up—until I get to the forest and a monstrous thunderstorm begins.

Waterfall-like streams of water barrage me from seemingly every angle, and thunder claps every couple of seconds. Then a lightning strikes a tree a few feet from where I'm passing, which makes me wonder if vampires can survive a hit from one.

Probably not.

A tree crashes to the ground in front of me next. Could a vampire survive *that*?

Also doubtful.

I do my best to traverse the muddy mess that the forest trail has become. Vampire or not, my muscles are beginning to ache in earnest now, but I ignore the pain and keep running.

The storm ends, and I pick up my pace again.

Finally, I see Godiva in the far distance.

As I get closer, I realize that the army has already entered the battlefield.

Crap.

In my vision, they were just finishing their march when Nero walked toward those giant boulders, which means it's now *after* that moment.

And when I look at the boulders in question, Nero isn't there.

There goes my plan to tell him not to go into the castle. He must've already entered the cursed tunnel.

Now I have to catch him before he gets too far.

Sprinting for the boulders with everything I have left, I listen for any signs of the battle starting.

Nothing yet—which means there's still hope.

On the off chance that vampires recharge their seer powers quicker than normal folks, I attempt going into Headspace.

Nope. Still in recovery mode and probably will be for a while.

By the time I get to the boulders, my heart is hammering against my chest.

Interesting.

I guess that *can* happen to a vampire if she runs fast enough, or worries about someone enough.

Steadying my finger, I draw the letter "zhe" on the smaller boulder and hold my breath.

For all I know, the passage might only open to dragons.

But no.

After a few excruciatingly nerve-wracking moments, the ground opens with the same screech as in my vision.

I climb into the hole and, straining my muscles, start running through the musty, bioluminescent-critter-lit passage. Before long, I reach the castle entrance.

Damn it.

The metal door has already been cut with the gate sword, and the guards are lying here dead.

Nero and his companions are clearly far ahead of me.

Frantically, I rush into the wine cellar, jumping over the dead bodies of guards as I go.

I'm running so fast it feels like I break the sound barrier on my way through the corridor with high ceilings. And as I swing open the door to the torture room, I hear the usurper say, "Looks like it's just us."

Oh no.

The brother dragons are already dead, and Nero is just about to join them.

I barge in and see that I'm right.

Everyone but Nero, Claudia, and the usurper are already dead.

"This is it for you." Gripping his sword tighter, Nero takes a menacing step toward the usurper just as Claudia gets within striking distance.

"Nero, watch out!" I yell, but in that very moment, Kit (who's pretending to be Nero) roars "Attack!" outside the castle, drowning out my scream.

I torpedo forward, but Claudia's blade is already slicing Nero's right forearm to the bone.

CHAPTER THIRTY-TWO

"SHE'S BETRAYING YOU!" I scream at the top of my lungs. "I had a vision. She's about to stab you in the back!"

No one seems to notice my arrival.

Just like in my vision, Nero grunts from the pain, and the gate sword slips out of his grip, hitting the floor with a clank as it deactivates.

And, like in my vision, the usurper slices at Nero's head—a strike that my boss dodges but just barely.

Then, like clockwork, Claudia thrusts her sword forward—but Nero isn't there to get stabbed like before.

So he *did* hear me. And—thanks to his truth-telling ability—believed me right away.

Seeing Nero sidestep Claudia's strike, the usurper swipes at Nero with his sword—which is when Nero catches his wrist and gives it a vicious jerk.

Yudo's sword flies to the side.

Claudia rushes forward to help her ally, but I'm finally there, and I slam my fist into her sword-wielding arm.

Dragons sure are sturdy.

Even with my vampire-boosted strength, I don't break her arm—but at least her sword goes flying.

"You bitch," Claudia growls, spinning around to face me as she throws a punch at my face—moving at a hundred miles per hour.

Amazingly, I dodge the punch and even have a moment to uppercut her in return.

Only when my knuckles connect with her jaw, it feels like it's made of steel.

The impact sends her flying about a foot in the air, but when she lands, she does so on her feet, and instead of passing out, she just gives me a murderous stare.

I leap at her, fist aimed at her jaw.

She blocks me with her right hand, then counter-punches me.

Her small fist rams into my cheek with a force Mike Tyson would envy. Stars explode in my vision, but miraculously, I don't pass out.

Angry growls and sounds of fists battering flesh can be heard from where Nero is going at it with the usurper.

I spare them a glance, but both are moving as blurs that are too fast to track. All I catch is Nero striking the usurper with his injured arm, but then I think he punches Nero back.

Using my distraction, Claudia tries to kick me, but I

side-step it and land a punch on her cement-like forehead.

She doesn't even blink, and I finally register the troubling truth.

I'm fighting a freaking dragon.

CHAPTER THIRTY-THREE

SWITCHING my eyes into glamour mode, I stare at Claudia intently and say, "Sleep."

She bares her teeth in a humorless smile. "Little vampire, I'm a dragon. Did you really expect that to work?"

Shrugging, I sweep at her feet, but she jumps over my leg, then rakes her talon-like nails over my face.

I jump back, crying out in pain, but then a confusing thing happens.

I feel the gash closing up and the pain dulling.

This is so cool.

I might not be a dragon, but I'm not a pushover either.

Maybe I'll actually manage to hurt her before she kills me.

She strikes at me again, but I block her punch, then land a fist into her jaw, which doesn't seem to faze her much.

The heel of her hand slams into my chest, and I fly back but land on my feet. When she leaps to attack me again, I kick her knee—sadly, not damaging anything.

Over the next two minutes, we go back and forth like that. I bet if anyone were watching, it would look like a mix between an MMA and a superhero fight. Between punches, kicks, and gouging out chunks of flesh, we throw each other at the torture equipment, but the only thing that breaks is said equipment and not either one of us.

A sudden spray of blood reminds me of the battle Nero is fighting. It's impossible to tell whose it is just by the look or smell of it, and I can't help but spare Nero and the usurper another microsecond-long glance.

Again, though, all I see is a big blur.

Capitalizing on my distraction, Claudia leaps for her sword.

Two can play that game, though. Using *her* distraction, I dive for the gate sword.

She gets hers first and charges at me.

I grasp the handle of my weapon just as her blade enters my back.

Asshole.

She loves stabbing people in the back, doesn't she?

Ignoring the burning agony in my back muscles, I activate my sword's shimmering plasma and swipe blindly at Claudia.

The pain almost makes me pass out—and at first, I have no idea if I got her. The gate sword is so light, and slices things so smoothly, that it feels like I missed her completely.

Only I didn't miss.

The first thing I register is the horrified expression in Claudia's eyes. Then a river of blood streams over her birthmark.

Staring at the bloody gash on her forehead, I realize what I managed to do.

I sliced off a hat-like chunk of her skull.

As she collapses, the top part of her head falls to the side, exposing the chopped-off brain underneath.

There's no healing from that. Even for a dragon.

As this realization dawns on me, I belatedly recall that this woman means something to Nero—and though I think she totally deserved her fate, he might have a different opinion.

Oh well, no time to worry about that.

I have to help Nero.

Though my back is healing rapidly, it still hurts as I grip my sword tighter.

Ignoring the pain, I turn to face the two blurring dragons.

Only Nero no longer needs my help.

With an angry growl, he picks up the wounded usurper from the ground and tosses him into the maw of the iron maiden.

Hundreds of sharp blades enter Yudo's body, and he roars in pain.

Face contorted in rage, Nero smashes down the lid

of the coffin-like device, piercing the enemy with hundreds more blades.

"Here." I disable the gate sword and toss the handle to Nero. "Make sure this is finished."

Nero catches the handle, activates the sword, and cuts the iron maiden into even halves. Then he slices each half into more halves, and keeps repeating it until all that's left are tiny pieces of meat impaled on the blades of the device—a kind of macabre dragon shish kebab.

Nero prods one particular piece with his foot, and a bloodied gold crown clinks on the floor.

Deactivating the sword, Nero turns to face me, his gaze filled with a mixture of fury and confusion.

"You died in my vision about this," I say, chewing on my lip. "I came to help."

Eyes narrowing, he opens his mouth to retort—but then his gaze falls on Claudia, and the sword drops from his hand.

With a leap that makes me jump back, he reaches the dead woman and kneels down.

Oh crap.

His limbal rings completely overtake his eyes, and his face is contorted with grief.

Despite Claudia's treachery, he's more than upset at her death.

"Why?" His hands clench on her bloodied dress. "Why? Why?"

I have no idea if he's asking me why I killed her, asking her why she betrayed him, or asking the uncaring universe why it likes to take everyone he loves from him.

I only know one thing for sure.

When Nero recovers his ability to think straight, he'll understand how Claudia came to be dead.

He'll realize I'm the one who killed her.

CHAPTER THIRTY-FOUR

THOUGH I SHOULD PROBABLY RUN, I approach Nero. And though I'm probably risking its loss, I put a hand on his shoulder.

He doesn't seem to feel my touch.

His powerful body is stiff, as if turned to stone. The blood dripping from his forearm paints the stone floor red, and the expression on his face is pure devastation.

"Why?" he whispers raggedly again. "Why did you do this?"

My chest feels like a herd of elephants is sitting on it. If I didn't know better, I'd think Woland is giving me another heart attack. Only it somehow feels worse this time, with the squeezing pressure echoed by the painful stinging behind my eyes.

I did this to Nero.

I killed the one person he seems to have still cared about.

"Nero," I say achingly. "I'm sorry. I really am."

He's still oblivious to my presence, all his attention on Claudia's corpse. Tenderly, he reaches out and wipes away the blood covering her face—and as he does, I notice something strange.

That birthmark of hers.

It seems to be smearing away, like makeup.

Like it was painted on.

In a flash, it all makes sense to me—and the magician part of me is grudgingly impressed even as fury boils in my veins.

Knees weak with relief, I sink to my haunches next to Nero, and he finally turns to look at me, his gaze uncomprehending.

"She's not Claudia," I say softly, pushing aside my turmoil as I reach out to clasp his hand. "Her birthmark is fake."

The limbal rings in Nero's eyes impossibly dilate, nearly taking over the white, and his hand curls into a fist within my grip.

"What?" His voice is barely audible.

"The usurper did to you what you did to him," I explain, releasing his hand. "You made everyone think Kit was you, but he made you think this person is Claudia. Look."

Nero turns his attention to the corpse as I spit on my finger and drag it through the smeared birthmark on the imposter's cheek.

It leaves a clean streak—and no trace of the birthmark.

The blood loosened the paint or makeup or

whatever, allowing my finger to easily wipe it away.

As he stares at my handiwork, Nero's face seems to roller-coaster through every emotion known to science, settling on a mixture of hope and rage.

"Where is she?" he growls, leaping to his feet.

"No idea," I say, in case he's asking me and not the corpse of the Claudia impersonator.

Without another word, Nero blurs out of the room.

I get up, and as I do, I notice that my back is feeling noticeably better. Picking up the gate sword, I run after him.

He's too fast for me to catch, so I follow the trail of broken doors and overturned furniture that he leaves behind.

When I reach the prison portion of the castle, I see multiple cell doors ripped out of the wall.

Farther in, I find Nero standing next to a giant cell with thick metal bars that remind me of the cage where the impostor Claudia awaited her "rescue."

I freeze in place.

The woman inside this cage is dressed in a plain dress that's identical to what the fake one wore, has similar long reddish-brown hair, and—of course—a birthmark in the shape of a cloud on her cheek. Her face, however, is quite different. Where the impostor was pretty, this woman is Helen of Troy airbrushed in Photoshop.

The kind of beauty men would go to war for.

Standing behind the bars, she's almost nose-to-nose with Nero. As I watch, she tries to bend the cage bars—but without any success.

"Your name," Nero demands, reaching out to grip her hands. "Tell me who you are."

Tears run down her face as she squeezes his hands. "I'm Claudia," she chokes out. "And you are my brother, Nero." She laughs shakily, and I exhale a big breath of relief.

Sister.

She's definitely his sister.

Until this moment, I didn't realize how tense I was, waiting for this confirmation.

"I can't believe you're alive," she continues. Then her gorgeous face contorts into a mask of fury. "That bastard Yudo—"

"Is gone," Nero growls. Releasing her hands, he grabs the bars of the cage and they both strain to bend them—but again to no avail.

"No matter how often I tried, I couldn't escape," Claudia says, then punches the bars in frustration.

Snapping out of my paralysis, I activate the gate sword and rush over.

"Step aside," I say, and when they do, I cut a hole in the cage that's big enough for Claudia to walk through.

As soon as I move aside, Claudia tackle-hugs Nero so viciously that if he weren't a dragon, he'd end up with a cracked rib.

They stand there embracing and murmuring to

each other, and I tactfully step back, giving them privacy. I feel like an idiot that I was jealous over Claudia—which I was, even if I didn't want to admit it to myself.

But they're brother and sister, so yay.

Extra glad I didn't kill the real Claudia. I'll have to use this sword very carefully around her in the future.

A sound of clanking metal to our right startles me, and I spin on my heel, activating the sword on autopilot.

About a dozen guards run in, armed to the teeth.

Nero reacts immediately, shoving Claudia behind himself. "Lay down your weapons." His tone is blade sharp. "Your master is dead, and a new regime is—"

Before Nero can finish, Claudia blurs forward, and in a split second, the guards are left in bloody shreds.

Wiping her hands on her dress, she looks up, her expression vaguely embarrassed. "They kept spitting in my lunch," she says, and I can't help but notice how the copious blood streaking down her face does *not* mess with her birthmark this time. "They—"

"You don't need to explain yourself." A smile touches Nero's eyes. "You've always had a bit of a temper."

Sure. Leave it to the guy who also shreds people who piss him off to call what she did "a bit of a temper."

I must've snorted because Claudia turns to me, her gaze lighting with curiosity.

"Who is she?" she asks Nero as if I'm not standing right there.

"This is Sasha," Nero says, then gives me a narrow-eyed stare for no good reason that I can think of.

She examines me closely, then looks at Nero's scowl, then back at me, a gleeful smile appearing on her lips.

"Are you my sister-in-law?" she asks, cocking her head.

I reel back.

Did she just ask if Nero is my *husband*?

I mean, he has a skilled tongue and all, but that is a ridiculous thing to suggest.

Ignoring her question, Nero says to Claudia, "Now that you're safe, we have to stop the bloodshed outside." Still scowling, he turns to me and barks, "Follow me."

Before either of us can ask him for details, Nero stalks back down the corridor.

I look at Claudia, and she grins, then makes her face eerily like Nero's when he's mad. In a perfect imitation of his voice, she says, "We better follow Mr. Grouchy's commandments."

I suppress a laugh. "Sure." Turning so she can see the wound in my back, I ask, "How bad is it?"

If the pain is anything to go by, the boo-boo should be just about gone.

"Knitting as I speak," Claudia says approvingly. "What are you?"

"A vampire," I say in a low voice. "But that's a recent development."

"What?" Nero growls from somewhere, then shows up in the hallway and gives me a blood-chilling stare.

Stupid dragon super-hearing. I didn't intend for him to learn about my new state of being just yet.

"I had some trouble with a few chorts back on Earth," I say. "One thing led to another, and I ended up drinking Lilith's blood. That's my mother, by the way," I say to wide-eyed Claudia. "Then Woland—the honcho chort—killed me, so I turned. Darian wasn't lying when he—"

"You will go over all this again later." Nero's face is thunder dark. "In great detail."

Before I can retort, he turns on his heel.

"You're in so much trouble," Claudia whispers, grinning. "I can't believe how little he's changed."

Grunting something unintelligible, Nero disappears around the corner, and when we catch up, he's picking up the bloody crown from the usurper's remains.

Shaking off the blood, he puts the crown on his head with a ceremonious gesture, and as soon as he does, the bone-deep gash in his arm heals, as do all the other cuts and bruises on his body.

"The imperial treasure is his now," Claudia explains when she sees my confused expression. "With all that wealth, he gains power."

Oh. This must be like when Nero healed on top of his treasure pile on Earth. This whole castle must count as his riches now—that or maybe there's an actual cave with gold and diamonds below us.

I wonder if that's what allowed the usurper to fight

Nero for as long as he did: he had all that extra treasure-powered mojo.

Examining the dragon kebab that is the usurper, Claudia smiles. "Serves him right." She then looks at fake Claudia's dead body. "His whore, too. The two of them had been gloating about their plan to me for days, ever since rumors of your return reached Yudo's ears."

Nero grunts and stalks toward the big doors through which the usurper and his minions originally entered the torture room, and we follow.

When we get to the giant doors that lead into the castle, Nero activates some mechanism, and the doors open with a deafening screech.

Outside, the battle is still raging. The strongmen and the werewolf guy are ahead of everyone, a sea of dead bodies behind them. Vlad is right on their tails, bent over one of the enemy soldiers, likely drinking his blood—which makes me realize I could use a little snack myself.

Everyone else is fighting just as furiously. Colton and the other giants are trampling people under their feet, the elf-like guy is drowning enemy soldiers in arrows, the cockatrice warriors are taking dragon and human lives left and right, and the centaurs are prancing around like horses in a game of polo, leaving death in their wake.

The only part of the fight that isn't going as well as it should is the sky battle.

Despite Kit's victory over the giant Zmey, there are

simply too many enemy dragons compared to Nero's allies.

"Dragons, hear me!" Nero roars in a voice that sounds like a mixture between a human's and a dragon's. "The usurper is dead." Taking off the crown, he lifts it high above his head. "You have two minutes to cease hostilities and live."

The sky battle stops instantly as every enemy dragon looks in Nero's direction.

It doesn't take them long to make the right decision.

One by one, they swoop down, assume their human form, and kneel before Nero.

"Order the humans to surrender," Nero growls at one of the bigger enemy dragons—who must be a general of some sort.

The guy barks out orders, and the human army stops fighting, staring around in confusion instead.

For the next hour, every dragon from Yudo's side approaches Nero and swears his fealty. A few—likely the ones who were higher up in the usurper's forces of evil—offer recompense in the form of a portion of their treasure or chunks of their territories.

Nero listens to them, stone-faced, and while he accepts their treasure, none of them walk away with the titles they'd held in his enemy's court.

Meanwhile, Claudia goes to speak to the human army, and though I can't hear what she's saying, the people appear relieved.

As I watch all this, feeling completely useless, my heart sinks lower and lower. Because I now have an answer to the question that had occurred to me after my Claudia-betrayal vision.

Is Nero planning to rule the dragon kind?

Yes, he clearly is.

Which brings up the bigger question.

What room can a dragon emperor have in his life for someone as insignificant as I am?

CHAPTER THIRTY-FIVE

"I'M GOING to go for a stroll," I mutter, but no one pays me any attention.

Which makes sense.

Why would they?

There's just been a revolution on this world, and I have nothing to do with anything.

Dispirited, I make my way to the battlefield as Nero continues doing his emperor-y things, distributing the lands and treasure he acquired between the dragons who supported his campaign. As I'm stepping over the corpses at the edge of the Godiva half-moon, I glance back and see that Claudia is now at his side.

"Sasha!"

Startled, I turn and see Kit coming toward me with Vlad and the rest of Nero's Cognizant helpers from Earth. "How are you here?" she asks, stopping in front of me. "Nero made a big stink about you staying out of this conflict."

"Did he? Well, I guess I'm not that easy to control."

"I'd say." Kit smiles, then peers at me closely. "Did you do something different with your makeup?"

"She turned," Vlad says with an unreadable expression. "She's now one of my kind."

"You're a vamp?" Kit exclaims excitedly. "How? Why didn't you tell me? When did this happen?"

"We need to see Nero," Colton booms through his giant larynx. "Maybe you can chat later?"

"You go and I'll catch up." Kit waves a dismissive hand at him.

Kit's companions go ahead, but Vlad stays behind.

"So," Kit says. "How did this happen?"

"It's a long story," I say. "And I wouldn't want his Imperial Majesty to have to wait unnecessarily."

"You might have a point," Kit says, missing my sarcasm completely. "How about we skip to the most important part?" Sensually brushing her hair off her neck, she turns with a languid motion, letting me get a good look at her temptingly pulsing carotid artery.

"Take a little sip," she says seductively. "You know you want to."

I look at Vlad in time to see him roll his eyes. Refocusing on Kit, I clear my throat. "Thank you, but I just had a huge snack back at the castle," I lie. "Maybe a raincheck?"

"I guess." Looking disappointed, Kit moves her hair back, concealing her neck. To Vlad, she says, "I guess we should catch up with the others."

"One second," Vlad says, then gives me an intent

stare. "If you want to act like a civilized person, never ignore the thirst."

I nod gratefully. I figured as much, but it's good to hear this info from the blood-drinking horse's mouth.

"Give me your phone," Vlad says, and when I do, he puts a number in. "That's my personal blood bank contact in New York," he explains. "Tell her I recommended you, and she'll set up deliveries."

Blood deliveries. Great. I wonder if they use Uber Eats.

"Thank you," I say, pocketing the phone.

"No problem," Vlad says. "Now, where are you going by yourself? Not back to Earth, I presume?"

"No, I just needed some fresh air after all the bloodshed," I reply. "Figured I'd take a stroll in the forest."

In reality, though, his idea is a good one. The vampire thirst is back now, and Kit didn't help matters with her proposition. On Earth, I'll be able to get in touch with Vlad's contact and get a meal, plus I'll be out of Nero's imperial hair.

"Fine, but don't stroll too far," Vlad says. "You don't know these woods, and it's getting late."

"No worries. I'll stick near here," I lie.

"We better go," Kit says, glancing up at the darkening sky.

"Right," Vlad says, and with one last warning look at me, he turns away.

As they hurry to the castle, I resume my walk, heading toward the forest where the thunderstorm caught me earlier. Nothing stops me now, as the weather is perfect, and with my enhanced vampire vision, I can see as well in the darkness as on a slightly cloudy day.

In general, with my boosted senses, the alien forest is a pleasure to explore. Purely by accident, I walk onto a meadow the size of a stadium and stop in awe.

Covered with some kind of bioluminescent moss, the place makes me feel like I'm walking in the starry sky.

Doing my best to put Nero out of my mind, I inhale the fresh air and try to figure out what the moss smell reminds me of. A mix between rose petals and passion fruit, I decide after another lungful.

How romantic.

A shadow blots out the sky, and my heartbeat jumps as I look up.

It's a dragon.

An angry dragon swooping down on me.

CHAPTER THIRTY-SIX

A DRAGON I was just trying to put out of my mind, in fact.

He lands on the moss and turns into a very naked figure with a furious expression on his chiseled face.

"Nero," I say, hyperaware of his nudity. "Don't you have a whole empire to boss around now?"

Even with him a few feet away, I can smell his clean, woodsy scent. And that's not all. My boosted olfactory system informs me that underneath is a warm, musky scent of something primitively male.

It takes all the willpower I possess to keep my eyes above his chest—though what I do glimpse looks beyond mouthwatering. Especially in ultra HD.

"You got between fighting dragons," Nero growls, advancing on me. "Again."

"And you got yourself killed in my vision, again," I retort, refusing to retreat. "Do you see *me* bitching?"

His muscles bunch dangerously as he leans in,

glaring down at me. "I forbade you to leave that apartment. How did you get out?"

"No one *forbids* me from doing anything. That goes doubly so for ungrateful assholes." I lift my hands to push him away, but he grabs my wrists in a grip that feels unyielding even with my new vampire strength.

"Darian said you would die." He squeezes my wrists. "I knew he wasn't lying. What did you want me to do?"

"Oh, I don't know," I say, every word dripping with a lethal dose of sarcasm. "How about *talk* to me? I know it sounds crazy, but—"

"Lilith has my blood." His gaze drills into me as if he's the one who can glamour people. "Talking to you would've meant giving you to her on a silver platter."

"Sure." I twist out of his grasp. "Is Lilith the reason you couldn't call me? Or text or video conference or attach a letter to the foot of a pigeon?"

"Rasputin gave me a very tight timeline," he says with a lot less anger. Inhaling deeply, he adds in a calmer tone, "But you're right. I should've personally asked you to stay home."

"Yes, you should've."

For a moment, we just stare at each other, and the stupid vampire thirst pulls my gaze to his neck. His strong, muscular neck with skin that looks so smooth and appetizing.

I lick my dry lips, forcing the dark urge away as I meet his eyes again.

"I'm not good with goodbyes," he says roughly, and

the warm male scent intensifies as he eyes my lips like he'd like to trace the path of my tongue with his own.

That scent is arousal, I realize as I feel his reaction against my belly.

A *big* reaction.

"So is *this* a goodbye?" I ask, my breath hitching as I take a step back, battling the urge to leap at him.

His eyes narrow. "This—right now—better not be a goodbye. I was talking about back on Earth. I wasn't sure I'd see you again and—"

Losing the battle, I reach out with vampire speed and wind my arms around his neck as I lock my lips with his.

Nero stiffens at first. Then, with a low growl, he kisses me back, his tongue dancing with mine, making alliances before it invades my mouth like a conquering army.

Heat blasts through my veins, liquifying my insides, and without pulling out of the kiss, I kick my shoes off my feet and wriggle out of my blazer.

"Wait." He tears his mouth away, and breathing heavily, steps back. "This is dangerous, even with you as you are now."

Dangerous?

I was stabbed in the back with a freaking sword today and survived. If he thinks I can't handle *his* sword, he's got another thing coming.

Running my tongue over my lips again, I begin stripping, taking off each piece of clothing as slowly and seductively as I can.

His limbal rings—and other things—engorge out of control.

When my bra hits the ground, Nero's control snaps. With a tortured growl, he blurs forward, and before I can blink, we're kissing again. Only this time, the experience is more ferocious, more overwhelming than ever, the combination of Nero and my enhanced senses messing with my mind. I can feel everything, taste everything… smell the very blood rushing in his veins.

And I want more.

I want everything.

"I'm willing to risk it," I whisper into his mouth. "Please."

With a sound reminiscent of a wounded animal, Nero pulls away from the kiss and bends his head, offering me his neck. "Drink," he orders hoarsely.

The hunger I feel as I look at the pulse beating under his tanned skin makes me stagger with its intensity.

It takes all my willpower not to attack him like a predator and to kiss his neck instead. He shudders, gooseflesh rippling over his skin, and his hands clench on my back, yanking me toward him.

My self-control evaporates, and with a moan, I sink my suddenly extended fangs into his flesh.

As the rich liquid touches my tongue, the pleasure slams into my brain, jumbling my consciousness like a tornado.

Time becomes jittery and thinking impossible.

Somehow, we end up on the moss—which is when I

feel Nero carefully enter me—and the pleasure explodes exponentially, turning what happens next into a hazy blur of violent ecstasy.

Sometime, somewhere, I hear Nero groaning in pleasure.

From even farther away, my own moans reach my ears, then escalate into orgasmic cries.

I'm dimly aware of crashing sounds and pain mixing with the mind-blowing pleasure, but the ecstasy trumps everything, and as more blood drips onto my lips, I lose myself completely, shattering over and over in his dark embrace.

AT SOME POINT, we must've stopped, because I gradually recover some portion of my wits. Opening my eyes, I find myself cradled in Nero's arms, my head pillowed on his shoulder and my leg draped possessively over his thighs. We're on the edge of the meadow inside a small crater in the ground, with fallen trees in the forest next to us.

Wow.

Was that the thunderstorm or us?

"Are you okay?" Nero murmurs as he strokes my back.

"No," I whisper in awe and scan my body for aches and pains—only to find the exact opposite. "I feel amazing."

It's an understatement.

I feel like I was rebuilt from the ground up using stronger, morphine-laced components.

"Good," he says, and when I raise my head to glance

at his face, I see a look of relief—and purely male satisfaction—stamped on his hard features.

I lay my head back down, hiding a grin.

Okay then.

I just had sex with a dragon and lived to tell the tale.

Being a vampire definitely doesn't suck.

Though I have to say, I do feel kind of tired. Maybe it's like an after-meal slump?

Glancing up at my meal's face, I catch him yawning, and I reflexively yawn in response.

Huh. So that didn't go away when I became a vampire. Good to know.

"You don't need to sleep anymore," he murmurs, as if reading my mind. "But do it anyway."

And tucking me against him in a spooning position, he hugs me like a body pillow and goes to sleep, his breath evening out within seconds.

I'm tempted to get up just to spite his Imperial Bossiness, but it feels too good to lie here. Closing my eyes, I let my muscles relax and begin counting sheep, just to see if I would drift into sleep if I tried.

On sheep number twenty-seven, my consciousness winks out.

———

WHEN I WAKE UP, Nero is still wrapped around me, his breathing warm on the back of my neck.

He's clearly still sleeping, whereas I'm as alert as if

I've had a triple espresso. Must be a side effect of not needing sleep in the first place.

I savor being enveloped in his powerful arms for a few blissful moments, then realize enough time has passed for my seer powers to have recharged.

Assuming I retained them when I turned into a vampire, that is.

My contentedness begins to evaporate, so I decide to put this question to rest.

Steadying my breathing, I settle into the state of required focus—and effortlessly find myself in Headspace.

Phew.

It's official.

I'm a seer *and* a vampire. A vampseer, as it were—or maybe a clairvampoyant.

Regardless of what I'll call myself, I now have one less thing to worry about—which leaves just a few million more to resolve.

Floating around, I focus on the soothing shapes that surround me. If I were to experience them, they'd undoubtedly show me luxuriating in Nero's arms.

As tempting as that is, since I'm here already, I might as well do something more practical—like checking on my friends.

It doesn't take me long to decide whom to start with.

Overeager to experiment with my glamour skills, I used them on Felix yesterday—so I should probably check to make sure the effect has worn off.

As I dwell on Felix's essence, a new set of shapes shows up.

Like the prior ones, these are pretty chill, which is great—the last thing I need is more Felix-related drama.

Reaching for a random shape, I let the vision start.

———

FELIX IS SITTING at a fancy kitchen table across from Ariel and Rasputin.

I recognize their surroundings. This is the digs Nero provided to Rasputin at his club. I once spied them sitting there, plotting.

Holding some Gomorran pastry that looks like a cross between pizza and a Cinnabon, Felix seems completely recovered, which relieves me greatly.

"A vampire," Felix says in English, his unibrow dancing a jig on his forehead. He then repeats the word in Russian—I guess with him around, Ariel and Rasputin don't need a translating gizmo to communicate. "She used glamour on me and put Eric into such deep sleep that he was still napping by the gates when I headed over here."

Eric is still knocked out? Oops.

"I can't believe it." Ariel frowns. "I don't *want* to believe it."

Oh no.

I know that expression. Ariel is deeply unhappy, and I realize why.

By becoming a vampire, I've turned into a walking, talking fix of her favorite drug.

Does that mean she can't be around me anymore? Or would she be okay if I just told her that she can never, ever have my blood?

"I can confirm this," Rasputin says after Felix translates Ariel's words. "I've seen the future where Sasha comes here, to Gomorrah, and she is, without a doubt, a vampire."

Felix bites into his pastry, then sips his tea. "At least she's fine in this vision of yours," he says to Rasputin after he swallows. "I was afraid she'd get herself killed saving Nero this time."

"Yes, she was perfectly okay," Rasputin says. "And before you ask, she was grateful for your research."

Felix looks confused, but Ariel makes him translate what Rasputin says anyway.

"What research?" Ariel asks Felix.

"What research?" Felix asks Rasputin.

"The phone stuff," Rasputin says. "I already had this conversation with you in a vision, you see. It's why you came here, is it not?"

"That's trippy," Felix says in Russian. Looking at Ariel, he explains in English, "I came here because I wanted Rasputin to seek out Sasha in Headspace and tell her about my findings as soon as possible."

"I already tried to reach her in Headspace," Rasputin says. "It didn't work."

I wonder what I was doing at that time… sleeping or Nero?

Of course, I could've also been out of juice.

"Can you tell me what this phone stuff is about?" Ariel says when Felix brings her up to speed and stops oohing and ahhing about Rasputin's foreknowledge and its implications.

"Sasha gave me a bunch of numbers and asked that I find out with whom Lilith spoke—and I did," he says smugly. "One of the numbers was Nostradamus, but the other was that Woland guy—the head of the chorts."

Rasputin cringes at the Russian word.

"Wait… what?" Ariel blinks at him. "Didn't you say Lilith saved you and Sasha from someone named Woland?"

"Exactly," Felix says. "But before she saved us from him, she disguised her voice and called the bastard." He grabs another piece of the pastry. "She told him that Sasha and I might have information about *his*"—he nods at Rasputin—"whereabouts. Then she told the chort where *I* could be found."

So it was Lilith. She was the "good authority" Woland kept mentioning during my torture. I can't believe that woman. She told me fairy tales about St. Petersburg probability manipulators sniffing out Rasputin's trail, but it was her all along.

"That makes no sense," Ariel says. "Why put you in danger, then save you?"

"To make Sasha think she's a good mom?" Felix suggests uncertainly. "Or maybe she wanted to make sure Sasha would become a vampire."

"Couldn't she have just forced Sasha to drink her blood and then killed her herself?" Ariel asks, and I can't help but notice how disturbed she looks when talking about her kryptonite. Clearing her throat, she says, "Lilith is powerful enough to do so, isn't she?"

"Maybe she didn't want Sasha to hate her more than she already does." Felix sips his tea. "You're asking me to get inside a very twisted mind."

"I think you're only partially right," Rasputin chimes in as if he understood their English. In reality, though, he must be relying on what he learned in the vision he mentioned. "I believe Lilith took Nostradamus's advice, and it was *he* who came up with the convoluted plan."

"But why?" Felix asks, then translates for Ariel.

"To lessen the chance that another seer would be able to thwart the outcome in a single counteraction." He waits for Felix to translate for Ariel, then continues. "I believe Nostradamus knew I was out of commission after giving Nero his war plans, and he must've tricked Sasha to run out of her seer powers at a critical point in this scheme. If Lilith's plan had been simply to attack Sasha, my daughter could've seen that coming and fled —plus, as you said, Lilith might want to retain Sasha's good opinion of her. The woman is certainly deluded enough to think such a thing is possible."

Wow.

My head spins as I process Rasputin's words.

Could Nostradamus really have planned such a thing?

There are clues that confirm it.

For example, he started the conversation about seers and then offered to "teach me something." Granted, I was the one who asked him how to target a specific time, but maybe he influenced even that by foreseeing different threads of that conversation in order to guide me where he wanted.

And he was definitely the one to urge me to test out the skill—which was how I later ran out of seer juice.

I bet if he didn't teach me what he did, I could've defeated Woland without dying.

I'm angry but impressed with Nostradamus's skills.

He was so confident in his plan, he even warned me that the skill uses up a lot of seer juice—no doubt so that I'd trust him more.

"I'm beginning to really hate seers," Ariel mutters when Felix translates the rest to her.

Yep. She stole that thought straight out of my nonexistent head.

"We are a meddlesome bunch," Rasputin says—again without needing a translation.

"Here's what I'm wondering," Felix says. "Now that Woland is dead, will you be able to come to Earth and spend some quality time with Sasha?"

It's a great question, but before Rasputin can answer, the vision terminates.

———

FINDING myself back in Nero's arms, I try to process what I've just learned.

Lilith and Nostradamus are the reason I became a vampire.

Though I should be furious with them, I can't help but realize that in doing what they did, they also inadvertently made sure Nero survived. Because if I weren't a vampire, there's no way I would've made it in time to save him from fake Claudia—let alone been able to fight her dragon ass.

Also, in a way, they might've given me my only chance at vampire life. I've been avoiding vampire blood like the plague because of Ariel's addiction, and if they hadn't tricked me into imbibing some of Lilith's, I would've continued to do so. So if someone had killed me, I would've been really dead.

Still, being thankful doesn't make me stupid.

Knowing what I know now, I'm going to stay as far away from those two as I can. Except…

My blood chills as I realize that they know about one of my major weaknesses—my adoptive parents. In fact, their plan relied on putting them in danger.

No. Surely Lilith isn't enough of a monster to—

What am I saying?

She's enough of a monster to do the worst thing I can possibly imagine.

With a sinking feeling, I jump into Headspace.

———

IGNORING the default shapes around me, I focus on Dad's essence.

A set of safe shapes show up.

Another *phew*.

Dad is okay in the near future, which is good.

But what about a few days from now? Or a week?

Well, I can use the "targeting specific time" technique that ended up costing me my first life.

Maybe to start, I should check to make sure Dad is alive in a month?

It sounds like a good idea, only I don't know how much seer juice this will cost me. Does seer mojo expenditure go up with the length of the time interval—meaning the vision will be thirty times more "expensive" than when I targeted a day ahead to see Nero's second battle?

Nostradamus didn't specify, but I guess it doesn't matter.

If there was ever a good place to run out of seer reserves, it might be in Nero's embrace, on a world he rules and where he has a huge army at his disposal.

If I'm not safe here, I don't know where I would be.

Continuing to focus on Dad, I do my best to conjure up the essence of a month—starting with the mental gymnastics I did for a single workday, then picturing twenty more like it. From there, I also visualize my weekends—doing something fun with Felix and Ariel, learning magic effects, binging on TV shows, and going to Orientation on Sunday.

Whatever I did must work, because the safe shapes go away, replaced by ones that are anything but.

Actually, I've never heard this flavor of creepy music before.

It's not so much danger they radiate but something like grief.

Anxiety spiking, I sprout an ethereal appendage and reach for the worst of the shapes.

CHAPTER THIRTY-EIGHT

I'M BODILESS, inside a familiar high-tech office that also doubles as Dad's meeting room.

There are schematics of the latest 3D printer up on the board in front of a big group of people—except they're not looking at it.

They can't... because they're all dead.

No, not just dead. They're mummified in the way I've seen recently.

They look like Tartarus sucked the life out of them.

No.

It can't be.

I must've made a mistake in my seer targeting, and this is the world I passed through on my way to dragon world —the one that seems so much like ours but is long dead.

Could that world have a Boston equivalent with an office that looks like Dad's?

It's feasible but for one huge problem.

At the head of the table is Dad himself—dried up, like the rest of his people.

Still, maybe—

———

I'M BACK in Nero's arms, on the verge of a panic attack.

There has to be some other explanation.

That can't be the future.

With great effort, I even out my ragged breathing enough to leap back into Headspace.

Once I'm floating among the shapes, I very carefully conjure up the essence of a month, then the essence of my mom. Then, for good measure, I do my best to focus on the essence of the Otherland known as Earth —the blue planet I've thought of as home all these years.

As a result of my efforts, a set of shapes shows up— emitting the same creepy vibes as before.

I go through the essence rigamarole even more carefully, but the result is the same.

I might as well get the horrific confirmation.

Like a masochist, I reach for the worst of the shapes once again.

———

I'M FLOATING in Times Square, New York.

Right. This is one of Mom's favorite haunts, Broadway show aficionado that she is.

And there I find her, clearly on her way to see *The Phantom of the Opera* for the umpteenth time.

Except she didn't make it.

She's lying on the asphalt, a raisin-like shell with life sucked out of her.

I wish I had a mouth so I could scream.

Despite the dried-out husk of her body, there's no denying that this is my mom. I recognize those perfectly tailored clothes and tastefully applied makeup.

And she's not alone.

Tens of thousands of tourists and locals alike have met the same fate, their bodies lying everywhere.

They must've died recently, as the enormous Times Square screens are all still working, showing ads and glimpses of life preceding the disaster.

On a few screens, however, the newscasters are the same dead husks as in the Square itself—as if they'd been struck by the plague mid-broadcast.

One seemed to have been reporting from China, one from Australia, one from Germany.

And in the background of those horrifying broadcasts, everyone is just as dead.

———

BACK IN NERO'S ARMS, I'm ice cold and shaking uncontrollably.

I can't deny it any longer.

In a month or less, Tartarus is coming to Earth.

My Earth.

And he is going to kill my parents.

He is going to kill *everyone*, like he did on so many other worlds.

Behind me, Nero stirs, his warm lips brushing against my neck, but for once, my body remains cold and stiff, locked in terror.

Because if everything I've heard about Tartarus is true, there's no stopping this Armageddon.

But there's no choice.

I have to try.

SNEAK PEEKS

Thank you for reading! I hope you're enjoying Sasha's story. The next book, *Smoke, Vampires, and Mirrors*, is coming February 18!

To be notified of new releases of my books, please visit www.dimazales.com and sign up for my mailing list.

Love audiobooks? This series, and all of my other books, are available in audio.

Want more exciting action and adventure? Check out:

- *Mind Dimensions* - the action-packed urban fantasy adventures of Darren, who can stop time and read minds
- *Upgrade* - the thrilling sci-fi tale of Mike Cohen, whose new technology will transform our brains *and* the world

- *The Last Humans* - the futuristic sci-fi/dystopian story of Theo, who lives in a world where nothing is as it seems
- *The Sorcery Code* - the epic fantasy adventures of sorcerer Blaise and his creation, the beautiful and powerful Gala

I also collaborate with my wife on sci-fi romance, so if you don't mind erotic material, you can check out *Close Liaisons*. Visit www.annazaires.com for more information and to get your copy.

And now, please turn the page for an exciting excerpt from *The Thought Readers*.

THE THOUGHT READERS

Everyone thinks I'm a genius.

Everyone is wrong.

Sure, I finished Harvard at eighteen and now make crazy money at a hedge fund. But that's not because I'm unusually smart or hard-working.

It's because I cheat.

You see, I have a unique ability. I can go outside time into my own personal version of reality—the place I call "the Quiet"—where I can explore my surroundings while the rest of the world stands still.

I thought I was the only one who could do this—until I met *her*.

My name is Darren, and this is how I learned that I'm a Reader.

———

Sometimes I think I'm crazy. I'm sitting at a casino table in Atlantic City, and everyone around me is motionless. I call this the *Quiet*, as though giving it a name makes it seem more real—as though giving it a name changes the fact that all the players around me are frozen like statues, and I'm walking among them, looking at the cards they've been dealt.

The problem with the theory of my being crazy is that when I 'unfreeze' the world, as I just have, the cards the players turn over are the same ones I just saw in the Quiet. If I were crazy, wouldn't these cards be different? Unless I'm so far gone that I'm imagining the cards on the table, too.

But then I also win. If that's a delusion—if the pile of chips on my side of the table is a delusion—then I might as well question everything. Maybe my name isn't even Darren.

No. I can't think that way. If I'm really that confused, I don't want to snap out of it—because if I do, I'll probably wake up in a mental hospital.

Besides, I love my life, crazy and all.

My shrink thinks the Quiet is an inventive way I describe the 'inner workings of my genius.' Now that sounds crazy to me. She also might want me, but that's beside the point. Suffice it to say, she's as far as it gets from my datable age range, which is currently right around twenty-four. Still young, still hot, but done with school and pretty much beyond the clubbing phase. I hate clubbing, almost as much as I hated studying. In any case, my shrink's explanation doesn't work, as it doesn't account for the way I know things even a genius wouldn't know—like the exact value and suit of the other players' cards.

I watch as the dealer begins a new round. Besides me, there are three players at the table: Grandma, the Cowboy, and the Professional, as I call them. I feel that now almost imperceptible fear that accompanies the phasing. That's what I call the process: phasing into the Quiet. Worrying about my sanity has always facilitated phasing; fear seems helpful in this process.

I phase in, and everything gets quiet. Hence the name for this state.

It's eerie to me, even now. Outside the Quiet, this casino is very loud: drunk people talking, slot machines, ringing of wins, music—the only place louder is a club or a concert. And yet, right at this moment, I could probably hear a pin drop. It's like I've gone deaf to the chaos that surrounds me.

Having so many frozen people around adds to the strangeness of it all. Here is a waitress stopped mid-step, carrying a tray with drinks. There is a woman about to pull a slot machine lever. At my own table, the dealer's hand is raised, the last card he dealt hanging unnaturally in midair. I walk up to him from the side of the table and reach for it. It's a king, meant for the Professional. Once I let the card go, it falls on the table rather than continuing to float as before—but I know full well that it will be back in the air, in the exact position it was when I grabbed it, when I phase out.

The Professional looks like someone who makes money playing poker, or at least the way I always imagined someone like that might look. Scruffy, shades on, a little sketchy-looking. He's been doing an excellent job with the poker face—basically not twitching a single muscle throughout the game. His face is so expressionless that I wonder if he might've gotten Botox to help maintain such a stony countenance. His hand is on the table, protectively covering the cards dealt to him.

I move his limp hand away. It feels normal. Well, in a manner of speaking. The hand is sweaty and hairy, so moving it aside is unpleasant and is admittedly an abnormal thing to do. The normal part is that the hand is warm, rather than cold. When I was a kid, I expected people to feel cold in the Quiet, like stone statues.

With the Professional's hand moved away, I pick up his cards. Combined with the king that was hanging in the air, he has a nice high pair. Good to know.

I walk over to Grandma. She's already holding her cards, and she has fanned them nicely for me. I'm able to avoid touching her wrinkled, spotted hands. This is a relief, as I've recently become conflicted about touching people—or, more specifically, women—in the Quiet. If I had to, I would rationalize touching

Grandma's hand as harmless, or at least not creepy, but it's better to avoid it if possible.

In any case, she has a low pair. I feel bad for her. She's been losing a lot tonight. Her chips are dwindling. Her losses are due, at least partially, to the fact that she has a terrible poker face. Even before looking at her cards, I knew they wouldn't be good because I could tell she was disappointed as soon as her hand was dealt. I also caught a gleeful gleam in her eyes a few rounds ago when she had a winning three of a kind.

This whole game of poker is, to a large degree, an exercise in reading people—something I really want to get better at. At my job, I've been told I'm great at reading people. I'm not, though; I'm just good at using the Quiet to make it seem like I am. I do want to learn how to read people for real, though. It would be nice to know what everyone is thinking.

What I don't care that much about in this poker game is money. I do well enough financially to not have to depend on hitting it big gambling. I don't care if I win or lose, though quintupling my money back at the blackjack table was fun. This whole trip has been more about going gambling because I finally can, being twenty-one and all. I was never into fake IDs, so this is an actual milestone for me.

Leaving Grandma alone, I move on to the next player—the Cowboy. I can't resist taking off his straw hat and trying it on. I wonder if it's possible for me to get lice this way. Since I've never been able to bring back any inanimate objects from the Quiet, nor otherwise affect the real world in any lasting way, I figure I won't be able to get any living critters to come back with me, either.

Dropping the hat, I look at his cards. He has a pair of aces—a better hand than the Professional. Maybe the Cowboy is a professional, too. He has a good poker face, as far as I can tell. It'll be interesting to watch those two in this round.

Next, I walk up to the deck and look at the top cards, memorizing them. I'm not leaving anything to chance.

When my task in the Quiet is complete, I walk back to myself. Oh, yes, did I mention that I see myself sitting there, frozen like the rest of them? That's the weirdest part. It's like having an out-of-body experience.

Approaching my frozen self, I look at him. I usually avoid doing this, as it's too unsettling. No amount of looking in the mirror—or seeing videos of yourself on YouTube—can prepare you for viewing your own three-dimensional body up close. It's not something anyone is meant to experience. Well, aside from identical twins, I guess.

It's hard to believe that this person is me. He looks more like some random guy. Well, maybe a bit better than that. I do find this guy interesting. He looks cool. He looks smart. I think women would probably consider him good-looking, though I know that's not a modest thing to think.

It's not like I'm an expert at gauging how attractive a guy is, but some things are common sense. I can tell when a dude is ugly, and this frozen me is not. I also know that generally, being good-looking requires a symmetrical face, and the statue of me has that. A strong jaw doesn't hurt, either. Check. Having broad shoulders is a positive, and being tall really helps. All covered. I have blue eyes—that seems to be a plus. Girls have told me they like my eyes, though right now, on the frozen me, the eyes look creepy—glassy. They look like the eyes of a lifeless wax figure.

Realizing that I'm dwelling on this subject way too long, I shake my head. I can just picture my shrink analyzing this moment. Who would imagine admiring themselves like this as part of their mental illness? I can just picture her scribbling down *Narcissist,* underlining it for emphasis.

Enough. I need to leave the Quiet. Raising my hand, I touch my frozen self on the forehead, and I hear noise again as I phase out.

Everything is back to normal.

The card that I looked at a moment before—the king that I left on the table—is in the air again, and from there it follows the trajectory it was always meant to, landing near the Professional's hands. Grandma is still eyeing her fanned cards in disappointment, and the Cowboy has his hat on again, though I took it off him in the Quiet. Everything is exactly as it was.

On some level, my brain never ceases to be surprised at the discontinuity of the experience in the

Quiet and outside it. As humans, we're hardwired to question reality when such things happen. When I was trying to outwit my shrink early on in my therapy, I once read an entire psychology textbook during our session. She, of course, didn't notice it, as I did it in the Quiet. The book talked about how babies as young as two months old are surprised if they see something out of the ordinary, like gravity appearing to work backwards. It's no wonder my brain has trouble adapting. Until I was ten, the world behaved normally, but everything has been weird since then, to put it mildly.

Glancing down, I realize I'm holding three of a kind. Next time, I'll look at my cards before phasing. If I have something this strong, I might take my chances and play fair.

The game unfolds predictably because I know everybody's cards. At the end, Grandma gets up. She's clearly lost enough money.

And that's when I see the girl for the first time.

She's hot. My friend Bert at work claims that I have a 'type,' but I reject that idea. I don't like to think of myself as shallow or predictable. But I might actually be a bit of both, because this girl fits Bert's description of my type to a T. And my reaction is extreme interest, to say the least.

Large blue eyes. Well-defined cheekbones on a slender face, with a hint of something exotic. Long, shapely legs, like those of a dancer. Dark wavy hair in a ponytail—a hairstyle that I like. And without bangs—

even better. I hate bangs—not sure why girls do that to themselves. Though lack of bangs is not, strictly speaking, in Bert's description of my type, it probably should be.

I continue staring at her. With her high heels and tight skirt, she's overdressed for this place. Or maybe I'm underdressed in my jeans and t-shirt. Either way, I don't care. I have to try to talk to her.

I debate phasing into the Quiet and approaching her, so I can do something creepy like stare at her up close, or maybe even snoop in her pockets. Anything to help me when I talk to her.

I decide against it, which is probably the first time that's ever happened.

I know that my reasoning for breaking my usual habit—if you can even call it that—is strange. I picture the following chain of events: she agrees to date me, we go out for a while, we get serious, and because of the deep connection we have, I come clean about the Quiet. She learns I did something creepy and has a fit, then dumps me. It's ridiculous to think this, of course, considering that we haven't even spoken yet. Talk about jumping the gun. She might have an IQ below seventy, or the personality of a piece of wood. There can be twenty different reasons why I wouldn't want to date her. And besides, it's not all up to me. She might tell me to go fuck myself as soon as I try to talk to her.

Still, working at a hedge fund has taught me to hedge. As crazy as that reasoning is, I stick with my decision not to phase because I know it's the gentlemanly thing to do. In keeping with this unusually chivalrous me, I also decide not to cheat at this round of poker.

As the cards are dealt again, I reflect on how good it feels to have done the honorable thing—even without anyone knowing. Maybe I should try to respect people's privacy more often. As soon as I think this, I mentally snort. *Yeah, right.* I have to be realistic. I wouldn't be where I am today if I'd followed that advice. In fact, if I made a habit of respecting people's privacy, I would lose my job within days—and with it, a lot of the comforts I've become accustomed to.

Copying the Professional's move, I cover my cards with my hand as soon as I receive them. I'm about to sneak a peek at what I was dealt when something unusual happens.

The world goes quiet, just like it does when I phase in... but I did nothing this time.

And at that moment, I see *her*—the girl sitting across the table from me, the girl I was just thinking about. She's standing next to me, pulling her hand away from mine. Or, strictly speaking, from my frozen self's hand—as I'm standing a little to the side looking at her.

She's also still sitting in front of me at the table, a frozen statue like all the others.

My mind goes into overdrive as my heartbeat jumps. I don't even consider the possibility of that second girl being a twin sister or something like that. I know it's her. She's doing what I did just a few minutes ago. She's walking in the Quiet. The world around us is frozen, but we are not.

A horrified look crosses her face as she realizes the same thing. Before I can react, she lunges across the table and touches her own forehead.

The world becomes normal again.

She stares at me from across the table, shocked, her eyes huge and her face pale. Her hands tremble as she rises to her feet. Without so much as a word, she turns and begins walking away, then breaks into a run a couple of seconds later.

Getting over my own shock, I get up and run after her. It's not exactly smooth. If she notices a guy she doesn't know running after her, dating will be the last thing on her mind. But I'm beyond that now. She's the only person I've met who can do what I do. She's proof that I'm not insane. She might have what I want most in the world.

She might have answers.

———

Visit www.dimazales.com to get your copy!

ABOUT THE AUTHOR

Dima Zales is a *New York Times* and *USA Today* bestselling author of science fiction and fantasy. Prior to becoming a writer, he worked in the software development industry in New York as both a programmer and an executive. From high-frequency trading software for big banks to mobile apps for popular magazines, Dima has done it all. In 2013, he left the software industry in order to concentrate on his writing career and moved to Palm Coast, Florida, where he currently resides.

Please visit www.dimazales.com to learn more.

www.ingramcontent.com/pod-product-compliance
Lightning Source LLC
Chambersburg PA
CBHW060622100726
47907CB00006B/1733